Chains of Blood and Darkness

FRENCH QUARTER VAMPIRE KING

M GUIDA

Chapter One

Serenity

I looked around my dorm room at Crescent Moon University, taking it all in. The clean, crisp scent of fresh linens and the faint aroma of coffee from the mug on my desk were in sharp contrast to the stench of stale beer and rotting food that had constantly permeated my childhood home. My mom passed away when I was fourteen, and with my stepfather's drinking and poker buddies always coming and going, it had been a constant struggle for me to keep the place clean.

I was excited. This dorm represented my chance at a fresh start, an escape from the chaos that had defined my life for the last four years. My eyes drifted to my poster of Captain America on the wall, his shield gleaming with the promise of justice and protection. It had been the first thing

I put up when I moved in. Growing up, I had always dreamed of meeting a hero like him, someone who could swoop in and save me from the villains that always seemed to surround me at every turn, even though in my eighteen years I had learned the hard truth—heroes didn't exist, at least not in my world.

Instead, I was stuck with my stepfather, Freddie, the leader of the pack of lowlifes that had taken over our home the moment Mom was in the ground. He was the kind of villain who didn't need any superpowers; his cruelty and manipulation were more than enough to make my life a living hell. But now, standing in this small, tidy room that was all my own, I felt a flicker of hope that maybe, just maybe, I could finally break free of him and start living life on my own terms.

I smiled at my best friend, Joy DuPont. "Can you believe it? I'm actually here."

Joy, her raven-black hair pulled back in a ponytail and dressed in pink sweatpants that made her look like an athletic version of Barbie, sat down next to me on my twin bed. "You worked your ass off to get here, girl. I don't know many people that could work three jobs like you," she said, leaning her head on my shoulder and gesturing toward my poster. "Just like Captain America—I can do this all day."

I let out a deep sigh and squeezed her hand tight. "Even better, I finally escaped Freaky Freddie's clutches." My heart sang at the idea of never having to lock my bedroom or bathroom door again or needing to constantly be looking over my shoulder.

Joy returned the squeeze with a thoughtful nod. "Yup.

On the scale of creepy dudes, Freddie tops them all. But hey, that's all behind you now. You're safe here, and I'm right by your side to make sure it stays that way."

I grinned, feeling truly free for the first time in ages. "And I never have to see that man again, thanks to you and your dad."

She winked playfully. "Having a family of cops comes with certain perks," she said, elbowing me gently. "Besides, my dad thinks of you as a daughter. Trust me, slapping that restraining order on Freddie totally made his day."

Freddie had beaten me countless times but had always weaseled his way out of getting arrested. He was friends with some corrupt cops, and they always made sure the paperwork disappeared...until Joy's dad made detective, that is. Then everything changed.

Her trademark smile lit up her face. "Let's celebrate. Classes don't start until tomorrow. Apparently, some of the girls on our floor are going to The Junction to get to know each other. I think we should go too. We haven't really met anyone on this floor, and it would be good to make some new friends."

The Junction was a restaurant across the street from our dorm and a popular local hangout for college students. It was rumored to have the absolute best pan-sized fresh baked cookies with homemade ice cream, beignets, and chunky bread pudding. I wasn't completely convinced on the bread pudding because that had been Mom's specialty. But I hadn't had some for a long time, and it sounded tempting.

I frowned, looking down at my dirty sweatshirt and pants. "I look like crap."

Joy giggled. "It's not for another hour," she said, giving me another playful nudge with her elbow. "Plenty of time to spruce up. Come on, it'll be a blast—and hey, who cares if we're a bit messy? We're going for the food, not a fashion show! Please?"

She batted her eyelashes, and I laughed. I never could deny her anything.

I leaned my head on her shoulder. "Okay."

"Yay!" Joy hopped off the bed, but her socked feet slid on the smooth wooden floor, causing her to lose her balance. She stumbled and hit her head on the floor with a loud thud.

I rushed over and knelt down next to her. "Oh my god, are you all right?"

Her smile was forced as she rubbed her forehead. "I think I saw stars for a moment."

I gently placed my palm on her forehead, and as soon as I did, the familiar tingling sensations rushed through my hand. My head snapped back, and...yep, there it was...my nose started bleeding. I dropped my arm and quickly grabbed a tissue. "Feel better?"

She rubbed her forehead. "Yes, much, thank you. I'm not dizzy or anything. Wow. You've definitely got the healing touch, girl," Joy said with a relieved smile, winking at me to lighten the moment.

My shoulders sagged, and I stared at the hardwood floor. "I wish I knew how I'm doing it." I blinked away tears. "And I really wish I'd had it when Mom got cancer." My voice caught, and I struggled to keep the tears away.

The memory of my mom's final, horrible days flooded my mind. Why couldn't I have already had this ability then?

Joy got up from the floor and pulled me into a tight bear hug. "I know," she whispered, her own voice shaking with emotion. "Your mom would have been so proud of you. But hey, I'm sure she's smiling down on you, seeing all the amazing things you're doing."

We held each other for a few minutes before she pulled away, wiping her cheeks. "Enough of this. We gotta get ready and head over to The Junction to meet up with everyone else on our floor. We don't wanna be late, right? It'll be super fun to finally get to know our neighbors better. Let's just throw on something cute and comfy, do a quick makeup touch-up, and we'll be good to go!"

I sniffed and took a deep breath, then held up my palms. "Okay. Okay. I don't want to think about Mom or what happened after she died, anyway. Those memories can stay buried. Let me just take out this last bit of trash, then I'll get dressed and we can go."

Joy laughed and clapped her hands. "Yay! I'll be out of the shower by the time you get back. I'm so excited to meet everyone. This is gonna be an amazing night, for sure!"

"No rush," I said as I picked up our trash can that was filled to overflowing.

Leaving the warmth and laughter of my dorm behind, I stepped into the cool evening air, the campus lights flickering softly in the distance. The normalcy of a task as mundane as taking out the trash felt grounding after the whirlwind of emotions I'd just experienced.

The dumpster sat just behind the dorm, reeking of rotting food and overflowing with garbage. As I approached, a prickling sensation crept up the back of my neck. The night was suddenly unnaturally silent and felt charged with a foreboding I couldn't place. A white van was parked too close for comfort, its windows dark in the dim light.

A shiver ran down my spine, the cozy dorm room suddenly feeling worlds away. I quickened my pace, eager to return to the safety of my room, to Joy's infectious laughter and the promise of a night out. It was then, as I was looking back toward the dorm, that I heard it—a voice, chillingly close, shattering the night's calm.

"He was right. You really are a beauty," the voice sneered.

I spun around. A strong hand covered my mouth with a foul-smelling rag. Adrenaline pumped through me, and I kicked and flailed my arms as hard as I could and thrashed my head back and forth, but I started choking on the fumes and my arms and legs went limp. My eyes fluttered shut, and then everything went black...

As I slowly regained consciousness, my eyes struggled to see in the dimly lit room. My forehead was throbbing, and when I instinctively reached up to touch it, I discovered my hands were bound behind my back. A thick cloth was also stuffed in my mouth, muffling any sound I tried to make. I was on a bed.

I twisted my wrists, trying to break free, but the bindings were so tight that my efforts merely made them dig harder into my flesh. Beads of sweat broke out all over my body as I thrashed around on the bed, trying to throw my bound legs over the edge, but my sweatpants stuck to me like a second skin, making it even harder.

I frantically looked around, trying to figure out where I was—a luxurious purple bedroom with a small window. Maybe I could hop over to the window and crawl out? But first, I had to get these damn bindings off.

The mumble of voices stilled my heart. Shadows flickered underneath the door. The voices got closer, and my blood ran cold. Using all my strength, I rolled off the bed and landed on my back with a thud, sending the air rushing out of my lungs. A fresh, sharp pain stabbed the back of my skull, and stars dotted my vision.

The door whipped open. A tall, broad-shouldered man in a suit walked in and stared down at me. I had never seen him before. "Ah, so you're awake. Good. I'm Simon." He stroked his beard, eyeing me in a way that made me feel like I needed a hot shower. "You will bring a good price...especially since you're so young. My customers like them young."

Fuckfuckfuckfuck

Dread lodged in my throat—followed by a fear that burst through my chest, crushing my heart. It was like a panic bomb exploding inside me—I could feel my blood rolling through my veins, pumping between my temples.

"Now, here's what's going to happen, Serenity." He circled me, giving me a cruel stare.

God, he knew my name?! I had to get the fuck out of here. I briefly considered swinging my bound ankles and knocking him on his ass, but just then a large shadow filled the doorway, smashing my hope. It was a burly man that could snap me like a twig.

Hope returned when I thought of Joy. She would have reported me as missing to the police by now, either officially or just by calling her father, Louis. God, please, please, please let them be looking for me already. Girls disappeared on the streets of New Orleans all the time, and I didn't want to be another statistic.

"Michael." He nodded his chin at the bulky guy who stomped into the room like a giant. I shook my head wildly, scooting back from him, not wanting him to touch me. But my head swam as I inhaled more of the harsh chemicals, and I choked on the rough texture of the gag pressed to my mouth.

The man grabbed me and tossed me onto the bed like I was a suitcase. I landed on my back and the pulsing pain increased on the back of my skull. Then he stood back, folding his arms across his chest and watching me. If I made any sudden moves against Simon, I knew this guy would make me regret it.

Simon sat next to me on the bed. He lifted a blonde strand off my head and sniffed it.

Grossgrossgross

I jerked my head, yanking my hair from his long, slender fingers.

He chuckled softly. "Such a fighter you are, Serenity. And such a pretty name. Your new master will teach you discipline. Like I said, here's what's going to happen. I'm going to send my assistants in here, and they will help you get ready for the auction tonight."

Simon patted my thigh, making my skin crawl. "You will do exactly as you're told." He grabbed my hair and jerked my head up next to his narrow face. His nose and chin were too sharp, reminding me of a ferret, and his breath was overly sweet, as if he just eaten a whole tray of pralines. "There's a way we can inflict pain without leaving a mark. My witch has perfected it. Nod if you understand."

I forced myself to nod. I knew all about pain, and Freddie had hurt me more times than I could remember without ever leaving a mark. But a witch? Seriously?

Simon released my hair, and I fell back again onto the bed.

Then two women barged into the room dressed in suits, looking more like businesswomen than jailers, their faces caked with heavy makeup that failed to hide their lines and wrinkles. One of them, who had a severe gray bun and sharp features, gave me a once-over with cold, assessing eyes that were gray like her hair. "You were right, Simon. She will fetch a high price if we can bring out her real beauty. Wouldn't you agree, Marsha?"

The bitch! She made me feel like I was a cocker spaniel she was prepping for a dog show.

Trapped, I sized up my captors. Their hands were empty and relaxed, with no weapons in sight. Maybe this was my chance. I've never been one to play the victim.

But even as I plotted my escape, the older woman opened a closet, revealing a selection of long gowns. "Since she's so young, Marsha," she mused, "we'll dress her in white. Yes?" She selected a sleeveless gown with lace detailing. "But first, we'll clean her up. Those wolves would never want someone who reeks."

Wolves? My heart skipped. Were they talking about

actual animals, or was that a metaphor for something more sinister?

Marsha's gaze on me was cold and devoid of pity. "Let's get her untied," she ordered, nodding at my bonds. "Quickly. We only have two hours to make her presentable."

The mention of wolves lingered in my mind, ominous and confusing. Why wolves? The question haunted me as I tried to mask my fear, my brain racing for a way out.

I lay perfectly still, pretending to be too scared to move. The gray-haired woman grabbed my arm and pulled me roughly to my feet.

My wrists and ankles ached as she untied them, but the second I was free, I immediately swung my arm and connected with her jaw, sending her staggering back. Blood gushed from her nose as she cried out in pain.

Marsha grabbed my arm and twisted it behind my back, causing me to cry out. I refused to give up. With all my strength, I slammed my head back into her face, breaking free of her grip.

I lunged for the nearby window, frantically searching for a way out of this hellish situation.

"*Éclat de Chaos*," Marsha cried out behind me.

Instantly, a wave of agony wracked my body, as if a fist had crushed me. I bent over, holding my sides, freedom just out of my grip.

Marsha gripped my hair with her fingers, her nails scratching my scalp. Tears of frustration streamed down my face.

"I assume Simon told you he had a witch." She gave me a

sinister smile. "That's me. And this is just one of my many spells that can cause you pain."

Simon stood in the doorway, watching with a cruel grin on his face. "I told you we could make you suffer, leaving no visible marks," he taunted as he approached me.

"*Lame Diabolique.*" Marsha released me and the pain ceased. But it had zapped all my energy, and I crumbled to the floor, landing hard on my knees and then falling forward onto my stomach.

In a desperate attempt to get away, I crept toward the window like a chastised dog, but glanced over my shoulder when I heard footsteps following me, only to find myself looking right into Simon's cold, calculating eyes. Fear turned me to stone. I had just made a grave mistake.

Chapter Two

Angelo

The door to my office creaked open, and I glanced up from my computer. The sight of Enzo Di Salvo, my trusted long-time enforcer and best friend, pulled my attention away from the screen. His heavy boots thudded on the hardwood floor as he took a seat in the leather chair facing my desk. He was dressed in one of his customary navy-blue suits with a white shirt and black tie, and his long, wavy brown hair was, as always, combed perfectly. Image was everything to him.

"What news do you have from the *Fondatori*?" I asked, my voice tinged with urgency.

Enzo met my gaze with worried, amber eyes. "There's been a big meeting on Seafarer's Island in Nova Scotia." His tone hinted at disaster, and I braced myself for the worst.

"One of the kings, Heinrich Rainer, managed to get himself beheaded in Germany."

This was the last thing I wanted to hear. I didn't respond until after several deep breaths. Yet another chess move that put my family in check. The loss of Heinrich Rainer could make our precarious house of cards wobble and perhaps topple. Vlad Țepeș, or Dracula as the humans called him, would be pleased with this new development. He was our number one enemy and wanted nothing more than to destroy our empire.

I sat taller in my chair. "Any idea who's behind it? And who's taken charge of Berlin now?"

"Leon Miller," he said with a grimace. "Seems like the Wolf King's allies might be involved, too."

Trystan Hunter, the Wolf King, was a thorn in my side, a constant threat to my family's territory in Crescent City. The possibility of his involvement in Heinrich's death, and what it might mean for our territory, needed immediate attention.

"We can't rule any of them out?" I pressed, the stakes of our situation growing ever higher.

"No, we can't," Enzo confirmed.

I knew the answer, but still asked it as I leaned back in my chair. "Any more news of Vlad?"

Enzo shrugged. "All we know is that he's here. Hiding in plain sight. He could be anywhere. You really need to watch your back, Angelo. He's coming for you first."

I dragged my fingers through my long hair. "Tell me something I don't know. And Dracula breathing down my neck isn't our only problem. On that note—do you still have men watching my sister?"

Enzo nodded. "Yes, I assigned three men to watch their place. Dimitri seems to be very protective of her, though. I don't think—"

"Keep the men on her," I said sharply. "Dimitri isn't as strong as we are."

Enzo cleared his throat. "He saved your sister twice."

I gave him a don't-mess-with-me-glare. "Don't press me."

"Okay." Enzo held up his hands. "But she won't be happy about us spying on them."

I grimaced. "She's not happy I made him my chauffeur, either. She's not happy about a lot of things."

Gianna, my younger sister, had defied me by marrying a vampire who was born, not turned, against my wishes. It was a bitter disappointment, especially since I had carefully arranged for her to mate with Anton Lange, an ancient and powerful vampire who now served as the headmaster of Legacy Academy in Colorado.

Despite my efforts to ensure her continued safety and status, she spurned the match I had so meticulously planned. Even when I offered for them to live at Crescent Manor, Gianna stubbornly refused, insisting on living with her husband in a townhouse near me that belonged to the family.

As a compromise, I "requested" that they visit me every Sunday. Dimitri, Gianna's husband, was well aware of the consequences should he fail to bring my sister to these weekly meetings. It was a small measure of control, but one I clung to fiercely in the face of Gianna's relentless defiance.

The conversation with Enzo shifted toward the night's business matters, including the auction at Crimson Stakes, a cornerstone of our empire, not just for its actual revenue but its value as a front for more covert operations.

As Enzo's footsteps faded away, leaving me lost in thought in the solitude of my office, my gaze drifted to the Aeternum Stone beside me. Its once-vibrant light now flickered weakly, a somber reminder of the encroaching darkness that threatened our world. The stone's magic, a gift from the witches that kept Dracula at bay and allowed our shadowy empire to thrive, was fading. Without the stone's power, our very survival was in jeopardy.

Memories of battles fought alongside Dracula, my maker and onetime brother-in-arms, haunted me. His shift away from our shared path, fueled by a love I had never known, had created a rift between us that was filled now with nothing but enmity. I had turned against him, not just to lead but to protect what we had built from his strange new beliefs. Yet I was now dependent on a magic that was fading as rapidly as my certainty.

The chill that swept through the room was a grim reminder of the evil presence I felt always lurking in New Orleans. Dracula's very breath seemed to brush the back of my neck, a sensation at once familiar and unsettling. I knew he was close, an ever-present threat to my city, my family, and to me.

I sighed and returned to my work as the day stretched

into evening, a blur of preparations and strategies. The sky outside my window gradually deepened into the velvet of night. Time to get ready for the auction where I hoped to procure magical items that might restore the Aeternum Stone's power.

Chapter Three

Angelo

As my limousine rolled up the winding driveway, I admired the elegant grandeur that was Simon Cartier's Ravenwood Estates. The sprawling white antebellum mansion stood proudly beside the murky bayou, surrounded by tall oaks and immaculately manicured gardens. Its facade boasted towering columns and expansive verandas, exuding a deceptive air of tranquility that masked the estates' true purpose. I had thought of buying this place and taking over Simon's venture so many times, but I'd never gotten around to making him an offer he couldn't refuse.

The moment I exited my car, I saw Trystan's signature blue limousine looming large, out of place in its gaudiness and clamoring for my attention. An involuntary grunt of annoyance bubbled up, and my eyes rolled. The damned wolves always had to show off their pack color. They weren't the only ones flaunting their wealth though—I noticed Simon's sleek red Ferrari parked a few spaces down.

I nodded to my driver. "Be ready for anything, Dimitri." I initially only tolerated my sister's marriage to Dimitri for her sake. I had always considered blood-born vampires to be weak. But he had quickly proved that notion to be nothing more than archaic thinking. He had risked his life for my sister—something I would never forget.

Enzo, too, considered Dimitri to be one of his most valuable enforcers—a testament to his unwavering loyalty and brutal efficiency. Even if he wasn't as powerful as a made vampire, he had proven himself to be useful—especially as my chauffeur.

I glanced at Dimitri. "You got that? Be ready for anything."

He caught my eye in the rearview mirror, a smirk playing on his lips. "Always ready, boss. It's like my middle name, right after 'Danger.'"

"By the way, you'll be at dinner this Sunday?"

Dimitri rolled his eyes dramatically. "Oh no, I thought I'd skip the weekly family drama for once. Of course we'll be there. Wouldn't miss it for the world...or an apocalypse."

I narrowed my eyes. "See that it stays that way. I need to know that my sister is safe."

Dimitri's expression softened, a mix of love and fierce protectiveness flashing in his eyes. "Come on, Angelo. She's not just your sister—she's my mate. I've already died twice for her. Third time's the charm, right?" His trademark grin returned, but there was an unmistakable intensity behind it.

"Besides, I draw the line at unicorn shifters. Too glittery for my taste." He met my gaze in the rearview mirror, all humor gone. "Your sister—my mate—has nothing to worry about. Never has, never will."

"Good." I scanned the grounds. "Stay alert."

He stood next to me as tense as a Doberman pincher ready to attack, but his tone remained light. "Sure thing, Captain Obvious. I'll make sure to keep my vampire senses tuned to 'paranoid overprotective brother' frequency."

Just then, a sleek gray limousine pulled up next to mine, and the dark Fae announced their presence with a flourish. Despite not being as powerful as the wolves, they still posed a threat to our kind and were a constant annoyance in our territory.

Keir Rankin, king of the dark Fae Mafia, climbed out of his vehicle with a regal air. The moonlight caught his long white hair and reflected off his sharp blue eyes as he glanced over at me. His smile was polite but lacked warmth. "Good to see you again, Santi."

I gave him a brief nod before turning toward the mansion. "Likewise, Rankin. What are you interested in buying tonight?"

He shrugged nonchalantly and adjusted his sleeve carefully. "The usual. Stock is low. You?"

I let out a tired sigh. "The same."

My agenda tonight was clear, if unspoken: acquiring new talent for Crimson Stakes; seeking out artifacts imbued with magic that might restore the stone; and adding to my private collection with art of unparalleled quality.

Simon always put on a lavish event at these exclusive

auctions, and only the kings of the supernatural world and their equivalents were invited. I think it made him feel like he was royalty himself. The other kings and I respected this rule and never brought non-royal guests, since Simon had a powerful witch loyal to him in Marsha Cadieux. She had threatened to make the Aeternum Stone go completely dark if the Santi family crossed Simon. And it wasn't just my stone she threatened; Trystan's and Keir's were in danger too. I had briefly considered kidnapping and killing her until I discovered that she would absorb the power of the stones and turn on us with a vengeance. Simon was playing a dangerous game. If Marsha ever left him, he would be at her mercy.

The last limousine to arrive was Maximo Barone's, don of the Barone empire. His family had come over from Italy in the early 1920s. The humans were not a threat to my family. They traded mostly in drug and human trafficking—neither of which threatened my business. Simon treated him like a king, but he would never be one in my eyes.

Keir and I turned our backs on the white limo and headed up the steps to the house. One of Simon's goons opened the door for us.

The warm, golden glow of a crystal chandelier bathed us in its light as we entered the grand dining room. A majestic red-carpeted staircase rose to a second level, where luxurious rooms awaited us in which we could indulge in lustful fantasies. I had partaken in such activities before, but none of the beauties dressed in long gowns caught my fancy tonight, perhaps because I had already been with each of them more than once.

My heightened vampire senses were on overload from all the tantalizing scents in the air—savory dishes, fresh blood, delicate perfumes. As always, Simon had a glass urn filled with Chosen Blood, donated by an elite group of humans who received longer lifetimes in exchange for their gift. It was delicious, but not quite as satisfying as fresh blood.

"Simon has truly outdone himself tonight," Keir murmured beside me.

I nodded, silently taking in the opulent spread of culinary delights before us. Each dish was a testament to New Orleans' rich gastronomic heritage. Towering displays of chilled oysters promised a briny kiss of the sea, while silver platters held succulent crawfish étouffée and tureens contained spicy duck and sausage gumbo. Elegant bowls cradled creamy shrimp and grits, topped with sharp green onion. Meanwhile, golden beignets dusted with powdered sugar beckoned for dessert, along with decadent bananas foster flambéed tableside.

Simon rushed over to us with his arms spread, then bowed slightly. He had on a tuxedo, making him look somewhat like a tall, bearded penguin. "King Keir and King Angelo, welcome to my humble abode."

Though I held the rank of king within the vampire Mafia, it was a mantle I bore with reluctance, unlike the kings of the Fondatori, who reveled in their royal status. My realm was not royal courts but the shadowed corners of New Orleans, overseeing the vampire syndicate far from their prying eyes. Up to now, their gaze had not turned toward the Crescent City, allowing me a certain autonomy within my domain.

Simon gestured toward the long table lined with silver trays and chafing dishes, beckoning us to indulge in the sumptuous spread of hors d'oeuvres. "Take your time," he said with a sly smile. "We won't start the auction for at least an hour. Trust me, I have some truly one-of-a-kind pieces that will capture your interest."

He glanced behind us. "Don Barone, welcome, welcome." He broke away from us and fawned all over Maximo.

A girl brought me over a goblet of Chosen Blood. She lowered her dark head. "Your Majesty."

I rolled my eyes at the salutation, but I didn't correct her. The title did allow me to get what I wanted—especially from Simon.

"Thank you," I said as I accepted the glass.

She offered Keir a goblet filled with a sparkling blue liquid—High Tempest. It was from the Fae's Starlight Kingdom and extremely powerful. One sip would make most humans drunk.

But not vampires.

It only gave us a slight buzz.

I inhaled the mouth-watering scent of a sizzling Wagyu steak. My eyes landed on the Wolf King, Trystan, seated at a table by himself, his fork expertly cutting into the perfectly cooked meat. One of Simon's lovelies stood at his side, a serene look on her heart-shaped face. Trystan's piercing blue eyes narrowed as they landed on me, and for a moment, I thought I heard a low growl rumble from his chest. I knew better than to challenge him here. Not with Marsha's threat of destroying the Aeternum Stone hanging over my head.

I picked up a plate and loaded it up with chilled oysters and a bowl of rice, over which I ladled duck and spicy sausage gumbo. I took a seat next to a window that looked out onto the bayou and turned firmly away from the Wolf King.

A woman with jet-black hair glided toward me, her hips swaying seductively. Her smile was sultry. "My, my, my. Angelo Santi. I've missed you." She nearly purred my name.

I ran my gaze over her and did my best to suppress an annoyed sigh. "Emily. You're looking good."

As much as I loved the taste of Emily Bastion's blood, I didn't want to get caught up with her right now. I had too much on my mind between the auction and the stone.

She lifted my chin with two fingers. "Why don't you forgo your meal and take me upstairs before the fun begins?" Her charms left me flat.

In my peripheral vision, I saw Simon's eyes following her every move. He probably thought if he tempted us not just with lavish food and drinks but with women as well, we would open our wallets for him.

She must have sensed his gaze on her because she leaned in even closer, fluttering her lashes and running her fingers through her hair. As she did so, the soft fabric of her low-cut gown slid off her shoulder, revealing a hint of creamy skin and lace lingerie. My gaze followed the line of her neck until I caught myself and looked away, focusing on my meal instead.

"Not tonight, Emily," I said firmly, trying to ignore the seductive sway of her body as she stood next to me. She threw a worried look at Simon before nervously fidgeting with her napkin.

I glared at Simon, who quickly looked away, then turned back to the temptress. "You should have something to eat and drink," I said with a forced smile, gesturing at the lavish spread on the table. "You look a little pale."

Emily left, pouting, then came back with a plate of chilled oysters and a Greek salad.

"So, tell me, Emily, what kind of surprises does Simon have for us tonight?"

She glanced nervously over her shoulder at Simon, then back to me. "I'm not supposed to say..."

I dabbed my lips. "But it's me. Tell me." I didn't have to use compulsion on her. She was always eager to spill Simon's secrets.

Emily dipped her small fork into the oyster shell and delicately pulled out the meat. She swallowed and then asked, "You want to know about the magical objects Simon plans to auction?"

"Please...Do tell," I said as a waiter drifted in to refill my glass with Chosen Blood, then drifted away again.

She looked around nervously, as if she was afraid someone was listening. "I'm really not supposed to tell, but he has a few objects you may want."

I looked at her over the rim of my wine glass. "Go on."

She licked her lips. "There's the Lumina Pendant, which glows in the presence of magic."

I flashed her an unimpressed look.

When I didn't respond, she tried again. "He also has the Chroniker's Hourglass. It can manipulate small pockets of time. You can use it to go into the future or past."

That definitely sounded useful, but I had no intention of telling Emily. She would go blab to Simon and the bastard would up the price. Once again, I played coy.

"There's also the Vespers Ring." She clasped my hand. "You can walk in the shadows unseen."

I rolled my eyes. "Emily. I can already do that."

She bit her lip. "Oh! There's also the Codex of Eldritch Lore. Simon says it's a rare and ancient tome containing spells and rituals lost to time, written by a coven of witches who vanished under mysterious circumstances. According to him, the book's pages are said to shift and change, revealing their secrets only to those deemed worthy." She was practically reciting the words like a rehearsed sales pitch. Simon had definitely ordered her to find out what I was looking for.

I had heard of the Codex of Eldritch Lore. It could prove useful too. I took another drink from my goblet, but again said nothing.

Her shoulders slumped, as if she was disappointed not to get the response from me she wanted.

"There's also the Eclipsing Mirror. That's a handheld mirror framed in moonstone with the ability to reveal the true nature of anyone or anything reflected in its surface. You can also use it as a portal to a pocket dimension for brief escapes or clandestine meetings."

Something else that might prove useful...very useful... but I didn't even smile.

I leaned back in my chair, the silverware clinking softly against fine china as I set down my fork. The rich aroma of rare steak lingered in the air, a poor substitute for what I truly craved. My voice was low, barely above a whisper, as I asked, "What about the Moirai's Mirror? Has it shown up yet?"

My fingers idly traced the stem of a crystal wine glass filled with a deep red liquid. I had possessed the mirror earlier, but it was stolen from me. The artifact could reveal half-truths of the future, but never the whole picture. It had been invaluable in helping me protect my sister when those mangy wolves had foolishly put a contract on her to get to me.

I suppressed a snarl, not wanting to disturb the quiet atmosphere of the dining room. Simon swore he didn't take it, but I suspected a witch might be involved—possibly even his witch, Marsha. My eyes narrowed as I considered the possibilities, the candlelight casting flickering shadows across my face.

She reached out, her hand shaking, and took a sip of her wine. It seemed to give her courage. "There's one last thing. I heard Simon has a young girl, most likely a virgin. A real fighter." She gave me a devious smile and laughed softly. "Apparently, she's already given Frances a bloody nose."

I cocked my eyebrow. "Really? A heavyweight boxing virgin? Now that sounds intriguing."

Frances was like the madam of Simon's girls and kept them in line. She was very strict with them, and sometimes I wondered if it was her or Simon that punished the girls when punishment was due. I scanned the dining room to see Frances herself waltzing in as if on cue, wearing a scowl as if she had just downed a whole bottle of buttermilk that only added to her surliness. I could see why. She had a fat lip.

She whispered something to Simon, and he slammed his glass of red wine down on the table, spilling its contents onto the white tablecloth.

Something was up.

Was the virgin giving Simon trouble? Fascinating. And I hadn't been fascinated by a woman in a long, long time. Maybe she could be a pleasant distraction from everything that was falling down around my ears.

Yes, I'd definitely buy her. I could use a little fun.

Chapter Four

Serenity

Marsha and the older woman, who I had discovered was named Frances, had dressed me in a stupid, long white gown and had put my hair up in a loose bun. I looked like a fucking princess.

Marsha cast her gaze over me. "Cleaned up, she's beautiful. Watch her. I need to check the other merchandise."

Did she mean other girls like me?

I remained docile on the surface, but I wasn't even close to giving up the fight. I waited until Marsha had made her way out of the dressing room, leaving me alone with Frances, then I shoved her as hard as I could. She slammed her head into the wall and slid down limply like a puppet. I ran out of the room and into the kitchen. I immediately grabbed a steak knife out of a wooden block.

"Dan! Help me," Frances cried as she stumbled into the kitchen after me.

A man—Dan, I supposed—suddenly appeared behind her. He was built like a grizzly bear, and his massive hands looked capable of crushing my skull with a single squeeze. They flanked me, cutting off any escape.

My heart banged wildly against my ribcage. Blood raged through my veins, turning my skin scorching hot. I tightly gripped the metal handle of the steak knife, cold in my sweaty palm. Strands of my blonde hair came loose from my messy bun and hung in front of my eyes. As Frances and Dan closed in on me, I slashed and lunged with the knife, keeping them at bay. I could hear Joy's older brother's words —"Always aim for the soft spots!"—ringing in my ears as I fought for my life. Steve had taught me how to defend myself with a knife after an incident with Freddie years ago. Right now, I'd take Freddie over this guy any day.

Frances glared at me. "Serenity, put the knife down. You're only making things worse for yourself. Simon won't be pleased."

Dan cracked his neck. "I've got her trapped. She ain't going nowhere. Go get Simon."

Frances stormed out of the kitchen in a huff.

I bolted in the opposite direction, slicing with the knife again and again. Dan was quicker than I thought and cornered me against the sink, an immovable wall of muscle, but I stood my ground.

I gritted my teeth. "Come near me and you're dead."

"You're going to regret this, bitch. The boss ain't going to take kindly to this at all." He picked up a white dinner plate off the counter and hurled it at my head like a frisbee. I ducked, and it shattered against the wall behind me, fragments falling onto my bare shoulders.

Panting, I pressed my back against the counter. "Stay away from me." My once-steady voice had turned shrill. I was reaching my limit.

Heavy footsteps thundered down the hallway.

Simon and Frances barged into the room, their faces frantic. Simon's eyes locked onto mine with fiery intensity, his hand trembling as he pointed at me. "You're pushing my limits," he growled through clenched teeth. He shoved Dan at me, his face contorted with disgust. "Get that weapon away from her, you idiot."

I lashed out with the knife again, narrowly missing Dan's arm.

"Looks like she knows how to handle it," Simon sneered, reaching into his jacket and pulling out a gleaming revolver. "I'll shoot you in the leg or the arm if I have to." His thumb cocked the gun. "Don't test me, bitch."

My heart pounded like a jackrabbit's in my chest as I weighed my options.

Marsha walked into the room and flicked her wrist. "*Rayon Sacré.*"

The knife instantly flew out of my hand and embedded itself in the ceiling above my head.

"Shit!" I shouted.

Dan lunged at me and pinned my hand against the wall.

"Stop struggling," he grunted as I kicked and thrashed against him.

Adrenaline shot through my arms and legs as I fought to

escape from the enormous man, kicking, twisting, and stomping on his foot.

He growled dangerously. He really did remind me of a bear.

"Take her to the bedroom," Simon ordered.

Dan tossed me over his shoulder, and I pounded on his back with my fists. "No, no, no!"

He slammed me down on the bed, pinning my wrists over my head.

Simon approached the bed, holding a syringe. With no warning, he jabbed the needle into my vein, injecting me with god knows what. My body tensed up, and sweat broke out all over my skin as I thrashed my head back and forth and arched my back, trying to get the mountain of muscle off me. But it was no use—the drug had already begun to take effect.

A wave of dizziness overtook me, my vision blurred, and my limbs went numb.

Simon stared down at me, his face going in and out of focus. "Don't worry. You won't pass out, but you won't have the strength to fight us off, and you'll be a fuck of a lot more compliant."

Dan slowly released me. I tried to sit up, but Simon was right. I couldn't muster the strength to even move my pinky. It was as if my arms had turned into lead.

Simon looked at Marsha and Frances. He clicked his tongue with impatient disapproval. "Get her cleaned up. She's a complete mess."

My brain told my muscles to clench and fight back, but my limbs were heavy and unresponsive. Dan's grip on my arm was firm, but not strong enough to leave bruises. He pulled me along, my feet dragging on the hardwood floor. We reached a large powder room, and he pushed me onto a stool facing a huge mirror. I tried to steady myself, but my body had turned into that of a lifeless puppet, and I fell to the ground. I landed on my right side, twisting my arm behind my back and slamming my hip on the floor. I cried out in agony.

"You idiot. She's drugged and doesn't have any strength. Hold her up," Marsha's voice rang out behind us, clearly disgusted by my lack of coordination.

Dan's hand closed around my hurt arm like a vice, hauling me up from the ground and shoving me back onto the stool, ignoring my pained whimpers. My head swam with disorientation, and I struggled to keep my eyes open; everything was a blur. Frances' sharp nails dug into my flesh, causing sharp pain to shoot through my arm. I tried to use my other hand to soothe the ache, but it felt like it was glued to the stool.

Frances scrubbed my face clean. "I can't believe I have to redo your makeup again, you little bitch. Simon better be right about you bringing in lots of money." She pinched my cheeks hard. "Don't do anything else stupid. I'm losing my patience."

Frances moved swiftly around me with a powder compact, tube of lipstick, and mascara wand. When she was finished, I barely recognized myself. I looked even worse than when they made me a princess. I had rosy-pink cheeks, thick mascara around my eyes, and sparkling blue eye shadow. I looked like a porcelain doll.

She pinched my arm again. "Stop laughing."

I don't know why I was giggling. Maybe it was the drugs.

Next Marsha tugged at my hair, pulling it into an unfamiliar style, her fingernails scratching my scalp. I winced, but she didn't care as she pinned it up higgledy-piggledy. As I looked at my reflection, it was like seeing a completely different person staring back at me—a woman who wore way too much makeup and with unkempt hair—not at all me.

"Her gown is stained from where she got her dinner all over it. I'll get her another one." The drugs were getting stronger, and Frances' voice sounded like she was talking in a bucket.

Marsha yanked my dress off right in front of Dan, and I could feel his gaze flicking over me. I wanted to die, but I was putty in their hands. What had Simon given me?

Frances and Marsha helped me get into another strapless white gown that I thought might have sparkled, but I couldn't focus enough to be sure. Marsha covered up the bruises on my right arm with makeup and bound my arms behind my back. My arms and wrists throbbed, and I hissed between my teeth.

No one cared. They forced me to sit on the floor with my legs spread out wide. I felt like a marionette for them to pose at will. Time ticked by, and I tried to blink my eyes to keep my gaze focused and steady, but it didn't work. Everything seemed fuzzy, as if I had chugged a bottle of beer too quickly. My stomach swirled uneasily, and I hoped I didn't lose the contents of it. Hadn't Frances mentioned me getting dinner on my dress? I couldn't even remember the last time I had eaten.

Dan yanked me up off the floor and dragged me out of the powder room and down a hallway, to where, I wasn't sure. Everything had turned into a kaleidoscope of flashing white, green, blue, and red. I squeezed my eyes shut tight, longing to get off the merry-go-round.

Dan abruptly let go of me, and I staggered as if I were drunk.

Frances hissed into my ear. "You will walk out into that room, and *you will not make a fool of me*, do you understand? You'd better hope someone buys you, because if they don't, you don't want to know what I'll do to you."

Her harsh whisper was like a dagger cutting into my heart.

I could barely breathe as I heard what sounded like doors opening.

"Now...move." Frances' curt voice spurred me on.

I concentrated on putting one foot in front of the other and prayed I didn't trip over the stupid gown.

"...And this is our last piece, my kings. She's a young girl, barely eighteen, possibly even a virgin, ready to be popped by one of you."

Popped? Seriously, did he just use that word?

Tingles swept over me, and goosebumps ran down my naked arms. Gasps erupted around the room, as if my appearance had stunned the lecherous buyers.

I clenched my fists. This was my worst nightmare. Tears stung my eyes as my last bit of freedom was ripped from me.

I had fought so hard to escape one prison only, to enter an even more nightmarish second one.

I blinked, trying to decipher who these buyers were who would steal a young girl's hopes and dreams.

"Shall I start the bidding at one thousand dollars?" Simon's unctuous voice made me want to scratch his eyes out.

"I'll bid a thousand," a man with a husky voice said.

"The bid is at one thousand to Don Barone, thank you. Do I hear more?"

"Five thousand," another voice growled.

Was he serious? It would take me two months working three jobs to earn that kind of money.

I looked in the direction of the voice, and I thought I saw a man in blue, but I couldn't make out his features.

"The bid is at five thousand to King Trystan. There must be another bid," Simon purred like a greedy cat counting its bowls of cream.

A king? There was a king here bidding on me?

"Ten thousand," another voice chimed in.

This was insane. If Freddie had known I was worth this much, he would have auctioned me off ages ago.

"Thank you. The bid is at ten thousand to King Keir. Do I hear anymore bids?" Simon was speaking more quickly now, eager to hit that big jackpot.

Tears sprang to my eyes and fear clawed at my chest. What did these men expect in return for these outrageous bids?

"One hundred thousand," a soft male voice said quietly. It sounded like he was right next to me.

I turned too fast, trying to make out his features. The room spun around as if I were on a Tilt-a-Whirl.

"Thank you, sir. The bid is one hundred thousand—do I hear one hundred fifty?" The eagerness in Simon's voice made me ill. "No? Going once, going twice..."

There were no more bids.

"Sold..." His voice faded from my ears as my eyes rolled back in my head.

The Tilt-a-Whirl picked up speed. My stomach dropped to my feet. The room spun faster and faster, and I shut my eyes, trying to get off the crazy ride. My legs betrayed me, and I swayed.

Excited voices erupted around me. Oh god, they were going to punish me but good for this. My body swirled around, my head tilted back, and I fell backward, waiting to topple onto the hard floor.

But strong arms caught me.

Someone whispered in my ear, "It's all right. I won't let anyone hurt you. You're mine."

"No..." It was all I could muster before the darkness closed in, rescuing me from the nightmare.

Chapter Five

Angelo

I struggled to keep my composure as I cradled the unconscious young woman in my arms. Her body radiated an otherworldly light, such a stark contrast to the darkness that had consumed me for so long. She was exactly what I needed. I studied her face, seeing remnants of angelic features, which confirmed her true identity—a Nephilim. She had been the most valuable item at tonight's auction, and now she was mine. Her power surged through me, igniting a fierce protectiveness in my heart such as I had never experienced. With her at my side, we could bring life back to the dying Aeternum Stone and restore balance to our world. I was certain of it.

I would never let her go. She was mine.

Angels rarely mated with humans, and when they did,

they kept any offspring well-hidden. How in the world had Simon stumbled upon this rare gem? Most humans couldn't see auras, and I doubted Simon, Maximo, or any of their goons recognized what she was. Even Simon's witch seemed not to know.

Unfortunately, my two rivals weren't so dense.

I could see the lust and desire in their eyes. Across the room, Keir's gaze cut through my tight chest, a silent challenge etched in his sharp features. Trystan, always the embodiment of stoic resolve, observed from a distance, his now-glowing golden eyes saying that he would do anything to possess the Nephilim.

Keir and Trystan slowly advanced toward me. For once, I felt like the prey instead of the predator. I flashed my fangs, warning them to stay back, but it had about as much impact as a three-year-old sticking out his tongue. Neither of them cared.

A ball of panic fluttered in my chest, something I rarely experienced. I had to get out of here before I had to fight Keir and Trystan for the Nephilim. Marsha would never stand for that, and I couldn't afford to have her cast some draining spell on the Aeternum Stone.

Simon rushed over, dabbing at his sweaty brow with a handkerchief. "King Santi, my most sincere apologies. She's been...problematic. I fear the diazepam dose was perhaps too generous," he stammered, the worry in his voice bordering on panic.

"You fool." I flashed my fangs again. "Carelessness with her life would be a mistake you'd soon learn to regret, Simon."

Sweat rolled down his temples, and the blood drained from his face. He swallowed hard, his Adam's apple bobbing up and down. My reputation as the Angel of Death preceded me.

My enemies approached me and my prize. I refused to back down and show fear—fear wasn't an option.

Keir tilted his head back and forth thoughtfully as he assessed the Nephilim. He drew his slender brows into a frown, then moved to put his palm on her forehead.

"Don't touch her," I growled instantly.

He stepped back. "Very well." He hovered his palm over her forehead but didn't make contact with her skin. "She clings to life, but just barely," he announced, concern lacing his tone. Clearly he was as desperate to save his people's Anchoring Obsidian as I was our Aeternum Stone.

Trystan sniffed and shook his head miserably. "A grave mistake, Simon. Her value is beyond measure." His voice was laden with a mix of sorrow and condemnation.

Simon's face paled, and a tense breath escaped him. "B-beyond measure?" He looked down at the girl as if trying to figure out what made her so special.

Maximo looked down at the girl with disinterest. "She's beautiful, but lovelies like her are a dime a dozen. She's barely breathing, Santi. Let her go."

"No. I won't let her die." I shouldered my way through the onlookers, parting them like the Red Sea.

I didn't want to admit it, but Maximo was right. She was barely conscious, her breathing getting shallower by the minute.

Using my vampire speed, I raced up the grand staircase. I

could feel her heart beating weakly against my chest. I kicked open a door to one of Simon's luxurious bedrooms and gently laid her down on a red canopy bed. Without hesitation, I bit open my wrist and pressed it to her lips.

"Drink," I commanded. My blood would heal her injuries but wouldn't turn her into a vampire unless I willed it. And that was the last thing I wanted to do. If she became a vampire, she would be useless to me.

She lay on the canopy bed, her skin pale against the brilliantly white sheets beneath her. A thin red line of blood trickled down her chin, leaving a trail of crimson against her ghostly complexion. She remained motionless, resembling a sculpture of the Roman goddess Venus.

My muscles tensed. I balled my hands into tight fists, and as I tapped into my powers of persuasion, the familiar prickling sensation ran over my skin, every hair standing on end. I focused all my energy on her still form.

"Drink." My low voice echoed around the bedroom. The air crackled with my power.

I felt a slight tug on my wrist, and the corners of my mouth pulled up into a grin. Her lips pressed against my skin and sucked and sucked. She coughed and choked, twisting her head back and forth on the pillow. I pulled my arm away from her grasp and watched as she groaned and gasped for air. She was still under the effects of diazepam, but she was alive, and the realization shot a spark of hope through my tight chest.

The sound of boots thudding down the hallway caught my attention, and I spun around with a low growl. The door crashed open, and Keir burst into the room. His face was tense, but he attempted to flash me a smile. His eyes flicked to the girl stretched out on the bed.

"You saved her?"

I bared my teeth at him. "She's mine."

"Perhaps you should speak with Trystan and Simon." Keir tilted his head. "Trystan has made a higher bid for her if she survives."

I stiffened. "Remember what I took care of for you?" When Keir first came here, he had used my services to eliminate a deadly enemy.

Keir nodded solemnly. "Yes. And I told you I owed you."

"Exactly. So watch her. No one, and I mean no one, comes in here." I pointed directly at the girl. "And don't touch her."

Keir nodded slightly. "I won't let anyone take her..." I could hear the hidden message in his voice. His type never did anything without expecting something in return, but he also wouldn't want to defy me, not after I had helped him.

I stormed down the stairs to find Trystan and Simon conversing quietly in the corner.

As soon as Simon saw me, he let out a terrified shriek and ran away like a scared rabbit—as if he could outrun the Angel of Death.

Trystan's blue eyes turned gold, warning me he was about to shift into a wolf. But I didn't care—he wasn't my intended target.

With an angry snarl, I seized Simon by the throat, lifting him off the floor. He squirmed and struggled, kicking his feet in the air, but I held him firmly in place. As I bared my razor-sharp fangs, his eyes bulged, threatening to pop out of his skull.

Bringing him closer, I hissed at him. "You declared her sold to me. Do you honestly think you can go back on that?"

"But...he..." Simon gasped for air.

I squeezed his neck tighter, causing his face to turn bright red.

Tears streamed down his cheeks and spit ran out the corners of his mouth as he choked out the words, "No...she's...she's yours."

I dropped him like a sack of bricks, and he landed on the ground with a loud thud.

When I turned around, Trystan had gone, but I heard angry voices upstairs. Adrenaline pumping through me, I rushed up the stairs two steps at a time. Keir stood in front of the canopy bed with a sword drawn. I had no idea where Keir had gotten a sword, but I didn't care.

"Stand down, Keir," Trystan growled, the undercurrent of desperation in his voice cutting through the tension. His eyes, usually such a stoic mask of resolve, now betrayed his desperation. "I want the girl."

It wasn't just a demand—it was a plea. The Luparion Crystal, the heart of their unity and strength, was also fading, its once-vibrant pulse now a mere echo of its former power. This weakening not only risked the pack's cohesion but left them vulnerable to the enemies lurking at their borders.

As Trystan stood there, a formidable figure of raw power and barely contained need, the importance of the Nephilim to his cause became abundantly clear. I knew I would have a fight on my hands, but when did I ever back down from a fight?

"I bought her, Trystan." I walked around him. "You can't have her."

Trystan whirled around, his golden eyes glowing and his fingernails lengthening. "Only because you threatened Simon."

I glared at him. "You didn't even want her until I saved her."

Trystan laughed menacingly. "I'm a wolf. You actually think I couldn't smell whether or not she was alive?"

The bedroom was shrouded in darkness, lit only by the faint glow of moonlight filtering in through the curtains. The air crackled with tension as I stood my ground.

I gritted my teeth. "You'll have to get past me first, cur."

Trystan broke into a deadly smile. "With pleasure, vampire." With that, he shed his clothing piece by piece until he stood before me in all his naked glory.

As our gazes locked in a silent challenge, he began to shift. His muscles lengthened and bones cracked, fur sprouting rapidly until he stood before me not as a man, but as a beast of legend—the Wolf King himself. His golden eyes burned with a primal fury that set every killing instinct inside me on fire.

I could shift into a wolf, but he was more experienced at fighting as a wolf, so I stayed as I was.

Keir watched from the sidelines, his expressionless mask of boredom concealing his true thoughts well. I guessed his plan without him saying a word—use the chaos to his advantage and escape with the one capable of saving us all.

Trystan took a step toward me, gnashing his teeth.

My fingernails lengthened and my muscles tensed as Trystan lunged at me, his large wolf form bristling with fury. We collided in a fierce clash of vampire and werewolf, ancient enemies locked in an ancient battle.

The sound of snarls and growls filled the air as we fought, our movements fluid and calculated. I sank my teeth into his neck as he clawed my face, leaving deep gashes. Stinging pain exploded across my cheek. Blood poured from the wound. I could barely breathe.

I could feel Keir's gaze burning into me from the edge of my vision. Keir stood motionless, arms crossed and lips pressed to a thin line, calmly watching us tear each other apart.

I bit, slashed, and punched Trystan as hard as I could. His fur flew around me in bloody clumps. Waves and waves of vampire strength pumped through me like roaring floodwaters. I would have easily killed any other wolf by now, but this wasn't any other wolf. This was the Wolf King. He met each strike with equal force—ripping into my flesh, crunching his powerful jaws into my bones, spraying blood across the walls. Agony pulsed through me, but I didn't back down.

Neither did he.

Exhaustion started to settle into my muscles, and my strikes slowed. Trystan was panting as he backed up from me, weariness and pain flickering in his golden eyes. I gasped for breath, resting my hands on my knees, trying to regain my strength. The stakes were too high for me to give up. The fate of my people and possibly our very existence depended on the outcome of this fight.

Trystan snarled and lunged again, aiming for my throat. His feverish breath brushed over my sweaty face. I summoned every ounce of strength and smacked his snout as hard as I could. He whimpered, but still he wasn't done. He circled me as I panted hard.

I followed his movements, preparing for another attack. His hackles stood straight up, and he pulled back his lower lip into a snarl. I glanced over his head to see Keir lifting the Nephilim into his arms.

I locked eyes with Keir and gritted my teeth. "She's mine."

Trystan snapped his head around. I drew on every strained muscle and in that split second, when he was distracted, pushed the massive Wolf King, knocking him to the ground.

I leaped over the fallen wolf and raced toward Keir who held the captive girl in his arms.

"Keir," I roared, the force of the anger raging within me causing my chest to tighten and my body to tremble.

He paused, a flash of panic crossing his features. I punched him square in the jaw. Blood spewed onto his pristine shirt. The impact sent him reeling backward, and in his surprise, he loosened his hold on the girl just enough for me to wrench her from his arms, a jolt of adrenaline bursting through me and lending me strength I scarcely knew I possessed.

I hoisted her over my shoulder and looked around desperately for a means of escape. Trystan had risen, blocking the door. Keir stood poised, fury flashing in his eyes as he advanced on me. The only way out was through the picture window.

Keir saw what I meant to do. "Santi, no."

The room around me turned to a blur as I charged toward the closed window that stood as the only barrier between us and escape. The fury surging through my veins screamed for action, not caution.

Trystan was getting closer, his hot breath burning the back of my neck.

I put my shoulder to the glass like a wrecking ball. The window shattered with a resounding crash, shards flying like raindrops whipped up by a tempest. We were airborne for a moment that stretched into eternity, the night air rushing to meet us as we descended, the ground zooming up toward us.

We landed hard, a jarring impact that I somehow managed to shield her from with my own body. The grass beneath us did little to cushion the fall, but it was the softness of freedom compared to the bloody fray we had left behind. She would have the power to save my family, if I could only get her back to Crescent Manor.

I hurried to my waiting limousine, the sleek black vehicle already idling at the curb. Dimitri revved the powerful engine as I climbed inside. The tires squealed as we peeled out of the driveway and left Simon's grand antebellum estates. With each ragged breath I took, fresh agony pulsed through me and blood spurted down my body from the long gashes from the Wolf King's claws. My flesh hung from my arms, exposing the very bone. Exhaustion and agony gripped me. It would take some time for me to heal, especially with the Aeternum Stone fading. What used to only take a couple of hours to heal would need at least a day. I glanced through the tinted back window. I could see Trystan, still in his wolf form, and Keir standing in the dust kicked up by my speeding limo. Their grim expressions told me that I had just declared war on both the Wolf and the Dark Fae Mafias.

Chapter Six

Serenity

Boom Boom Boom

I groaned as I woke up with a pounding pain in my head. Sunlight pierced through gaps in the thick red curtains, and I cupped a shaky palm over my eyes to block it out. It felt like my head might split open at any moment.

My mouth had turned bitterly dry, and I couldn't swallow. Water, I needed water. I scanned the unfamiliar surroundings. Wow. If this was a prison, it was nicer than any prison I'd ever seen on tv. The bedroom looked like it was something out of a five-star hotel. Rather than being handcuffed to a chair, a plush goose down comforter enveloped me. My gaze drifted over the room, taking in the opulence and timeless elegance that surrounded me: High ceilings adorned with intricate moldings. Walls hung with tasteful art. A floor covered in a lush, deep red carpet that looked like it would swallow the sound of any movement. The air was perfumed with a subtle scent, an intoxicating blend that both comforted and soothed my pounding head.

But this was still a prison, and I was still someone's captive.

I forced my aching muscles to stretch and sat up on the bed. My mind was still hazy as I emerged from the deep sleep I'd been in. I sat on the edge of the bed, trying to collect my thoughts—a fragment of memory floating back to me of a deep, gravelly voice whispering in my ear, *"It's all right. I won't let anyone hurt you. You're mine."*

The words should have been comforting, but they filled me with a sense of impending doom. I had to escape this place, whatever it was, before it was too late.

I wiped the beads of sweat from my brow with a trembling hand. Beside the bed, a set of French doors stood slightly ajar, leading to freedom. Maybe this was my chance. I could jump out the window or possibly scream for help.

I flipped the quilt off me—

Crapcrapcrapcrap

I was completely naked. How did I get like this? My breath caught in my throat, and my racing heart pumped against my ribs as tears pushed against the back of my eyes. God, was I destined to be somebody's whore? I clenched my fists. Not happening. Not after I had escaped Freddie's hell.

I wrapped myself in the comforter, dragging it behind me like the train of a wedding gown as I edged toward the

French doors. A loud clink made me stiffen and glance over my shoulder. On a nightstand, there was a single glass of red wine next to a crystal decanter. I hadn't even noticed they were there, and somehow the edge of the comforter had caught the stem of the glass. Anger shot through me like a flaming arrow. I gritted my teeth. Had some creep been watching me sleep? Whose wineglass was that? Did it belong to the same pervert who stripped me out of my dress?

I headed over toward the nightstand, but the comforter pushed the glass again, clinking it against the decanter and sloshing the wine back and forth.

I held my breath, afraid someone would burst through the door, but nothing happened. I disentangled the comforter from the nightstand and headed back toward the French doors. My hand shaking, I reached for the handle, determined to find help.

"You can't escape," a male voice said behind me.

Shit

I forced myself to turn to look at the perv who thought he had bought me. Probably some shriveled up, elderly dude. But I froze and my breath left me as I gazed up at the towering figure that seemed to blend the wildness of nature with an unmistakable air of genteel nobility. His long, dark hair framed a face that was both rugged and hauntingly beautiful, with stormy, deep-set green eyes. His muscular physique, visible even beneath his casually elegant attire, spoke of strength and agility. There was an intricate tattoo on his neck that snaked toward his jawline; its inky lines almost pulsing with a life of their own. Blood droplets blended seamlessly into a vine with roses that bloomed in shades of a deep crimson, their beauty contrasting against the danger represented by their sharp thorns. My gaze landed on his cheek where there were deep scratches. They only made him look more rugged. This was a man who clearly lived on the edge of danger.

And he terrified me.

"You can't escape," he repeated, his voice deep. It resonated not with malice but a certain seriousness. It made me realize it wasn't a threat—just a simple statement of fact.

My chest constricted, and I fought to take a deep breath. "Why? Because you think you bought me?"

He cocked an amused eyebrow. "Think? Oh, I can assure you, you belong to me." His words hung heavy in the air between us.

I lifted my chin, trying to hide the quiver in my voice and ignoring the way my hands were shaking at my sides. "I won't be your whore."

My words actually came out stronger than I felt.

He casually lifted a shoulder. "Never said you would." His nonchalant attitude only made me angrier.

He brushed past me and shut the French doors, forcing me to back up and preventing any means of escape. As he went by, I inhaled his spicy scent, one that reminded me of cloves and ancient forests, a captivating blend that evoked thoughts of autumn woods veiled in mist and the warmth of a secluded cabin. His forceful presence was both intriguing and intimidating, and his aroma enveloped me in an unexpected sense of security amid my turmoil.

"Who are you?" I asked, instinctively inching away from

him, my back pressing against the cold wall. My only protection was the thick comforter still wrapped around me.

His rugged features were shadowed by the dim lighting in the room. "Angelo Santi," he said with a hint of smugness in his voice. He leaned against the door frame, casually crossing his arms over his chest as if he had all the time in the world.

The name sounded familiar, but my still-sluggish mind couldn't place it. I rubbed my sleek forehead as I tried to think of where I had heard it before. Something I saw on television, perhaps? My brain was too foggy to remember.

"You are free to roam around my home. But know that all my servants and guards are fiercely loyal to me. No one will help you escape."

That didn't mean I wouldn't try. I knew Joy would have reported me missing by now. I glanced at the French doors. Maybe if I screamed my head off, I could draw some policeman's attention and get the hell out of this place that way.

As if my reading my thoughts, his lips pulled into a sinister grin, and my heart skipped a beat. "If you even think about trying to escape, your dear friend Joy DuPont will pay the price." My blood ran cold at the mention of her name.

I narrowed my eyes. "How do you know about Joy?" Hatred laced every word.

"In my business," he put his hands behind his back and strolled around me, "I make a point of learning everything there is to know about a person. Their strengths, wants, weaknesses...In your case, she's a weakness."

"No, she's not. She's like—" I stopped short.

"Like a sister?" He gave me a knowing smile.

Anger nearly choked me. Joy was even more than that. She was the one that had helped me get away from Freddie—yes, she asked her brother to teach me how to use a knife, but she was the one who taught me how to fight. She was a black belt in karate. I wasn't nearly as good as she was, but I was no slouch either. "Stay away from Joy. She's not part of this."

He gave me a cool stare. "If you don't want her to become part of this, don't try to run away. You were lucky to escape Simon's auction. Your friend might not be so fortunate."

"I didn't escape the auction at all! According to you, I'm your property!" I couldn't keep the bitterness out of my tone.

"True, but you're lucky you're with me. There are others, such as Maximo Barone..."

That name I knew. My face paled and I could barely form the words, "The gangster?"

He looked amused. "If that's what you want to call him. If he had bought you...or if he were to buy your friend...I'm afraid—"

I held up my palm. Tears flickered in my eyes as my chest tightened and defeat crawled down my dry throat to settle in my gut. "All right. All right. Fine."

The fear of anything happening to her gripped my heart with icy terror.

He gave me a curious stare. "Fine? Fine, what?"

My shoulders slumped. "Fine, I won't try and escape."

He took a step closer, his breath reeking of copper and sulfur. "I'm sure you understand what will happen if you break your promise. Your friend will either end up sold or dead. The choice is yours." He lifted my chin with a sharp fingernail, causing me to tremble under his touch. His eyes burned into mine as he spoke.

"So, we have an accord?" His soft words stabbed my heart.

"You're a monster."

He cocked his eyebrow. "That's no answer."

"Yes, damn it. We *have an accord*," I spat. I couldn't stand the way his touch made me feel, but at the same time, there was something undeniably alluring about him. What was wrong with me? He was my captor, my enemy.

"Not a monster, by the way," he smirked, his green eyes flashing with red. "A vampire." He bared his razor-sharp fangs in a wicked smile.

"That's impossible," I protested, shaking my head in disbelief. "Vampires aren't real."

He became a blur as he crossed the room; the flick of a light switch seemed like an eternity in comparison. "Are you so sure about that?"

My heart thrashed in my chest like a wild animal desperate to escape. Oh, my god. How had he done that? I licked my lips nervously. "Yes. But even if they were real, based on what I've read, vampires can always heal their wounds. If you're a vampire, why do you have red scratches on your face?"

"I got into a scrape with a wolf," he purred, leaning in closer. "All the nightmares you have heard about—wolf shifters, Unseelie, Fae, witches, dragons, demons, vampires —we're all real."

He had to be insane. Those were just fairy tales and myths. What twisted game was he playing? Then it hit me that he hadn't answered my question about why he hadn't healed. Was he hiding something, or just plain lying?

"How long have I been here?" My voice was small, the question hanging between us.

"Two days," he answered, leaning closer. "You've been unconscious. The diazepam Simon administered took its toll, along with certain...other factors."

"Other factors?" I echoed, confusion lacing my voice.

He paused, as if choosing his next words carefully. "The process of healing you was not without its...complexities. But you're safe now, Serenity. You're in my home—Crescent Manor—in the French Quarter of New Orleans."

I stood my ground, refusing to back down despite the fear churning in my gut. "Safe?" I spat. "I'll only be safe when I'm out of here."

His piercing green eyes locked onto mine, his gaze boring into me like a target. "No, you won't. I wasn't the only one interested in buying you, Serenity. The minute you step out of here, they'll be after you."

My throat tightened as fear nearly choked me. I reached up and rubbed my forehead, trying to ease the tension that was building. "This is just one big, fat fucking nightmare." The frustration and despair in my voice didn't light a bit of compassion in his cold eyes, which seemed to be able to see into my very soul.

Angelo's intense gaze never faltered. "No nightmare. You're here, Serenity, because you hold the key to something far greater than you can imagine."

His use of my name felt intimate, like a lifeline to keep me grounded in a chaotic situation. But he wasn't a lifeline; he was the enemy who had taken my precious freedom away and threatened to hurt the ones I held dear.

I broke my gaze from his steely one and allowed my eyes to wander around the lavish bedroom again, taking in every detail. There was a painting on the wall of a two-story structure with wrought-iron balconies adorned with trailing greenery and flickering gas lamps that cast a warm, inviting glow. As I stared at it, a sense of déjà vu washed over me. I had seen that building before...on television, maybe? Yes! That was Crimson Stakes on Bourbon Street, one of the many gambling houses Freaky Freddie frequented. And it was owned by someone called Angelo Santi.

My heart sank as realization set in. This man in front of me was the head of one of the most notorious Mafia families in the city. The mere mention of his name struck terror into hearts, his ruthlessness the stuff of legend, which had led to him being known as the Angel of Death. Every hair on my body stood on end as the horrifying connection clicked into place. "Wait, you're Angelo Santi? You're ruthless, evil," I blurted. Fear shook my voice when I realized what I just said.

A smirk tugged at the corner of his lips. "Ah, so you have heard of me."

"Are you going to kill me?" My resolve was shattering.

He cupped my cheek. While repulsed, I was too scared to move. "Not at all, Serenity. I need you."

I swallowed the dread in my throat, wondering what he meant by that, aside from thinking I would be tastier than a McDonald's Happy Meal.

He dropped his hand. "My servant, Madame Elena Moreau, will assist you. Don't be foolish enough to think she will help you escape. She's been with me for years and her loyalty is unwavering."

He left me standing there, my back plastered against the bedroom wall, as I waited for Elena to come. God, she had to be a vampire too. She'd be a thousand times worse than Frances or Marsha.

I glanced around the room, looking for some kind of weapon. I picked up the wine glass, all set to throw it at her head. If Elena thought she could treat me like vampire chow, she'd be sorely disappointed.

A graceful figure swanned into the room, her silver hair styled in a chic bun and fastened with a single pearl pin. She wore a crisp white blouse tucked into a flowing red floral skirt, and her feet were clad in elegant red kitten heels. A warm smile played on her lips, revealing a dimple on her right cheek. She had a tattoo on her neck similar to Angelo's.

"*Bonjour, mademoiselle,* I am *Madame* Elena Moreau. Please, call me Elena," she greeted me in a soft French accent. Her piercing blue eyes swept over me with motherly concern. "I apologize for leaving you in such a state, but your attire was beyond salvaging. The master had me order new clothes for you, and they have only just now arrived. I hope they will meet with your approval."

I cleared my throat as I slowly put down the wine glass on a dresser. "Are you the one who undressed me?"

"*Oui.* The master insisted. Don't worry, he didn't come in here while I was cleaning you up. Chef is making quite a feast for you." She headed over to a door and opened it, revealing a luxurious bathroom. "Would you like to shower before I bring the clothes in?" She gave me a sympathetic look. "I think it might make you feel better." Her tone sounded genuine, but I wasn't sure I could trust her.

I wished I had a blade to defend myself. I would feel a million times better. But then again, what would a blade do against vampires? I needed a stake, not a knife.

Misery rolled over me at my plight. I had no choice but to follow Elena's suggestion. I was their prisoner, with no allies, and if I tried to escape, Angelo's threat had been clear: I would condemn my best friend to a life of horrors or even worse, Angelo could kill her. His enemies had a way of disappearing. She was more than a sister. She was my savior who had helped me to escape Freddie's clutches, and I would do anything to protect her—even if it meant staying in this nightmare willingly.

Chapter Seven

Angelo

I stepped out of the Nephilim's bedroom, my fists clenched and pulse racing, and focused on putting as much physical distance between me and Serenity as possible. Not because I was angry with her, but because I had to remember she was a means to a precious end. And yet she was also a flame, calling to me.

I didn't want to get burned.

I rubbed the scratches on my face. She was right—they should have completely healed by now. As the day grew to evening, the sun cast deeper shadows into my home. Each one seemed to whisper Vlad's name, a constant reminder that I was never truly alone.

My long strides took me down the hallway to my office. The antique sconces cast a flickering light that danced like the jazz musicians in the Quarter's lively night scene. Every step I took on the aged hardwood floors echoed the rhythm of my beating heart. No woman had had this effect on me in centuries.

As soon as I walked in, I saw Enzo perched in a leather armchair facing my desk. I studiously avoided his curious gaze. He would detect my rapid heartbeat and notice the beads of sweat that had broken out across my forehead immediately and want to know why. Nothing ever got me riled up like this except hunting an enemy.

He raised an eyebrow at me. "Is she awake?"

"Yes." I kept my face carefully arranged as I walked toward the large mahogany desk and took my seat behind it. My fingers clenched the armrests as I tried to calm the emotions roiling inside me.

"And?" he pressed.

I switched on my laptop. "And what?" My words came out crisper than I intended.

He let out an exasperated sigh and rolled his eyes. "Did you take the girl?" His tone was laced with irritation.

"No." I shook my head and pulled up the reports on our family enterprises, particularly the casino.

Enzo's jaw dropped and his eyes bulged. "What do you mean, no? She has the ability to activate the Aeternum Stone." He could barely keep his anger in check.

I glanced only quickly at Enzo before returning my attention to the reports in front of me, detailing recent disturbances at our gambling house. "The Nephilim must willingly offer herself to me for the stone to work. If I force her or use compulsion, her power won't be released, and we'll be no better off than we are now. No, I need to seduce her into truly wanting me." I sighed and rubbed my temples, trying to focus on the task at hand. "What's the latest update on Crimson Stakes?"

Enzo's lip curled into a sly grin, his eyes shining mischievously. "Do you really want me to go over the mundane reports, or would you rather talk about the Nephilim down the hall?"

I glared at him, my jaw tensing as I tried to contain my frustration.

He frowned. "I haven't seen you this upset since the Unseelie and the dark Fae moved into the French Quarter."

I refused to divulge anything to him, even though he was my closet ally and like a brother to me. I couldn't show any weakness, not even to him.

"Enzo. Tell me the reports on Crimson Stakes."

"What's going on outside it, you mean? The cops, including our friend, Detective Louis DuPont, have been making inquiries up and down Bourbon Street about the Nephilim."

I leaned back in my chair, puzzled. "Why does DuPont care about a missing girl? He's homicide." We'd tangled before and he considered me to be the devil incarnate. Maybe I was.

"Apparently, his daughter is this Nephilim's best friend. His daughter has been putting up missing person flyers all over town."

I cursed under my breath. I had been so focused on Serenity I hadn't had my people check Joy's activities. Not a mistake I would make again.

DuPont was a bulldog, and now his daughter would be a yapping chihuahua nipping at my heels. Wonderful. "I want you to watch the girl. See if she learns anything."

"And if she does?"

I shrugged. "Then...Serenity will have her best friend at her side."

Enzo tapped his fingers on the armrest meditatively. "There's something else. Two more murdered girls have been discovered in the French Quarter. Their bodies were found close to Crimson Stakes."

I narrowed my eyes. "That's not us. Who is doing it?"

He shrugged. "I don't know. DuPont is determined not only to find Serenity but to find out who's murdered these girls. I think DuPont believes Serenity might be the next victim. He also got wind of the auction at Ravenwood Estates and has become more than curious."

That wasn't good. "Does he know of our world?"

He shook his head. "Not yet. But the man's persistent."

I gnashed my teeth like a wolf. "We can't let him discover our world. That would bring Vlad out of the shadows and make him come after us with a vengeance." The mere thought of Dracula's looming presence made every hair on the back of my neck stand straight up.

He met my hard gaze. "What do you want me to do if DuPont gets too close?"

I shrugged. "Detectives die in the line of duty all the time. Just make sure it looks like an accident."

I wasn't sure, but I thought I saw hesitation in Enzo's eyes. And he never shrank from an assignment.

I steepled my hands and put my elbows on my desk. "What do you know of these girls?"

"Not much. I have an informant. He may know something about who is killing those girls—one of them may have come from Simon's stable, but I'm not sure. He's really paranoid and will only meet with me."

I sat back. "So meet with him. We need to know who is murdering these girls, especially if they are pinning the crimes on us." Suddenly I felt a need to have everyone I cared about close to me. Someone was setting me up, and it would be only a matter of time before they managed to hurt people I loved. "Tell Dimitri that he and Gianna need to come and stay here."

"She won't like it."

"Doesn't matter. Just tell them."

Enzo nodded. "Done—but, by the way, DuPont isn't the only one curious about these deaths."

I rubbed my forehead tiredly. "Let me guess. Palazzo and Tarus?"

"Yup. I suspect they'll be wanting to set up a meeting with you soon."

King Nico Palazzo was the actual king of the vampires. He had sworn allegiance to Vlad years ago and decreed that vampires follow Vlad's rules of not killing humans. But that decree wasn't observed by me and my family organization. We were a constant thorn in his side because of it.

Costin Tarus, meanwhile, was the headmaster of Red Rose Academy. He and the king were thick as thieves, and the headmaster frowned whenever one of his graduates forsook what they learned and switched their allegiance by joining my family.

They would love nothing more than for the Aeternum Stone to grow dark, thereby causing my organization to come crashing down.

I locked eyes with Enzo and gritted my teeth. "We can't let them know about Serenity's true power. The last thing we want is for them to prevent Serenity from revitalizing the Aeternum Stone."

Enzo's nod was grim and determined. "Agreed. But you won't be able to avoid taking a meeting with them unless you want to be at war with them too. I would have thought the wolves and the dark Fae were enough there."

I pondered the recent murders, massaging my stubbled jaw. "Do we have any leads? Could it in fact be the wolves or the dark Fae behind these gruesome deaths?"

Enzo gave me another helpless look. "I've reached out to our usual sources, but no one knows anything yet. Maybe my informant will have news today. Based on previous interactions, I highly doubt it is connected to the Barone family. But I'll do some digging, just to be sure."

There was a knock at the door. One of my guards, Lorenzo, peeked in hesitantly. Usually no one disturbed my meetings with Enzo, so this must be urgent.

"Summons for you, Angelo," he murmured quietly. "It's from King Nico. He's requesting that you meet him at Fandor Citadel."

Fandor Citadel was King Nico's plantation. It looked like any other plantation in New Orleans, but a wall surrounded it, keeping out the curious. I had no intention of going anywhere near it.

"He knows better than that. Tell the king's messenger that I will be happy to meet with him at St. John's Tavern tonight for dinner."

St. John's Tavern was a restaurant that was frequented by tourists and in which I was a silent partner. We would both be quite safe there.

My guard bowed slightly and left.

Enzo lifted his eyebrow. "Do you think the king will agree to that?"

"If he doesn't, we don't meet. Simple. Now, has Simon sent the three magical objects I bought at his auction: the Eclipsing Mirror, the Codex of Eldritch Lore, and the Phoenix Feather Quill?"

Enzo's brow furrowed as he shook his head. "N-no," he said uncomfortably, crossing his beefy arms over his chest. "Simon is holding your shipment hostage until you pay for the damage to his bedroom window."

I clenched my fists angrily. "He should know better than to try that. Send some of our guys to talk to him and make an example of the idiot. Meanwhile, I want you to meet with your informant."

A wicked grin spread across Enzo's face as he stood from his chair. "Consider it done," he said with a menacing glint in his eye. I knew Simon would soon regret making such a foolish demand.

As Enzo's heavy footsteps faded down the hall, I returned to my desk and sifted through the casino's financial reports. I scanned the list of names and numbers, mentally calculating all the interest that was piling up on these delinquent debts. It never ceased to amaze me how some people thought they could gamble away money they didn't have and then refuse to pay up when their luck ran out. A few strong-armed men would need to be sent out to collect what was owed.

"Angelo?" Madame Elena stood in the doorway. "You wanted me to let you know when Serenity was ready. She is in the dining room, and Chef is about to serve her lunch, if you would care to join her."

"Thank you, Elena. Did you have any trouble with her?"

"None at all; she was very polite. I must say she's very beautiful, but still, I detected that life hasn't been that easy for her."

Over the years, I had come to listen to Elena's impressions. She had a knack for reading people, and that ability had helped me out more than once.

I frowned. "What do you mean?"

She avoided my gaze and looked down at her red kitten heels as if they were the most interesting thing in the room.

"Elena?"

She lifted her gaze to me and wrung her hands. "I didn't want to tell you, but the poor girl has dreadful scars on her lower back."

"From Simon?" The words came out as a growl. My jaw clenched tight and my fists curled, ready to deliver the punishment that bastard deserved.

She shook her head. "No. They're not that recent."

"I see. Thank you, Elena."

Translation: be gentle with her. Well, I would be more

than gentle. I would find out who did this to Serenity, then pay them a little visit.

I stood up from my desk, the wooden floorboards creaking under my weight as I followed Elena out of the office. Serenity sat at a small round table in the dining room, the sunlight streaming in through the window behind her and casting a warm glow on her blue sundress. White daisies were embroidered all along the neckline, and her blonde hair cascaded down her back in gentle waves. Her eyes met mine warily, as if trying to decipher my intentions.

I flashed her one of my most charming smiles. "You look stunning."

"Thank you," she replied softly, but there was a hint of sadness and defeat in her voice.

As I took my seat across from her, I felt an unfamiliar sensation stirring within me—a mix of attraction and unease that I couldn't quite shake off. Ridiculous. I had been with countless women before, each one a forgettable conquest. Yet there was something about the Nephilim that made me feel off-balance, like I was fighting for control in uncharted territory.

I tried to maintain my composure, to view her as just another nameless woman that I would discard when she no longer served any purpose, but even as I told myself this, I found myself drawn to her in a way that unsettled me. Her presence ignited a desire I couldn't ignore, a longing I was determined to keep carefully concealed behind a mask of indifference.

Chef Gaultier had outdone himself today. He had prepared lobster rolls, their tender meat exuding the rich, succulent scent of the sea and lightly dressed in a delicate, lemon-infused mayonnaise that added a tangy freshness, all nestled within a freshly baked brioche bun. Beside them, the shrimp Greek salad offered a medley of crisp flavors—cucumbers and tomatoes freshly picked from the garden, mingled with the briny sweetness of the shrimp and the sharp bite of red onion. The olives and feta cheese, generously interspersed throughout, added depth with their earthy and salty notes, while a drizzle of olive oil and oregano finished the dish with an herby fragrance.

Chef Gaultier dished up fried potatoes, golden and crunchy, that added a comforting, homey smell to the meal. Each piece was a perfect blend of crispy exterior and fluffy interior, seasoned with a hint of rosemary and sea salt that made them irresistible. The sound of their sizzling as they were laid out on the serving platter still echoed faintly throughout the room.

Yet despite the sumptuous feast that lay before her, Serenity remained motionless, her expression filled with dread and apprehension.

I picked up a napkin and put it on my lap. "Aren't you hungry?"

She shook her head slightly and looked down at her lap.

"I assure you, the food isn't poisoned or otherwise doctored. With the drugs that Simon so foolishly gave you, you'll feel better sooner if you eat something."

"I'm not hungry," she said quietly. Such a lie. I could hear her stomach grumbling miserably from here.

I picked up a lobster roll with a pair of tongs and placed it on her plate. "Eat."

She lifted her eyes to me. "Is that an order?" Her voice was soft, but it still held a challenge, a challenge I couldn't back away from.

"If you'd like to take it that way. I can't allow you to damage yourself. You're too valuable to me."

She glared at me as if she would like to throttle me, but despite her apparent anger, she delicately picked up the lobster roll and took a bite. As she swallowed, her demeanor softened noticeably, a contented sigh escaping her lips as she savored the taste. The way she delicately handled the roll, the thoughtful pause as she appreciated the flavors, the relaxed ease that washed over her—it was a moment of pure gastronomic delight, captivating in its simplicity.

I watched transfixed as she continued to eat, each bite an alluring display of her enjoyment. Her slender fingers gripped the roll with a gentle yet firm touch, guiding it to her mouth with a grace that I found utterly mesmerizing. Within a few minutes, she had cleaned her plate, leaving me with a hungry desire, not just for the food, but for the woman before me.

My guard, Jacques Girard, came into the dining room and murmured into my ear, "Detective DuPont is waiting for you in the parlor."

Serenity snapped to attention and her eyes lit up like two firecrackers.

I patted my lips with a napkin. "Jacques, please return Serenity to her room. And make sure she stays there."

Serenity jumped up from the table and raced toward the hallway. "Louis!" she cried out.

Jacques grabbed her arm, and she unexpectedly back-handed him across the face. He snarled, revealing sharp teeth.

A raw, primal rage surged through me, fueled by a possessive instinct I had never experienced before.

"Never touch her again." My hands shook as I grabbed Jacques' throat, lifting him effortlessly off the ground. His face turned purple, and his eyes bulged as he struggled for breath.

"Louis, I need your help. Where are you?" Serenity ran out of the dining room.

Drawing on my vampire speed, I easily caught up with her and lifted her into my arms. Her heart was beating as wildly as mine. She kicked and screamed, her fear turning angry as she fought to escape. But I didn't care. All that mattered was keeping her safe. In a desperate attempt to silence her, I impulsively pressed my lips hard against hers, tasting the sweetness of her mouth and feeling an over-whelming desire to devour her completely. Her fists pounded against my chest, but I held on tighter, knowing that now I could never let her go.

Chapter Eight

Serenity

Angelo swept me into his arms, carrying me like I weighed nothing at all as he strode down the hallway. I struggled in his iron grip, but it was like trying to bend steel with my bare hands. His body was an unyieldingly solid mass of muscle and power that easily overpowered my own. As he held me closer, his lips descended upon mine, devouring me with a hunger that left me breathless.

His kiss was possessive, arrogantly claiming me as his. I gasped for air, both terrified and excited by the intensity of his desire. When we reached my door, Angelo shifted his hold on me, freeing one hand to turn the knob before carrying me inside and kicking the door shut behind us. He pressed me against the wall, his body pinning me in place as his hands began to roam hungrily over my curves.

I stumbled backward, falling onto the soft mattress of the bed. A shiver of terror ran through me as I looked up at him, his lips pulled back to reveal two long, sharp fangs glinting in the moonlight.

"N-no," I gasped, pushing against his chest with every ounce of my strength. But I might as well have tried to push a mountain aside or stop a freight train with my bare hands. It was as if he were carved from granite, unyielding and indestructible, a superhuman entity that defied the very laws of nature.

"DuPont!" I screamed for help, but my voice came out thready and weak.

There was no way he would hear me.

In a flash, Angelo's fangs pierced my neck, and I tensed, anticipating an agonizing onslaught of pain. But instead, an unexpected wave of euphoria washed over me, a pleasure so intense and all-encompassing that it threatened to unravel my very being. It was as if molten desire was coursing through my veins, setting every nerve ending ablaze with a blissful fire that consumed my entire existence.

My resistance crumbled faced with these overwhelming sensations. It was as if all my fears, doubts, and reservations had been incinerated, leaving behind only the desire to submit to him completely. My eyelids grew heavy, weighed down by the sheer force of pleasure engulfing me, and I found myself surrendering to Angelo in a way I would have never thought possible, my very soul laid bare before him.

"DuPont..." I mumbled again, drawing out his name. "Please...don't...let...him...kill me." My words faded away to nothing.

Angelo's tongue licked over my neck where he had bitten me, and he whispered low in my ear. "Sleep, little one. Know that no one will ever touch you again but me. I will protect you always. I will never let you go. You're mine." His soft voice welcomed me into a safety net that I never thought I would have again.

Not since Mom had died...

I found myself walking through the familiar landscape of my childhood. The vibrant color of azaleas, camellias, and crepe myrtles in full bloom filled my vision as I walked through my mom's garden.

The sweet fragrance of magnolia flowers surrounded me, bringing a sense of peace. I sat on the old swing hanging from the magnolia tree and watched my mom carefully pruning the lemon and orange trees. Behind her rose the majestic oak tree with its long branches draped in Spanish moss. As a small child, I used to imagine all sorts of fearsome creatures hiding in its shadows, but now it just brought back fond memories of outdoor picnics and playing tag with Joy and her brother, Steven.

Mom was pruning her favorite orange tree as I approached her.

"Mom." I rushed over to her.

She put down her clippers and embraced me. "Oh darling, I've missed you so much."

"Me too," I choked out as tears streamed down my cheeks.

She pulled away and cast a fond gaze over me. "You've turned into such a beautiful young woman."

I almost wished I hadn't. Maybe then I wouldn't be in this mess.

The words tumbled out of my mouth like a runaway train. "Mom, I've been kidnapped and sold at an auction." My voice quivered as I wiped away another tear.

"I know, honey." She squeezed my hand.

"And I can heal people now. How can I do this? You couldn't."

"Oh, Serenity." She cupped my face. "There are so many things I wish I'd had the courage to tell you."

I frowned. "You mean like about my father?" The question had haunted me for years.

My mother's eyes held a mixture of sadness and love. "Your father was a man caught between worlds, much like you yourself are now. His story is a piece of your puzzle, but not the one you need to solve it just yet."

"What does that mean?"

"Just know I loved your father with all my heart. You were my greatest joy after I lost him."

"Why...Why did he leave us?" It was a question I had asked her so many times, and she always avoided answering, but maybe now she would finally tell me.

She rubbed my arm. "You will find out in due time."

I wanted to scream.

"And another thing—if you loved my father so much, why did you marry Freddie?"

Her expression softened. "I married Freddie out of a misplaced hope and a desire for stability—for us. He wasn't always the way he is now. You might not remember that. But some gamblers are destined to lose, sweetheart. I see now. I should have bet on our strength together, yours and mine. I'm sorry."

As the dream faded, I found myself chasing other happy memories with her, reliving happier days...and then I drifted back to darker times...

Chapter Nine

Angelo

The coppery taste of Serenity's blood lingered on my lips, and I savored it with each languorous lick of my tongue. As the tingling sensations coursed through me, I could feel my strength returning. My wounds began to heal, as if a wave of power was rolling over me. It was unlike anything I had ever experienced before.

Not even with the Aeternum Stone.

I straightened my back, taking slow, measured breaths as I approached the living room. Despite my determination to push her out of my thoughts, Serenity's intoxicating aura lingered and teased at the edges of my mind. Enough! She was a distraction I couldn't afford to have. Distractions meant I wouldn't be at the top of my game, and in my world, that could prove deadly. Yet her blood called to me like a drug, and I couldn't shake the addiction.

No one would ever take her from me. Not Trystan. Not Keir. Definitely not the police. And if anyone dared to try, I would unleash an unstoppable fury on them that would leave a trail of broken bodies in its wake.

I set those thoughts aside as I entered the living room and saw Detective Louis DuPont standing in front of the marble fireplace. Clad in a tailored blue pinstripe suit that accentuated his athletic build, he turned his piercing blue eyes on me, his gaze intense in the dim light. His dark hair, styled in a neat cascade, added a youthful vigor to his sharp, chiseled features. Despite his relatively modest height, he carried himself with an undeniable command; the man had the sort of presence that filled the room without a word being spoken. His scowl, angry and deadly, flashed as he turned toward me, suggesting I was in for a stormy meeting.

I put on my best plastic smile. "Detective DuPont, to what do I owe the distinct pleasure?"

"Cut the crap, Santi. We need to talk about Serenity Bryce," he growled, his tone accusatory, hatred simmering beneath his words.

"I'm not quite sure who you're referring to," I said, moving to the buffet table. "Drink?" I offered, pouring myself a glass of red wine.

He declined with a curt shake of his head, refusing to play along. "You know damn well who that is. My investigation points directly to you being involved with her disappearance."

Interesting. Someone had a loose tongue and needed to be silenced—permanently.

Maintaining a neutral expression, I took a small sip of the Chianti. "Allegations require proof, Detective. And I doubt your supposed investigation has any. You seem to be grasping at straws."

His calm facade cracked slightly, a flicker of anger in his eyes. "Don't underestimate me, Santi. The truth has a way of coming out, and I won't stop until I expose you."

I met his gaze levelly. "Then I suggest you focus on facts, not fantasies. When you do, you'll find I have no part in this."

"What about the two murdered girls found in the French Quarter?" His question was designed to catch me off guard. It didn't work.

"Girls? What girls?" I asked innocently.

His jaw clenched, a mixture of frustration and determination. "They were found naked, beaten, and murdered in cold blood. Do you really expect me to believe you know nothing about this?"

"I assure you, Detective, my family is not involved in such barbaric acts. How exactly were they killed?" I asked, hoping he would reveal more. Compulsion was a tempting option, but it came with risks. When I had used it on the police in the past, their behavior had drawn unwanted attention from their superiors, leading to a flurry of questions I thought it best to avoid. Overusing it would only put my family under greater scrutiny.

No. I had other, more subtle ways to extract information.

DuPont hesitated, weighing the consequences of sharing more. "The circumstances surrounding their deaths are...unusual. What's even more intriguing is what we discovered with the bodies." He let the statement linger, a baited hook dangling in front of me.

If I didn't bite, I'd look guilty. "And what might that be?"

DuPont's eyes narrowed slightly, a hint of a smile playing at the corners of his mouth, as if he appreciated the game of cat and mouse we were playing. "Curiosity can be a double-edged sword, can't it, Mr. Santi? Let's just say, the details surrounding their unfortunate demise were...intriguing. One of the girls, Nancee Cruise, was a blackjack dealer in your casino. Did you know her?"

He looked at me, waiting for a reaction. I gave him an amused smile. "You don't think I do the hiring of blackjack dealers personally, do you?"

"I suppose not. Well, among the girls' belongings, items were found that raise more questions than answers. Items that could, hypothetically, connect several dots in ways one wouldn't expect. Ways that might conceivably lead to you, Mr. Santi."

I could practically feel him tightening the screws on me, trying to get me to tell him everything. Problem was, honestly? I was as much in the dark on this as he was. I didn't like it.

He paused, letting the implication hang in the air, a silent challenge to see if I would react or divulge any information that confirmed his suspicions. "But of course, I'm sure you wouldn't know anything about peculiar items found at crime scenes. After all, your establishments have quite the reputation for being—exclusive."

Shit. It sounded like someone was going out of their way to frame me and my family. It had to be either Trystan, Keir, or possibly even Maximo. Not Simon—even he wouldn't be dumb enough to do this over a broken bedroom window.

No, this was something else. This had to be some elaborate plan for them to get their hands on Serenity. Something I would never let happen. She was mine.

"I'm sorry you to disappoint you, Detective, but you're wasting your time here. Like I said earlier, my family doesn't have anything to do with the deaths of those poor, unfortunate girls, or with the missing girl." I gave him a curt smile. "If I hear anything, I'll, of course, be certain to pass it along to you."

"See that you do." He gave a nod, more to himself than to me. "Just remember, the longer this takes, the worse it is for everyone involved." He headed toward the front door then glanced over his shoulder. "And as for the girl...let's hope nothing happens to her."

Trust me, nothing will.

After he left, tension hung in the air, a silent acknowledgment of the dangerous game we were both playing.

Enzo entered the living room just as I was pouring myself another glass of wine. "I take it you want me to find out who has been singing to the police?"

I downed the crimson liquid, the burn of the alcohol warming my throat. My thoughts were consumed by Serenity and her blood, how I longed for more. "Yes, find them," I hissed through clenched teeth. "Bring them to me." As I spoke, my hands twitched with the urge to touch her body, to bring her pleasure.

"I will. While you were meeting with DuPont, I set some of my men to find out more about those murdered girls. As soon as I find out anything, I'll report back to you." He glanced at his watch. "I need to leave to meet with my informant right now, actually."

"Ask him about what the police know. Find out what it was that pointed to us."

He nodded curtly and left, and I headed back to my office to research more about these dead girls. Enzo said that they may be part of Simon's stable. Maybe I did have a lead there. Serenity had also been in Simon's clutches briefly. Maybe she saw or heard something. If she did, it could mean she had a target on her back.

I climbed the stairs to return to my office and research the girls. But before I could find any information on them, I came across a missing person report on Serenity, describing her kidnapping at the college. She had been taking her trash out when she'd been abducted. Her roommate, Joy, called tearfully for her to be returned. This was all news to me. Had Simon really become so desperate he'd started kidnapping girls off college campuses? There was more to this story, and I intended to find out what it was.

After Serenity's missing person story, I found newspaper articles briefly mentioning the two murdered girls, but the police reports provided little information. Their names, Nancee Cruise and Stella McClain, were given. They were both young women under the age of twenty-five, following an eerie pattern of unresolved stories. Nancee was discovered in the early morning by a jogger, her body lying between Jackson Square and the Moon Walk, her blonde hair fanned out like a grim halo in the grass near the famed tourist attractions.

Stella's story was equally disconcerting, found as she was by a local fisherman at dawn in City Park, amid the serene setting of ancient oaks and tranquil ponds. Her presence there was also an unnatural blemish on the landscape's beauty, her blonde locks mingling with the morning mist. Close to her was a cryptic note, partially soaked by the morning dew, with an enigmatic message that the police had not yet released to the public.

Their striking resemblance to each other had been noted, and they also bore a remarkable similarity to Serenity. This recurring detail of their blonde hair, now a haunting motif, seemed too pointed to be a mere coincidence. The reports made no real mention of their last known activities, only that they were both last seen at locations not far from where their lives were tragically cut short.

As I stared at Nancee's picture, the memories suddenly came rushing back like a tidal wave, threatening to drown me in a sea of guilt and regret. I remembered her now—a one night stand. She hadn't been part of Simon's stable. She'd been a blackjack dealer at Crimson Stakes. I remembered the way her blood had called to me, the way I had taken her in my arms and sunk my fangs into her soft, yielding flesh. I had tasted her essence, savored it like a fine wine, and then cast her aside.

She was just one of the many such encounters I had in my long life, but I hadn't killed her. Leaving a trail of bodies would stupidly draw attention to me and my family.

As the head of the Santi family, I had a certain reputation to uphold. I couldn't afford to let my past indiscretions come back to haunt me, but it seemed someone was determined to do just that. Was it DuPont who had discovered my secret? Was he trying to frame me for Nancee's murder in some kind of twisted power play?

I stared at Stella McClain's picture. I had no recollection of her being one of my conquests. But there was something about her...I had seen her somewhere...According to Crimson Stakes' personnel records, she'd never worked for me. Maybe I had met her on Bourbon Street at another bar? Or during Mardi Gras? Or possibly Simon's? I could have fucked her, fed on her, and not remembered it, possibly even killed her. But if I had done that, I would have buried her body where no one would have discovered it.

No, this was different. Sloppy. Someone was leaving a trail of dead bodies pointing to me as the killer. I had to find out who was behind these murders and why they were trying to frame me.

As a vampire, I was no stranger to death, but this was different. This was a threat to my family, my power, everything I had built. I wouldn't stand for it. I would hunt down the killer and make them pay for daring to challenge the Santi family.

I pinned my hopes on Enzo and his informant to unearth more clues. The pieces of this particular puzzle were scattered everywhere, and I needed to fit them together before Detective DuPont did.

I needed answers, ones that only the shadows whispered. Picking up my phone, I dialed. Keir answered on the first ring, his voice a calm, cool breeze in the stifling heat of my concerns.

"Santi. I didn't think I would hear from you after the auction." His tone was a combination of annoyance laced with begrudging understanding.

"I wouldn't be calling unless I was forced to, Keir," I growled, cutting straight to the heart of the matter. "I assume you've heard of these two dead girls?"

"I have. Detective DuPont made a house call to me. From what I understand, he also paid a visit to the wolves."

I flipped through the security camera coverage at Crimson Stakes, hunting for past footage of Nancee. According to the newspapers, she had been killed five days ago. "Did you learn anything from him?"

A brief silence followed, not of hesitation but of consideration. "Only that one of the dead girls was a dealer at your Crimson Stakes, and the other was a waitress at Trystan's Lunar Majesty."

I stopped scrolling and sat up. "Was she a wolf?"

"Trystan's not saying. You know how wolves are about protecting their pack."

Maybe Trystan wasn't involved, not if one of his own had been killed. Trystan was fiercely loyal to his pack and didn't kill innocents. I frowned. If it wasn't us, and it wasn't the wolves, perhaps I was talking to the one who had ordered the murders right now.

As if reading my thoughts, Keir sighed. "In case you're wondering, it wasn't me."

"How do I know that's true?"

"I guess you're going to have to trust me."

Like I did at Simon's, when you tried to steal Serenity from me?

I held my tongue, deciding to focus on the matter at hand. "Did you tell DuPont anything about the auction?"

"What, and incriminate myself?" Keir's tone betrayed no surprise, only a readiness to delve into the depths of the problem. "Do you suspect there's more at play here?"

"Exactly. There are connections I can't see yet, chess pieces missing from the board. And there's DuPont, sniffing around like a dog who knows where all the bones are buried," I said, my frustration mounting. "I need your sight, Keir. The kind that sees through the veils in a way that others can't."

His chuckle was soft, almost inaudible, yet it carried the confidence of one who held many cards in his hands. He would definitely deserve a favor from me in the end, but if he thought that favor was Serenity, he would be sorely disappointed. "Your trust in the dark Fae is not misplaced, Angelo. Let's see what we can uncover together. The shadows often speak more truthfully to those willing to listen. This time, however, you will owe me."

"I understand that. I wouldn't be calling if I had anywhere else to turn. The police are getting too close, and I can't afford any missteps. I must warn you, though, if I suspect a betrayal on your part against me, my family, or the Nephilim..."

"Understood." I could hear the note of fear in his voice, much as he tried to hide it. "Give me some time to...consult my sources. I'll find out what I can about the girls and why the police suspect you."

"Thanks, Keir. Like you said, I owe you one." The last thing I wanted was to owe a favor to the dark Fae King. Knowing him, he would try to wiggle something out of me that he wanted, like Serenity or one of the magical objects I possessed, or request I give up some territory to him. He had always wanted Crimson Stakes for its prime location. I might be willing to bargain with a magical object, but Serenity and Crimson Stakes were off the table.

If he pushed for either of those, most likely a war would break out between us. I would die protecting what was mine.

"Perhaps," he said, a hint of amusement in his voice. "But let's not count debts just yet. Talk soon, Santi." His smooth tone didn't do anything to dispel my suspicions.

The call ended, leaving me sitting silently in my office, the weight of the unsolved mystery pressing down on me. At least with Keir now on the hunt, the shadows that obscured the truth might become less impenetrable. I would also soon find out if he was an ally or an enemy.

I went back to studying the security tape at Crimson Stakes, losing all sense of time as I watched Nancee's every movement. She had done her job as a blackjack dealer well— she smiled, dealt cards, and made money for the house. There was some light flirting, but nothing out of the ordinary. I had to be missing something, something right under my nose.

Hurried footsteps pounded down the hallway. Lorenzo burst into my office, panting, his eyes huge. "Sir, Enzo's been attacked. I think...I think he's dying."

Chapter Ten

Serenity

Someone was shaking me gently. "Serenity, Serenity. Wake up, *mademoiselle*."

My eyes fluttered open. Tears streamed down my face, and I couldn't stop trembling. Not from fear, but from missing my mom. It had seemed so real...but I guess not.

Elena's face hovered over me, her face filled with concern. "*Mademoiselle*, what's wrong?"

"Nothing, just a bad dream," I grumbled. I didn't want to talk about my mom with her or anyone. The only person who really understood how I felt was Joy. But I couldn't reach out to her, since Angelo had as good as threatened to kill her if I did.

"*S'il te plaît*, you must come with me immediately." Her tone was tense and serious.

A chill ran down my spine as I noticed the wild look in her eyes. Why? Was Angelo hungry? Or did they all plan to feast on me? Here, I was nothing but prey.

I immediately put my hand over my neck and scooted away from her. "I'm...I'm not going to let anyone suck my blood."

Including Angelo.

She cast me a startled look. "*Mademoiselle*, no one would dare feed on you against your will." She put her hand on her chest. "Angelo has given strict instructions to that effect, and no one defies him. No, we have someone injured and Angelo said you might have the power to heal him."

Like a beast with sharp teeth, doubt gnawed at my gut. I didn't trust her or anyone else in this bloodthirsty place.

She cast me a pleading look. "Please, *mademoiselle*...He's dying."

I sat straight up in bed. "Who?" What did she mean, a vampire was dying? As in staked through the heart?

"Enzo. Please, come." Her voice choked on those three little words.

Elena's earlier warm and friendly demeanor had vanished, replaced by a sense of desperate urgency that sent my nerves jangling. She led me through the dimly lit hall-ways, her pace brisk and purposeful, as if every second counted. My mind raced with possibilities, each one more terrifying than the last. Who was this Enzo? How badly was he hurt? Why did Angelo think I could help him?

As we approached the bedroom door, I steeled myself, my heart pounding against my ribs like a caged bird desperate for escape. Elena pushed the door open, and I held my breath, bracing myself for the worst—perhaps the sight of a vampire covered in blood, his life hanging by a thread.

Even so, when I entered, a gasp flew from my lips, my body reacting before my mind could fully comprehend what I was seeing. A half-naked man lay sprawled on the bed, his chest a mangled mess of torn flesh and glistening crimson. Three deep, jagged gashes ran from his collarbone to his abdomen, weeping rivulets of blood that pooled on the sheets beneath him.

But the true nightmare was the gruesome wound on his neck. Blood spurted from the gaping hole, pulsing with each weakening beat of his heart. It cascaded down the side of his throat, painting his deathly white skin a sickening shade of scarlet. The metallic scent of blood hung heavy in the air, so thick I could almost taste it on my tongue.

My mind reeled, unable to comprehend the sheer brutality of what I was seeing. This level of violence was something I had only ever witnessed on a movie screen, a fictional horror that I could distance myself from. But now, confronted with the raw, visceral reality of it, my sanity teetered on the edge of the abyss.

Ohgod Ohgod Ohgod Ohgod

A scream bubbled up in my throat, but I clamped my hands over my mouth and nose, desperately trying to hold it back. My heart pounded against my ribs, and bile rose in my throat as the coppery stench of blood assaulted my nostrils again. I wanted to run, to tear my eyes away from the nightmarish scene, but I was rooted to the spot, transfixed by the horror of it all.

Angelo's piercing gaze locked on mine, his green eyes cold. "This is my enforcer, Enzo. You need to heal him." The ice in his voice matched the frostiness of his stare.

As my chest heaved, I gulped the air like a fish out of water. Did he really expect me to heal these wounds? If I couldn't, would I be lying next to Enzo in an equally bloody mess? I glanced around the room, frantically searching for any semblance of medical supplies. But all I saw was a wooden table covered in blood and various sharp objects scattered on the floor. He lay on the bed, his body battered and bruised, looking like a victim of Michael Myers. My stomach churned as I realized how serious this situation truly was.

I looked over my shoulder. The guard stood in the doorway like an immobile statue. I swallowed the terror in my throat. "How?" My meek and soft voice didn't melt the coldness in Angelo's eyes.

"I know of your ability," he said simply. "You need to draw on it to heal him." His low voice was a challenge, and I wondered again if I would end up like Enzo if I failed.

I watched in horror as the man lying on the bed struggled to breathe. He moaned, his throat making wet gurgling sounds and his body convulsing in pain. He was a vampire, stronger than any human. When I saw the panic in his eyes and the way he threatened to lose consciousness, my heart and lungs turned cold. I had only healed small aliments like when Joy bumped her head on the floor. "But he's...he's a vampire. Can't he heal himself?"

Angelo arched an eyebrow. "Does it *look* like he's healing

himself?" Angelo's tone was surprisingly calm, but I could see the agitation in his green eyes.

My eyes burned, my throat squeezed, and a sob bubbled up from my chest. "Angelo, I can't heal him. He needs a hospital."

He rested his hand gently on the poor man's shoulder. "No, Serenity. He needs you." He lifted his cold gaze and locked onto mine. "This is why I bought you. You have a unique ability, and you're more powerful than you probably even know." His words spread over me like a bitter frost, freezing my heart, my lungs, and my will to move.

And there it was. The reason why I was a slave in this place. He'd bought me because he thought I was some mage or sorceress. If he only saw the marks on my lower back, he would know that wasn't true. I couldn't even heal my own wounds.

And yet he was Angelo Santi, the Angel of Death. If I disobeyed him and didn't heal his enforcer, I wouldn't be of any further use to him, and I would become one of his countless victims. Terror finally got my shaking legs to move. I stepped back like a doe ready to bolt to safety, but instead I ran into Jacques. There was no way I was getting out of here.

Elena clasped my arm gently. I looked at her wildly; I'd forgotten she was even here. "Serenity, please, you can do this." Her soft voice couldn't douse the panic flickering inside me, ready to explode into an inferno.

Angelo stepped around the bed like a panther stalking his prey. I could barely breathe. God, he was going to bite me again, rip my throat out until I looked like the poor man on the bed.

I wriggled my arm free from Elena and stood there quivering, a lamb ready to be slaughtered.

His eyes burning red, he grabbed my shoulders firmly. It was enough to startle me out of panic, but not enough to cause pain. Why were his eyes red? Was he going to suck my blood again?

"You need to believe in yourself, Serenity. You can do this." He stepped aside, clearing a path to the injured man.

If I didn't at least try, I knew my punishment would be even greater. I had no choice but to indulge in his delusion.

I forced my wobbly legs to move closer to the man and stretched out my trembling hand. I drew on my power—power that I knew wasn't strong enough to heal him. But I wouldn't give up. That wasn't in my nature. Even if this man was a vampire and had committed unspeakable acts, he didn't deserve to suffer like this.

Squeezing my eyes, I placed my palm on his arm. As I feared, nothing happened.

Please please please help him

I repeated the words in my mind, calling out to that small healing ability I had, but I was met with silence. Just as I was about to give up, a quiver rippled through me, starting at the base of my spine and spreading through me like wildfire. Nothing like this had ever happened before.

The tingling sensation danced across my skin, growing stronger with each passing second. I wanted to pull my hand away, but something kept it locked to the man's arm. Something was pulling the power out of me, something unknown, something that terrified me. Warmth rushed over me as if I was bathed in sunlight. But then my teeth chattered, and my body shook violently and uncontrollably. Tears streamed down my face and wetness gushed from my nose. Unable to control my movements any longer, I snapped my head back as the overpowering energy flowed through me.

Strong arms caught me and lifted me off the ground.

"See what you did?" Angelo whispered in my ear. I couldn't tell if he was angry or disappointed or happy.

Gasping for breath, I opened my eyes. The man had stopped bleeding and making that horrible gurgling noise. His chest moved up and then down, and I thought it looked like he could breathe normally, but I wasn't sure. His white, ashen color had faded, replaced with a normal hue. Angelo guided me to a red velvet Queen Anne's chair that I hadn't even noticed was in the room and sat me down.

"I don't understand how I could have done this," I whispered. "I can't even heal myself."

Elena rushed out of the bathroom with wet towels and wiped away the dried and caked blood on his chest and neck. His gaping neck wound had healed, but he still had three nasty cuts across his chest. I trembled in the chair, wondering numbly if Angelo was going to beat me, because I had failed to heal Enzo completely.

Angelo took one of the damp towels and wiped the blood off my upper lip. "Does this usually happen when you heal someone?"

I frowned as I tried to process his unexpected question. "What?" The word fell from my lips, barely more than a breath, as I struggled to comprehend the sudden shift in his demeanor.

He reached out, his fingers surprisingly tender as they brushed against my skin, wiping away the dampness on my face. The gentleness of his touch sent a shiver down my spine, so unlike the fear and tension that had consumed me mere moments ago. I found myself leaning into his touch, craving the comfort it provided, even as another part of me recoiled at the thought of finding solace in my captor's touch.

As he withdrew his hand, I noticed the crimson stains on his fingertips. "Do you get a bloody nose after you heal someone?" he asked, his voice softer now, almost concerned.

I nodded. "Yes." It was all I could muster.

Please don't bite me again.

"You saved my enforcer's life." Angelo looked down at me, his face was still hard as a stone, not a crack of emotion coming through. "Not just my enforcer. My closest friend. I will not forget that."

I wasn't sure where this was going. "Meaning?"

"Meaning thank you. I am in your debt. Is there something I can do for you? Other than granting your freedom, of course. I'm afraid that's not possible."

"Please don't bite me again?" I whispered. The plea was worthless. He was an ancient vampire, and I was just food for him.

Elena blinked, as if she couldn't believe what she was hearing.

Angelo's look was calm, but there was a hardness there, the same hardness I had seen when he first attacked me. I had struck a nerve somehow, one that could involve punishment.

"I suggest you think of something else." Meaning he would feed on me at will?

I let the question that had been haunting me escape my lips: "How about information, then. Did you kill Detective Louis DuPont?"

He studied me curiously. "He's important to you?"

I hated giving him the slightest bit of intel about me, but I had to know that he hadn't killed that sweet man. "Yes. Did you?"

A small glimmer of surprise flickered in his gaze before his eyes hardened once again. "No, he's alive. He hasn't crossed me...yet."

My heart thudded as I took in his words, realizing that this powerful mobster and vampire had control over the life of a man I cared about deeply. I narrowed my eyes. "But if he does, his life is forfeit?" The sharp words stung my mouth like a wasp.

He held my gaze steadily, not saying a word. My blood thumped in my temples as I waited for his answer. Finally—

"He will pay the ultimate price, yes." His words cut through the tense silence like a knife.

A twinge of anger pricked me at the unfairness of it all. "He's a cop. You're a mobster and a vampire. Of course he's going to cross you."

A slight smirk formed on his lips. "Detective DuPont and I have played this game of chess together for quite some time. The only thing that would cost him his life would be if he tried to take you from me."

With Angelo threatening another person that I cared

about, now both Joy's and her father's lives were at stake. I sagged in defeat, refusing to cry, much as I wanted to.

"Is there anything else you desire? Something I can actually grant you?" His offhanded question sent rage swirling through me. Two could play this game. I'd make him think that I was a meek and mild victim.

I swallowed back a sharp retort and instead forced a demure smile, trying to mask the turmoil raging inside me. "Could I please have a small television in my room?" My voice sounded distant, as if it belonged to someone else. I looked down at my trembling hands, still stained with Enzo's blood. The crimson streaks stood out starkly against my pale skin, reminding me of the horror I had just experienced.

My gaze then drifted to my blue sundress, once a symbol of innocence, now marred with the same sickening red. The blood had smeared across the fabric, leaving what looked like macabre finger-painted flowers. The sight made my stomach turn, and I fought the urge to rip the dress from my body.

"And I need to take a shower right now," I added, my voice barely audible. I couldn't bear to look at the blood any longer, couldn't stand the feel of it drying on my skin. I needed to wash it away to cleanse myself of the physical reminders of the nightmare—even though I knew no matter how hard I scrubbed, the memory of healing Enzo would be forever etched into my mind.

Angelo's face softened. "I'll escort you to your room." He turned to Jacques. "Send someone to purchase a television for Serenity."

Jacques immediately left to carry out the order.

I glanced up at Angelo's wooden face. He wasn't looking at me, but at the man stretched out on the bed. I couldn't believe he had granted my small request so quickly. Maybe this was my way out. If I continued to please him, maybe... just maybe...he would grant me my freedom.

Chapter Eleven

Angelo

Guilt slid down my throat as if I had swallowed vinegar, the bitter taste of my selfishness consuming me. Enzo was like a brother to me, yet I hadn't revealed to him, or indeed anyone else, that it was Serenity's blood that had healed my wounds. If he had fed on her, her blood would have healed him and made him even stronger, but I couldn't bear the thought of even my best friend feasting on her. She was mine and mine alone.

My family was growing desperate; I feared they would attack her to survive, draining her dry. That couldn't happen. I had to protect her.

I had suspected that, as a Nephilim, there was another way Serenity could heal someone besides her blood, and I was right. When she touched Enzo's shoulder, I had watched transfixed as a stream of white light flowed from her and into him. Even in his unconscious state, he was still surrounded by a soft, white glow that matched Serenity's own aura. I couldn't believe what I was seeing—her healing abilities were beyond anything I had imagined.

She sat on the velvet chair, her once-vibrant energy now almost completely depleted, visibly struggling with a bloody nose. The guilt of using her in this way weighed heavily on my conscience, but there had been no other option. Her life —and Enzo's—had depended on it.

She had mentioned she couldn't heal her own wounds. That was something I would have to investigate. Was she referring to the scars on her lower back?

Granting her small request for a television and access to a shower seemed trivial compared to what she had done for me.

Serenity stared at Enzo as if in a daze. "Who did this to him?" She looked at me inquisitively, waiting for me to expand, but it was better that she not know.

So I only gave her a reassuring smile. "Someone who will regret what they did." Something in my voice must have frightened her. Fear crept into her eyes, and she looked away. Her face grew pale, as if she was about to pass out. What was wrong with me? I was terrifying the poor girl. I had to get her out of here.

She sighed and glanced down at my enforcer, concern in her eyes. "W-will he live?" Her voice shook as hard as her body.

I took a deep breath, forcing the turmoil inside me to settle, and plastered a smile on my face. "Enzo will be in good hands with Elena. She's as skilled as any healer in our ranks." I winked. "Well, except for you." My words were calm and confident, but inside, my emotions were swirling like a storm.

Elena wiped Enzo's face with a damp cloth. "*Oui, bien sûr*, I will take care of him."

I gestured with my hand toward the door. "Please, come with me. I'll take you to your room so you can have that shower."

Serenity got out of the chair but swayed as if she was about to topple over. I clasped her arm to steady her, and she placed her hand over mine. As her fingertips, smeared with Enzo's blood, brushed against my skin, a jolt of electricity coursed through my body. The centuries-old walls around me began to crumble, and I felt more drawn to her than I ever had to any other woman.

We walked in silence back to her bedroom. I stole a sidelong glance at her. Such a young girl, with such power pulsing within her, though she remained unaware of it. Her blood was like a gift from the gods. I cursed my foolishness. Of course it was. Her father was an angel. I just didn't know yet how truly powerful her blood was.

We stopped in front of her door. "Are you going to be all right?"

"I'll be fine," she mumbled as she opened the door.

"Come back out here when you're finished."

She glanced warily at me, then shut the door behind her.

I waited outside Serenity's room for her to finish her shower, wishing I had used the word please. Barking orders was so routine to me, I had forgotten to who I was talking.

Several minutes later, the door opened and Serenity emerged, now wearing a pair of jeans and a loose black T-shirt and smelling clean and fresh, like a summer breeze over the ocean. Somehow the casual attire made her even more enticing to me.

Her eyes were still dazed, as if she was not yet done processing what had happened. She was clearly still in shock over what had happened to Enzo and her ability to heal him.

I gave her a warm smile. "Feel better?"

She nodded. "I guess..." But I could hear the hollowness in her voice and see the way her hands still trembled.

I clasped her shaking hand. "Come with me. I have a surprise for you." I tried to soften my voice, so it sounded more like a request than an order.

She followed me without question.

I led Serenity down the hallway. "Shall I tell you how you did this?"

Her steps faltered, and she looked up at me, her eyes searching. "You know?" I couldn't miss the wariness in her voice.

"Yes, I do," I chuckled as I opened the door.

Serenity's breath hitched as I led her into the immense library, her gaze filled with astonishment as she beheld the grandeur surrounding her. The floor-to-ceiling shelves were filled with books, their spines adorned with intricate designs and gold-embossed titles. Our steps echoed through the expansive space as we walked.

My collection was more than a mere display of wealth or status; it held rare tomes and manuscripts that could not be found anywhere else. The room was filled with the intoxicating aroma of aged paper, and the silence was broken only by the sound of our footsteps. Looking at my vast library, I couldn't help but feel a sense of accomplishment; these books held not only incredible stories but also told the tale of my own journey through time. This was my sanctuary, where I could escape and continue my never-ending quest for understanding and knowledge, a quest that spanned centuries.

"Oh my gosh." She released my hand and ran her fingertips along the book spines. "This is incredible."

I headed over to a shelf filled with particularly ancient tomes and pulled out a thick book. "I have something you may find interesting."

She peered over my shoulder, leaning in for a closer look. "Is that a book about angels?"

I inhaled her delicate fragrance of dewy roses which lingered in the air. It made my mouth water.

"Yes, it is," I said, a small smile forming on my lips. "I want you to discover your heritage."

She let out a laugh as she straightened back up. "Angels?" She put her hand to her chest. "You think my healing ability has something to do with angels?"

"I do. And I think you need to discover it for yourself."

Her arms immediately crossed over her chest defensively. "I loved my mom, but she was no angel."

I looked at her patiently, waiting for the penny to drop. "And your father?"

The amusement in her eyes disappeared and was instantly replaced with pain. She shook her head and looked away. "I don't want to talk about him."

I studied her. "Is he the one that left marks on your back?"

Her cheeks flushed. "I thought you didn't see me naked."

"I didn't." I cupped her chin, brushing my finger over her cheek. "Elena told me."

She pulled away from me, tears forming in her eyes. "No, it wasn't my father."

"Then who?"

She wiped the tears that were now rolling down her cheeks. "Why do you care?" The pain in her statement touched me.

"Because I protect what's mine. I promise you, whoever did this to you will never hurt you again."

She lifted her chin in defiance. "He hurt me when I was younger, but not anymore." Still she kept who hurt her a secret, but that wouldn't last for much longer.

I ran the back of my hand down her wet cheek. "Maybe it's time you let someone take care of you."

"Someone like you? As you keep saying, I'm a prisoner here. I'm not sure that's the same as being protected."

She deserved honest answers on what she truly was. "Hiding from your past and your true nature won't help you, Serenity. In fact, it could be dangerous. In these books, this one in particular, I think you will find the answers to questions you never got answered." I brushed a lock of her hair off her face and felt her tremble beneath my touch, whether from fear or something else, I didn't know. "Face your past, Serenity."

"I think you're wrong." But I could hear the doubt in her voice. And the curiosity.

"Serenity, I want to offer you knowledge. Knowledge about who we are, about your power, about how you fit into this world that's so new to you," I said, hoping to bridge the gap between us with understanding and trust.

She considered my words, the tension in her shoulders easing slightly. "If I find out you're wrong, then will you promise me no more secrets? No more half-truths, either." She held my gaze, daring me to take up her challenge.

"No more secrets," I agreed, feeling the weight of my vow more than any other oath I'd sworn before. I extended my hand, and we shook on it.

But I wasn't ready to tell her about the Aeternum Stone. Not yet.

Chapter Twelve

Angelo

There was a discreet tap on the door. I glanced around to see Petar Dragan, Dimitri's father, standing in the doorway. He had had a hand in introducing my sister to her husband. As usual, his hair was slicked back, and his eyes were shifty. Petar had a habit of switching allegiances to suit his changing purposes. He had sworn allegiance to Grayson Allen, who defied Dracula's rules. Grayson had wanted to kill King Nico and had even made a deal with a demon in an attempt to seize the crown. But his plans had backfired, and Petar had been caught in the crossfire. I had found him dying in St. Louis Cathedral. He had been supplying me with blood ever since and proved useful in other ways as well.

He held out a note. "Excuse me sir, you have a message from the king."

Serenity lifted a skeptical brow. "Just how many kings are there in New Orleans, anyway?"

I took the note from Petar and scanned it. Good. King Nico had accepted my invitation for dinner at St. John's Tavern. The meeting was in less than an hour. "Technically, King Nico is the only real king. He's the king of the vampires. The rest of us are kings over our Mafia families—Trystan Hunter is the Wolf King and Keir Rankin is the dark Fae King." I slipped the note into my jacket pocket.

Jacques approached and coughed discreetly. "Sir, Serenity's television has been installed in her room as you requested."

"Good. I'd like you to stay and guard her while she looks through the library. She has access to anything she wishes."

Serenity looked at me in confusion. "Where are you going?"

"I have a dinner meeting I must attend. If you get hungry, let Jacques know, and he'll have something prepared for you. Perhaps when I return, you and I can discuss what you've learned."

She crossed her arms. "How do I know I can trust you?" I could see that faith in me wouldn't come easy for her. Unfortunately, I needed the Nephilim to have just that.

I lifted her stubborn chin and caressed her soft flesh with my finger. "That is something you'll have to figure out for yourself."

She studied me with blue eyes that reminded me of the deep sea. I released her and, without another word, left her to discover her heritage.

"Petar, come. You'll accompany me to St. John's." I

didn't completely trust him, especially around Serenity, since he had such a deep-seated hatred for the angels.

His presence at dinner would also definitely unnerve King Nico and Costin, making it easier for me to obtain information from them. Together with me and my family, he was number one on their list of enemies.

Dimitri pulled the limousine up next to St. John's Tavern, then opened the door for Petar to get out of the car. Their relationship was a strained one. Petar held higher rank in my family because I needed his connections for human blood, despite Dimitri actually being married to my sister.

I glanced at Dimitri. "Keep an eye out for any trouble, especially from the wolves and the Unseelie or the dark Fae."

"Yes, sir."

The tavern was directly across the street from Crimson Stakes. With its rustic brick exterior and welcoming, antique-lamp-lit entryway, it offered an inviting contrast to its neighbor's flashy presence. Also, in contrast to the casino, it was a legitimate business, not a money laundering operation.

The tavern was busy, but Petar and I went straight to the head of the line, bypassing people who were waiting to get inside.

The maître d', Jean-Pierre, bowed slightly. "Ah, monsieur, your usual table is waiting for you, as always."

I scanned the restaurant, looking for King Nico and Costin. "Have my guests arrived?"

He grabbed a couple of menus. "No, not yet. This way, please."

Petar and I followed Jean-Pierre through the crowded

tavern to the private dining room I had on the second-floor balcony, with a window from which I could look down and observe the various comings and goings of the tavern. It was always kept ready for me—no one else ever sat there. I inhaled deeply, the rich aroma of Creole cuisine filling my nostrils, and enjoyed the live jazz, the heart and soul of the Quarter drifting through the cozy, wood-paneled dining rooms.

We took our places at the table and didn't have to wait long to see King Nico and Costin Tarus arriving. Like me, they hadn't come alone. The king had his son Dante plus a guard with him, while Costin was accompanied by his manservant, Ethan. Ethan might look like a butler as he followed Costin at a respectful distance, his eyes down, but I knew better. Beneath his submissive appearance, he was a powerful vampire in his own right, and his skills were legendary.

Luckily, the table was always set for at least eight of us.

I glanced sternly at Petar as I unfolded my napkin and placed it in my lap. "You will contain yourself this evening. I need to know that I can trust you at all times." The implication was clear. If I couldn't, he was dead.

Besides Petar, I had guards stationed throughout the establishment just in case I needed them, but I knew my guests wouldn't try anything here, not with innocent patrons around. Like me, they didn't like to draw too much attention to themselves.

The maître d' appeared at the entrance to the private dining room and gestured for my guests to enter before retiring and shutting the door. They took their seats, and while most of them maintained a calm demeanor, Dante's expression darkened when he locked eyes with Petar. A tense silence fell over the group, but no one flinched or showed any reaction.

I bowed my head slightly as they all got settled. "Good evening, Your Majesty. Gentlemen."

"Santi." Costin nodded curtly. I had no doubt he would be the spokesperson for the group. He always was.

I waved my hand and a waiter materialized with a bottle of Chosen Blood and filled everyone's glass.

I cut to the chase. "I assume by agreeing to meet me so promptly, you think I have something to do with the two recently murdered girls?"

Costin sniffed his glass, then took a sip. "Their bodies were completely drained, so..." His cold tone had already convicted me.

Drained? This was news to me, but I hid my surprise well. "I assure you, my family didn't have anything to do with it."

King Nico finally spoke. "How can you be so sure?" His gaze wasn't on me—it was on Petar.

"Because no one does anything in this family without my blessing. If you're worried about Petar, I can assure you, he's being watched."

Petar blinked and stiffened, as if offended. "I am?"

I didn't answer him and focused on the others.

Costin put down his empty glass. "The other problem is ownership of the Nephilim. King Trystan claims she's his. We can't afford another war."

I swirled my glass, the blood sloshing against the sides.

"Trystan only wanted the girl after I saved her. That fool Simon had nearly overdosed her on diazepam. Simon agreed to my price, then tried to double-cross me." That still rankled. It was something he would regret. I wasn't done with him yet.

King Nico held my gaze. "My sources say that your men were ambushed, and your enforcer was badly wounded, nearly fatally. Is this true?" His voice was filled with apprehension.

I would have to discover who had such a loose tongue. I clenched my jaw, determined not to show any weakness in front of the king and Costin. "Your sources are mistaken. Enzo is perfectly fine."

Costin pointed at the empty seat. "Then why isn't he here?"

Showing that we were vulnerable was out of the question. I forced a smirk to my face. "Because I have another task for him tonight that doesn't pertain to this discussion."

"It's not just the two drained girls. Another girl has just been found murdered. My sources say that you had a liaison with her—Camila Alto. Witnesses report that you were seen with her as recently as last night." Costin's voice was tight as he leaned in, his eyes searching mine for any sign of guilt.

"The witnesses are mistaken. I wasn't with Camila last night. Our relationship ended months ago."

My breath had stilled at her name. Obviously, Costin and the king didn't know I'd had a dalliance with Nancee. It had only been brief. But Camila was another matter. She had been a waitress at Crimson Stakes and my favorite lover for quite some time until she went to work for the Barone family. If Costin and the king found out I had a relationship with both girls, they would fabricate some "evidence" and declare me guilty, I was sure of it.

Costin pressed a crumpled photo of Camila's dead body into my hand. Blood soaked her long black dress and terror reflected in her lifeless, staring eyes. As I gazed at her, I realized she looked like Serenity.

"I wasn't with her last night. I was with the Nephilim. Where was she found?"

He tilted his head. "In the alley behind the tavern."

King Nico raised an eyebrow, his expression bored. "You say you were with the Nephilim? Bring her to us, Santi, so we may question her ourselves."

I shook my head, my fists clenching angrily at the thought. No way in hell was I going to let them take her away from me. She was mine, and I would protect her with everything I had.

Costin locked eyes with me. "If you choose to not bring the Nephilim to us and another girl dies, you'll pay the price, Angelo. Not your family. You personally. Do I make myself clear?"

Crystal clear. I would not only be at war with the wolves and the dark Fae, but with the born vampires, the king of the vampires, and Costin himself. My enemies kept mounting, leaving me with little chance of escape.

Chapter Thirteen

Serenity

After Angelo left, I didn't have much choice but to roam around the library, especially with Jacques watching my every move. Curiosity welled up inside me to read these books and to actually learn about my heritage. Was I really descended from an angel? How was that even possible?

I plopped down in a chair and picked up the book Angelo claimed would answer my questions. It hummed, and I immediately dropped it onto the desk again.

Jacques' brows furrowed as he studied me. "Is there anything wrong?"

I hesitated, unsure of how to explain. "The book...it's... it's humming."

A petite woman with long, thick, black hair and deep green eyes came up behind Jacques. She cast an amused gaze over me, and I broke out in goosebumps. "So you're the one everyone's been talking about and why I was dragged here from my home?"

Jacques immediately got out of his chair. "Princess, you should be back in your room."

I blinked. "Princess?"

The woman sat down across from me and rolled her eyes. "Such an exhausting title. They only call me that because I'm Angelo's little sister. Gianna. Hi."

Angelo had a sister? I guess vampires could have an actual family. I thought they just called each other that, but as I stared at her, I saw her eyes were the same shape and color as his. She was definitely related to him. I wondered if he had other family members that were vampires too.

Jacques frowned. "Princess, you really should—"

She flicked her hand, as if accustomed to getting her way. "Leave us, Jacques. I want to get to know her."

He let out an exasperated sigh. "I will not be far away."

It amazed me that a big, muscular Mafia soldier obeyed such a petite woman. She definitely wielded her power well.

"Whatever," she mumbled pettishly. She glanced down at the book in front of me. "Did I hear you say this book was humming? I'm not surprised. Some of the books are magical, and you need to be careful handling them. However, Angelo wouldn't have given you anything to read unless he thought it was safe."

I stared nervously at *The Celestial Hierarchy: A Compendium on Angels*, not sure if I should pick it up again. It was bound in a supple, midnight-blue leather that had felt warm to the touch, as if holding the faintest pulse of life.

The cover was embossed with intricate silver filigree images of various angels in flight, their forms shimmering with an ethereal glow when caught by the light.

She laughed. "Don't worry. It won't bite. Your name is Serenity, isn't it? And you're the one who healed Enzo?"

I nodded. "Yes," I whispered quietly.

She gave me a sympathetic look. "You don't have to fear me, Serenity. I'm a prisoner here, same as you."

I tilted my head in shocked confusion. "What?"

Her lips curled into a sardonic smile, revealing pointed fangs. "Oh yes. When you're the sister of a Mafia king, you're always well-guarded. Sometimes too well-guarded. We have many enemies, and my brother doesn't trust anyone to protect me, especially not my husband."

I furrowed my brows. "Why not?"

"Because Dimitri is a born vampire, and therefore, according to my dear brother, not as powerful as made vampires like us."

"Born...made... What does that mean, exactly?" Maybe I could find out something that would eventually help me escape from here.

"Really? No one has told you about our world? So typical of my brother, Mr. Man-who-keeps-secrets. Okay—there are two kinds of vampires—made vampires, meaning we were born human but then turned at some point, and then born vampires, which is...well, just how it sounds. Made vampires are practically immortal, and we become even more powerful as we age. We're much stronger than the born vampires."

"So you're a—"

"Made vampire, yes. My brother turned me centuries ago." There was a hint of resentment in her tone that made me want to ask about that, but after seeing how Jacques had reacted to her, I didn't think questioning the princess was a good idea.

She narrowed her eyes. "However, my husband isn't, so my wonderful brother made him his chauffeur, even though Dimitri really is powerful in his own right."

If I wasn't so terrified, I would have laughed, but Gianna didn't seem to have a sense of humor about her husband being treated like a servant, so I kept quiet.

Luckily, Gianna changed the subject as she glanced around the room. "I take it you're doing research." She studied me. "Do you know what you are?"

"I'm...human?" I ventured, still not ready to believe I was anything else.

"Your parents were both human, then?"

"Yes...well...I don't know. I'm not quite sure what to believe." I just met this woman, and here she was asking me all kinds of personal questions. Normally, I shied away from those, especially ones about my father. It was too painful to talk about him. I glanced down at the way I was wringing my hands. It was something I always did when I got nervous.

She leaned back in her chair as if she was conducting a job interview. "Tell me about your parents."

I didn't want to share my whole torrid family history with her, so I just told her the basics. Hopefully, it would appease her and keep her from attacking me. "I never knew my biological father. He left before I was born. Then Mom married my stepfather, and he's the only father I've ever known."

Silence fell over us like a blanket. I opened the book, not wanting to dive into family history with Gianna any further.

I dug into the book, hoping the interrogation had stopped. I had just finished reading a chapter when she suddenly spoke, breaking my concentration.

"Is your stepfather the one that gave you the marks on your lower back?" Her voice rippled with genuine kindness... kindness I wasn't ready to accept yet.

I gritted my teeth. "God, is there a flipping newsletter circulating about my body? Remind me never to tell Elena any secrets." Bitterness laced my words.

What was I thinking? Elena and Gianna were both vampires and could easily kill me for being disrespectful. I needed to keep my anger in check better.

But Gianna didn't seem to get annoyed. Instead, she gave me an understanding smile like my mother used to do when I would get mad. "Don't be angry. Elena is worried about you, that's all. She's a real mother hen and wants to protect all her chicks, even my husband."

"And now I'm another one of those chicks?" A sharp edge crept into my voice like an icicle shattering on the pavement.

She gave me a warm smile. "I'm afraid so." She stretched her arms over her head. "Do you want some help researching?"

She seemed kind, but then again, she was Angelo's sister. "You would help me?"

"Sure, I don't have anything else to do except file my

nails for the millionth time." She came over and looked at my book. "Angels, huh? What specifically about them?"

"I'm not sure. Maybe healing powers. Unless you have a better idea?"

She shrugged as she got up and brushed her fingers over the spines of the book. "No, that sounds like a good place to start." She pulled out another angel book and returned to her spot across from me. "Anything specific?"

"Start with just healing in general. Maybe there's a particular type of angel that heals. Oh! Or one that has a penchant for loving humans and leaving a trail of broken hearts—an angel deadbeat dad."

"That narrows it down some, but not much. Just so you know."

"Great," I mumbled. "It's going to be like looking for an earring in the dark."

I flipped to a page filled with meticulously written long-hand, each letter a work of art in itself. The words were inked in a deep, rich hue that shifted and changed depending on the angle of light. Turning each leaf, I was struck by the beauty of the stunning hand-painted illustrations adorning the margins, each piece a velvety canvas come to life that pulled me deeper into this world. I couldn't believe someone had created this entire masterpiece by hand.

As I turned the pages, memories of Sunday school started flooding back. The words on the page were reminiscent of sermons I had heard as a child—stories of angels watching over us, delivering messages from God, and battling demons in the spiritual realm. But this book delved far beyond that and into angelic lore, revealing a complex society with its own hierarchy and a purpose beyond just guiding humans toward salvation or, conversely, passing judgment. My eyes were glued to the pages as I soaked up every detail.

Angelo had definitely left me breadcrumbs on who I was, and I was eager to learn.

Every once in a while, I heard Gianna turning page after page, almost as if she were speedreading.

After what might have been a couple of hours, she glanced up at me. "I'm curious...if your father was an angel, how did your mom end up with this stepfather who obviously hurt you?" Her soft voice echoed with concern, as if she'd been pondering it ever since we discussed my back.

"I don't know." Or I didn't—until I had my dream in which Mom had claimed she married Freaky Freddie for stability. Freddie must have really pulled the wool over her eyes. He was nothing but a monster, and the memory of what he did to me still haunted me.

I returned to poring over the ancient text, my eyes widening in horror at the intricate drawings of winged creatures with twisted horns and sharp fangs. The hairs on my arms prickled as I read about their deceptive ways and their desire to corrupt humans. A knot formed in my stomach as the realization slowly dawned on me—these were not just mythical beings, but actual, living creatures. And some angels fell from grace and became evil demons.

Gianna gazed at me and put her finger underneath her chin. "You found something that troubles you?"

I glanced up from the book. "What?" I squirmed in my seat. "No, nothing."

Her lips parted, revealing her fangs as she chuckled quietly. "Your face is pale, and I can hear your rapid heartbeat. Tell me. What's wrong?"

"I'm just...excited about what I found," I lied, and immediately returned to my book. How could I tell her that my father might possibly be a demon? That would make me twice as evil as any vampire.

Out of the corner of my eye, I could see Gianna studying me, but then she shrugged and returned to her reading.

What had Mom been keeping from me? She'd always been evasive about my real father. Did my father have horns and dance around with a pitchfork? Demons were evil, and I didn't want to end up like my deadbeat dad in Hell, chanting 'Satan is our pal.'

And what about Freddie, my stepfather who couldn't keep a secret to save his life—did he know the truth about my father? Is that why Mom chose him? Because in my book, he was just as evil as any demon father. My stomach turned sick at the thought.

I heard murmured voices, but I was so engrossed and horrified by what I was reading I ignored them.

"Enzo!" Gianna snapped her book shut. "You look so much better."

Startled, I jumped in my seat, banging my knees against the table. My heart beat a rapid rhythm in my chest as I fought to maintain a calm demeanor in the face of Enzo's piercing gaze.

"Surviving, is more like it." Enzo leaned against the door frame with one hand on it, as if to prop himself up for support.

Gianna got up and hugged him briefly. "I'm so glad."

I thought I saw tears in the corners of her eyes, and her voice cracked as if she cared about him. Enzo was definitely handsome, and I wondered briefly if maybe they had a thing before she met her husband. Somehow, I didn't think Angelo would allow that. Maybe they were more like brother and sister?

He stumbled over to a chair, his movements unsteady and uncertain.

Gianna clasped his arm to prevent him from falling.

He gritted his teeth. "I can do it."

She glared at him as she helped him sit down. "No, let me help you, Enzo."

He fixed me with a look. "Serenity, can we talk alone?" he asked, his voice laced with vulnerability.

"I'll leave you be." Gianna slid out the door.

I almost wanted to beg her to stay, but I didn't want to get on the bad side of Angelo's enforcer. With my luck, I'd jump straight to the top of his hit list.

Chapter Fourteen

Serenity

A sense of helplessness washed over me, knowing that I couldn't possibly refuse Enzo. I forced a tight smile to my lips. "Of course," I replied, trying to sound reassuring.

"I just wanted to thank you for saving me," he said slowly, his dark eyes searching mine for some kind of acknowledgment.

A small smile tugged at the corners of my mouth. "You're welcome. Honestly? I was surprised I could do it."

"You're very powerful. It's a power that others are desperate to possess."

I stared at his handsome face. His dark eyes reflected the pain still within him. If these people could do this to a vampire, I didn't want to think about what they could do to me. "The people who want this power...Are they the ones that attacked you?" I couldn't keep the fear out of my voice.

He held my gaze. "Just know that you're safer in here than out there. Angelo won't let anything happen to you."

"Really?" I wasn't sure if Enzo knew Angelo had fed on me.

Enzo's eyes flicked to the leather-bound book resting on the table in front of me. "Did Angelo give you that?" His tone was laced with suspicion, and I could tell he was hiding something by the way he changed the subject so quickly.

I nodded, running a hand lightly over the book. It was still humming. "Yes. It's...unique."

He chuckled, his brown eyes lighting up and a smile spreading across his face. "Many of the books in here are magical and strange. You wouldn't believe the lengths Angelo has gone to acquire some of them. He's literally traveled to the farthest corners of the earth for them."

I gazed at the books in fresh wonder. "Really?"

"Yes. And you should feel honored. Angelo is quite secretive about his collection. Very few have been allowed inside this library."

"Why?"

His smile broadened, bringing a warm, infectious glow to his face. "That's a question you'll have to ask him yourself."

There was a knock at the door. Elena poked her nose in and gave me a big smile that was at odds with the weariness in her blue eyes. "*Chère*, you've been in here for the last few hours. You must be hungry by now. Chef Gaultier has prepared dinner for you." She came up behind Enzo and put her hands on the back of his chair. "*S'il te plaît*, you need to eat too, Enzo."

Enzo sighed. "You won't give this up, will you?"

"Never," she said softly.

He put his hands on the table then pushed himself up with shaky arms. "Fine. I'm coming. I'm coming."

She stuck out an elbow, and Enzo reluctantly took it. I followed as they shuffled in front of me. I kept thinking of the fallen angels and the people who wanted me. The real question was: did they want me because they thought my dad was an angel, or because they thought he was a demon?

In the dining room, an array of silver chafing dishes awaited us, each one promising culinary delight.

Gianna was already seated at the table. "I hope I'm not going to be banished to my room to eat, Enzo," she smirked.

"No, no. You're welcome to eat with us," Enzo said as he slid into a dining chair.

I noticed a distinct difference in the way Jacques and Enzo treated Gianna. Jacques deferred to her, but not Enzo. He was definitely the one in control.

I inhaled deeply, the spicy scent of étouffée tantalizing my taste buds.

Elena gestured to the already set table. "*S'il vous plaît*, sit."

The crystal decanter on the table was filled with a thick, dark red liquid. When Elena poured it into Enzo and Gianna's glasses, my stomach lurched as I realized it wasn't wine at all—it was blood. Then Elena picked up a different bottle and poured for me. I wrinkled my nose and refused to take a sip, but Elena reassured me with a light touch on my shoulder. "Don't worry, *chère*. It's just pinot noir."

Pinot noir or not, I was hesitant to drink. After watching Freddie drown himself in alcohol to forget his misfortune, I limited how much I drank. I didn't want to become like him.

With a flourish, Elena lifted the lid off the main silver chafing dish, revealing the étouffée. The steam rose, carrying with it the mouth-watering aroma of succulent shrimp and crawfish simmered in a rich, roux-thickened sauce. The holy trinity of onion, celery, and bell pepper perfumed the air as hints of garlic and thyme, together with a generous splash of Louisiana hot sauce, added layers of complexity and warmth to the soulful New Orleans dish. My stomach rumbled as I eagerly waited for her to fill my plate.

There was a smaller chafing dish of white rice which she added to my plate before spooning the étouffée over it.

The scent of spicy roux and tender seafood wafted from the steaming bowl in front of me, causing my stomach to growl. I eagerly scooped up a spoonful of étouffée and savored the rich flavors bursting in my mouth. Trying to distract myself from the sight of Enzo taking slow sips from his glass of blood, I focused on the intricate design of the tablecloth.

After a few minutes, a soft voice interrupted my thoughts, "Are you enjoying your dinner, Serenity? You're so quiet."

My head snapped up when I heard Gianna's voice.

I blurted. "Yes, I'm just hungry."

Enzo's face had previously still been drained of color,

but now it had regained its natural hue, and his once lifeless eyes now sparkled with renewed vitality. The decanter on the table was empty, and I couldn't help but gaze at it.

"To answer your unspoken question, yes, the blood healed him," Gianna said gently.

My heart raced as I silently processed this information, taking an uncharacteristically large gulp of wine in an attempt to steady my nerves.

Enzo's smile grew, a hint of dark amusement playing across his features. "Do you have any questions about vampires?"

"I've already told her about the difference between made and born vampires," Gianna piped up as she pushed her plate away from her.

Enzo tipped his head from side to side. "I think she still has more questions."

Did I ever! I was dying to ask a hundred questions about vampires, angels, and demons. The need to understand my enemy drove me to speak up. I figured if I understood them and discovered any weaknesses, maybe I could find a way to escape. "Does blood always heal you?" I asked hesitantly.

His expression turned guarded, clearly considering how much to reveal. "Most of the time," he finally answered.

My curiosity piqued. "What do you mean by most of the time?"

He fiddled with the stem of his wine glass, avoiding eye contact. "This recent attack on me was particularly brutal, and I needed more than just blood to recover. That's where you came in."

I glanced at Gianna, who nodded.

"It's true," she said. "Whoever did this was determined to kill him, even though he's an ancient vampire."

Since he'd opened the door to satisfy my curiosity, I blurted a question that had been burning in me for a while. "How long have you been a vampire?"

"Since the plague," he replied calmly.

I looked at Gianna. "And you?"

"The same." She poured herself a glass of wine.

A jolt of shock coursed through me as the realization of just how old they were hit me like a ton of bricks. "But that's hundreds of years ago! That's...incomprehensible to me."

A smirk tugged at his lips. "Yes, it can be quite overwhelming to think about."

Suddenly, a thought struck me like lightning. "Was it Angelo who turned you into a vampire?"

Gianna's bitter words sliced through the air. "He turned us both."

Enzo remained silent for a moment. Finally, he gave a small nod. "We were both dying from the plague when he offered us a choice." His simple answer froze my blood.

Gianna's eyes darkened. "You mean he offered you a choice."

"He loved you, Gianna. He couldn't watch his sister die."

A chill rolled down my spine. If he hadn't given Gianna a choice, where did that leave me? I didn't want to become one of the children of the night. Would Angelo take this choice away from me like he had from his sister?

"If you'll excuse me..." Gianna got up from the table and stormed out of the room.

My throat tightened, and I pressed a hand to my chest, feeling the rapid beating of my heart. "What did she mean, you had a choice?"

He merely shrugged. "Just as it sounds. I would have died if I hadn't drunk his blood. And whether Gianna wants to admit it or not, she would have too."

Maybe so, but I had a feeling she would have rather died than become a creature of the night.

"Gianna mentioned that her husband is a born vampire. What does that mean? Are they born in the same way humans are?" I was still trying to wrap my head around the differences between the two.

Enzo's uproarious laughter echoed around the room as he tossed his head back, his fangs glinting in the dim light, his pain momentarily forgotten. "Oh, you mortals. Such wild imaginations," he chuckled, fixing me with his piercing gaze. His otherworldly eyes, an unnatural shade of amber, seemed to see right through me.

I shifted uncomfortably under his scrutiny, feeling a mix of fear and fascination. The rational part of my brain screamed at me to run, but I was rooted to the spot, entranced by his gaze.

"Yes, to answer your question. They are the descendants of Vlad the Impaler and his human mate," Enzo continued, his voice smooth as silk. "They enter this world the same way humans do—squalling babies covered in blood and amniotic fluid."

My breath caught in my throat. "You mean Dracula is real?"

"Not just real—still alive and in the flesh." He leaned

across the table, his upper body fluid and predatory. The air between us practically crackled with an unseen energy. "The difference is, even as infants, they possess an innate thirst for blood, a hunger that only grows stronger with time. It's woven into the very fabric of their being."

I swallowed hard, my throat suddenly dry. The reality of the danger I was in sank in. I had to get out of here before I was sprawled out on the dinner table like a prime rib done extra rare.

I thought of all the Dracula movies and how those vampires were always transforming into either a wolf or a bat. "What about bats or wolves? Can you change into those?"

He smiled. "All vampires can change into bats. There are only a select few that can change into wolves like Dracula can. Only those bitten directly by him can do that like Angelo."

"So, Angelo can shift into a wolf? It was Dracula who turned him, right?"

"Yes. Unlike shifters, our vampire magic allows us to change into bats—or a wolf, in Angelo's case—and back into our human form without ripping through our clothes. It also allows us to carry our weapons. Shifters can't do any of that."

I thought of Angelo changing into a bat or a wolf. Since he was the head of the Santi family, I bet he was bigger and scarier than any other bats or wolves. I also bet it would scare me out of my shoes.

I held up my hand and swallowed the dread in my throat. "Wait. Shifters?"

"Wolf and dragon shifters. They tear through their clothes when they shift into their beast."

I rubbed the spot on my neck where Angelo had bitten me. "Can vampires control their blood lust?"

"Newly made vampires struggle to do so because they are ravenous but born vampires and older made vampires can control the hunger."

"How long does it take for an 'older made vampire' to get control of this blood lust?"

"Depends on the vampire." *That's not a freaking answer, Enzo.* I was about to give him grief for dancing around the question when I realized he wasn't looking at me but at someone behind me.

I spun around, and my eyes locked with Angelo's. He had emerged from the shadows of the dining room. His pupils were two bright, fiery orbs of red, and my skin prickled with goosebumps at the sight. How long had he been listening to our conversation? My heart raced as I waited for him to say something.

Enzo motioned to Angelo's cheek. "Your scratches. They've disappeared. The stone?"

Angelo shrugged. "It seems it still has some power."

Stone? This was the first I'd heard about any stone. Was it a magical heirloom, like in *Lord of the Rings* or the Marvel Universe? Definitely something I had to find out more about.

Enzo's expression changed from curious to skeptical as his eyes narrowed. "So how did the meeting go?"

Angelo hesitated, glancing first at me then back to Enzo before answering. "We need to talk." His soft tone indicated that something was off, and I had a sneaky feeling it was about me.

The tension in the room increased; whatever was going on between them was serious. I didn't want to be left out of their conversation, especially if it was about me.

Suddenly a blood-curdling screamed pierced through the house, cutting off my breath.

Enzo jumped up, toppling over his chair. "That was a woman's voice."

My heart plummeted into my stomach as Enzo's words echoed in my head.

Pleasepleasepleaseplease don't let anyone have hurt Elena or Gianna

Angelo's hand gripped my arm tightly, pulling me out of my chair. "Stay close to me," he ordered, his voice firm and commanding.

Like I wanted to wander around here by myself.

"It sounds like it's coming from the courtyard," Enzo said, fear in his voice.

Angelo led us toward the source of the disturbance, his movements swift and purposeful. I was tightly sandwiched between Angelo and Enzo's large forms. Our footsteps rang throughout the once-peaceful corridors, the only sound in the oppressive silence that had descended over the house. My heart pounded in my chest, each beat a deafening reminder of the unknown danger that awaited us.

There was no turning back now. The woman's scream had shattered any illusion of safety, even though Angelo was the head of the Santi family and Crescent Manor should have been unassailable. I glanced at my companions, their faces reflecting the same grim thoughts that I felt in my own heart.

As we drew closer to the courtyard, the temperature seemed to drop, turning my blood ice cold. The walls of the house now felt even more like a cage, trapping us in a labyrinth of fear and uncertainty. My hand trembled as I clutched Angelo's arm.

I held my breath as we headed closer to the courtyard. It stretched out before us, bathed in an eerie, unnatural light. There, in the center of the stone-paved expanse, was the cause of the scream, a sight that made my blood run cold and my bones rattle with a terror I had never known before.

As we reached the doorway to the courtyard, we saw Elena hunched over on the ground, her face buried in her hands as she sobbed uncontrollably.

Gianna was clinging to a striking vampire, his presence both alluring and dangerous. His dark, piercing eyes looked as if they held countless secrets. Unruly, raven-black hair framed his face, giving him an untamed appearance that suggested a rebellious nature. The intensity of his gaze, paired with a mischievous smirk, hinted at the complexity of his soul, and a heart that seemed to teeter between the edge of darkness and the desire for redemption.

That had to be Dimitri.

More of Angelo's guards were gathering around Dimitri, Gianna, and Elena.

In the center of the courtyard, Jacques lay motionless on the ground, a pool of blood seeping out from under his body and growing larger by the second. His head had rolled a few feet away from his body, his lifeless eyes staring up at the midnight sky. Written in blood—his blood, I realized with a wave of sickness—were the words *Give up the Nephilim.*

He was dead. Not just dead. *Headless.*

A switch shut off inside me, stopping my lungs and heart. Everything disappeared but the terror swirling in my quivering belly. It boomed like a mushroom cloud, charging up my throat, blocking out every sound around me.

Angelo was saying something to me, but I couldn't hear him. The terror was followed by a piercing scream that erupted out of me.

The next thing I knew, he was whirling me around, his arms enveloping me tightly as if to shield me from the horrors of the outside world. His powerful embrace felt like a cocoon of protection, and I couldn't help but melt into it.

"I'll keep you safe," he promised, his deep voice rumbling like distant thunder.

Keep me safe? How could he say that when he himself had fed on my blood? Who would protect me from him?!

My fists balled in his shirt, tears streaming down my face, trying to forget what I had just seen.

But I never would. The image would remain seared in my brain forever.

I didn't want this life. It was brutal, heartless, ghastly.

But no matter how much I wished to escape this never-ending nightmare, it appeared I was trapped.

Chapter Fifteen

Angelo

I stroked Serenity's hair, my hand shaking with fury. My blood boiled with anger as I thought about the intruder who had not only murdered one of my best men, but also had threatened Serenity by his very presence. Crescent Manor had only been breached once. No one had ever dared to violate my family's home.

I was the Angel of Death, and this would not go unpunished.

No one would ever threaten Serenity in my presence—she was mine to protect and cherish, and whoever dared to cross that line would face my wrath. Like Vlad had done in 1462 to keep his enemies from pursuing him, I'd drop them down on a stake, make them suffer, and watch their body slowly writhe in pain as they slipped further down the pole in perfect agony.

"Petar, search the grounds. If you find the intruder, bring him to me."

Petar bowed slightly. "Yes, sir." This was a job I would usually assign to Enzo, but he wasn't at full capacity yet, and I had no intention of losing him too.

I turned to my sister's husband. "Dimitri, set up stakes in the courtyard. People will see what will happen if they cross swords with me." The intruder would wish he'd never been born once I was through with him.

Dimitri nodded, flashing his fangs. "It will be my pleasure."

I flashed him an evil smile. Sometimes my brother-in-law's thirst for vengeance ran as deep as my own.

Serenity looked at me with tears glistening in her eyes. "Stakes?"

I didn't answer her. She'd find out soon enough.

"And Dimitri, before you do that, have Gianna and Elena brought into the dining room."

I had to get Serenity away from the ghastly scene. She buried her face into the crook of my neck, her blonde hair shielding poor Jacques from her view. I lifted her into my arms and carried her back into the dining room.

A guard brought a sobbing Elena into the room directly after us, and she collapsed into a chair. She put her head down on the table, still weeping.

Dimitri helped Gianna into a chair and kissed her on the lips. "Stay here, my love."

She looked up at him and smiled weakly. "I can protect myself."

"I know you can." He brushed his finger down her wet cheek. "But let me be the one to do it." The statement was more for me than my sister, I thought. He was still trying to prove that he was worthy of being in the family. It did win him a small appreciative nod from me.

My sister glowered at me, but I wasn't going to get into another debate with her over Dimitri.

I stared into Enzo's cold amber eyes as he stood by my side. "Stay here with Elena, Serenity, and Gianna," I growled through gritted teeth.

He hesitated for only a moment, then nodded quickly. "Yes, sir. I'll protect them with my life."

I was sure that Enzo would be able to handle anyone who came near the three women, but as I turned to leave, Serenity reached out and touched my arm, her tearstained eyes filled with fear and confusion. "You're leaving me?" Her voice cracked with emotion.

My heart caught in my threat. Did she care for me even though I had fed on her? Regardless, I would take whatever acceptance or encouragement I could get from her.

I took a deep breath and clasped her shoulders firmly. "I promise I will return. You'll be safe here with Enzo. My family was attacked, Serenity. And I am the head of the family. The Angel of Death cannot let this attack on us go unpunished."

She winced at my words, but it was important for her to know who I was and what I was truly capable of. I needed her to know how far I would go to protect what's mine—

including her. More tears fell down her cheeks, and in that moment, I realized how innocent she was and how much I had forgotten about innocence in my line of work.

It took everything I had to leave her, but I had to find out who had murdered Jacques. I went to my office and grabbed my sword, which was deadly to supernaturals, and strapped it in its sheath around my waist. Then I headed out into the courtyard where one of my men was cleaning up the blood. Jacques' body had already been moved and would be burned in a vampire warrior's funeral.

But not tonight. Tonight was about avenging his death.

Petar landed next to me and shifted back from his bat. "We searched the streets but didn't find anyone suspicious."

"Keep trying. I want answers. We'll go to Simon's now. Be prepared for an ambush."

I shifted into a bat and flew high over the courtyard toward Simon's. This time, he would pay with his life. He had to be the one behind this.

I soared through the night sky until Simon's Ravenwood Estates came into view. Fog enveloped the sprawling property, the ethereal mist creating an otherworldly cloak of mystery. From above, I noted grimly that the fog would provide a perfect cover for any ambush that might be waiting for me. It was a thick blanket of silence and secrets, shrouding the sanctuary in an eerie atmosphere. The rolling mist, creeping in from the surrounding bayou, blurred the lines between the meticulously manicured gardens and the wild, untamed beauty of the nearby swamp. The grandiose mansion came looming out of the fog like a nightmare, its presence unsettling and foreboding. With each flap of my wings, I couldn't shake the feeling that this fog had something almost magical about it—as if Simon's witch had created an impenetrable veil.

Ancient oaks draped with Spanish moss came into view, their twisted forms adding to the eerie ambiance. Despite being muffled by the dense fog, I could hear the faint sounds of wildlife below, emphasizing the isolation of this place where reality and superstition blended together seamlessly. I searched for traces of wolves or dark Fae but couldn't detect anything—perhaps magic was concealing their presence from me.

I saw that the window I had jumped through had been repaired.

Too bad.

I dove toward it and burst through the windowpane, sending glass spraying into the bedroom. A man and woman in the bed screamed in terror. I glanced at the man and grinned. I recognized him. He was Dan Jenkins, one of Simon's enforcers.

Dan sprang out of the plush bed naked, scrambling for his gun on the dresser. I lunged forward, getting my steely grip around his throat before he could even lift his weapon. His eyes bulged in terror as I tightened my grip, his windpipe shattering beneath my inhuman power.

With a swift yank, I tore out his throat and savored the metallic taste of his warm blood as it spilled onto my lips and down my chin. It was nothing compared to Serenity's unique essence, but it still fueled my hunger.

The woman had fled to the corner where she shrieked and thrashed against the wall, her wild screams piercing through the air like a siren. But I paid her no mind. She was just another meal to come later.

Just then, Simon burst into the room with some of his lackeys. I hurled Dan's lifeless body at their feet, relishing the terror etched across Simon's face as he took in the scene before him.

"Don't hurt me," he begged, his voice trembling with fear.

"Don't make me." He had something I wanted—answers. And he would either give them willingly or suffer unimaginable pain at my hands.

I crashed through his circle of pitiful men like they were bowling pins, knocking them down. Their screams were drowned out by the sound of my raging heart. I easily caught him up and held him with one hand, his arms and legs flailing. "Marsha," he squeaked.

I doubted the witch could hear him, and even if she did, I didn't care. I had learned something. Her magic wasn't as strong as everybody thought it was. Not only that, Serenity had the power to rejuvenate the Aeternum Stone, and Simon had made the deadly mistake of declaring war on me.

"I want answers, Simon, and I want them now."

My grip tightened on his throat. His eyes bulged from his head and sweat streaked down his face.

"Anything, your grace, anything. Just, please, don't kill me."

I dropped him to the ground in a heap and circled him slowly, like a predator stalking its prey. "Who gave the order for the hit on Crescent Manor?"

Simon squirmed like a worm trying to escape, his lips trembling as he spoke. "I...I don't know."

"*Don't know?* Do you think I won't use compulsion on you? I will find out everything you know. And if I discover that you're lying to me, I'll cut out your black heart with my teeth...slowly." I let the threat hang in the air as I leaned in closer.

His eyes begged for mercy. I could smell the fear emanating from him, mixed with the stench of stale sweat and betrayal. "It wasn't us. I swear. We wouldn't dare betray you, my king." His words meant nothing to me. I knew Simon would sell his own mother to get a pretty piece of coin, and Serenity was priceless.

"Talk, Simon." I edged closer.

He cowered against the wall, his hands shaking in front of his face. "I've heard things..."

"What things?"

"There's been talk about plots...revenge...angels. But angels...they're just a myth."

A bitter laugh escaped my lips. Humans were so naïve to think that vampires, wolf shifters, dark Fae, and other supernatural creatures were just myths, when here we were, lurking in the shadows, ruling over them like gods.

I grabbed his hair and lifted him clean off the floor, his feet dangling in the air. "What *kind* of angels?" The question tore from my throat, my lips curling back to bare my teeth, revealing the true monster that I was.

He writhed in my grasp, his body drooping, as if all the fight had left him and he was accepting of his fate. "There have been rumors of a fallen angel among us..." His voice trailed off as he saw my fangs descend.

But before I could strike, he forced out a bombshell. "It's the girl...Serenity! They say she's the fallen angel."

"You're trying my patience, Simon." I brought my head closer and tilted my neck, baring my fangs as if I were about to feed on him.

"Wait, wait! I know somebody...they might know who ordered the hit. I swear it wasn't me." He burst into tears. "I swear it wasn't. Please forgive me. I'll do anything...just... Please don't kill me."

I shook him hard. "Tell me who it is. I need answers. If you lie to me, I'll know."

Through rattling teeth, he blurted, "Her stepfather— Freddie Evans. He's the one who sold her to me, to pay off his debt."

A wave of rage surged through me. Her stepfather was supposed to protect her, not sell her to cover his own fucking hide. Before I paid Freddie Evans a visit, I rapidly but thoroughly searched Simon's mind. His lips parted in a silent gasp, his gaze growing distant and unfocused as I sifted through his memories, plucking out essential details.

The snake hadn't been lying to me.

So I would let him live...for now. I didn't want his damn witch casting a spell on the Aeternum Stone. I tossed him aside, sobbing and crying, curled up in a ball.

Dimitri was waiting for me at the stairs. His chin was just as bloody as mine. Simon's men had had their throats ripped out and were scattered like drained husks. Dan's girl was still in the corner sobbing as Petar approached her.

"No. Leave her be," I ordered.

The naked girl looked at me as if she couldn't believe I had protected her. But I had no intention of going to war with King Nico and Costin, and yet another dead girl would sign my death warrant.

Petar stopped immediately. No one disobeyed me unless they wanted to end up like one of the bloody corpses piled in the room.

Dimitri quirked an eyebrow, a smirk playing on his lips. "Well, well. Look at you, playing the hero. Should I start calling you Saint Angelo?" His tone turned mockingly serious. "Or wait, is this some new strategy? 'Save the naked girls, avoid the wars'? Because I've got to say, I like it better than our usual 'kill first, ask questions never' approach."

"Listen up." I scanned my men. "We have another visit to make. Follow me." I leaped out the window and shifted into a bat. As I flew over the bayou and then through New Orleans' dark streets, my blood boiled with rage and a thirst for revenge. Freddie Evans had dared to hurt Serenity, and now he would not live to see another sunrise.

Chapter Sixteen

Serenity

Still sitting frozen in the dining room chair, I stared at the door through which Angelo had disappeared with some of his men. My heart raced as I tried to process the shocking revelation. Someone was out to destroy Angelo, or at least someone in the Santi family. Was this over me, or something else? The thought of being the cause of this danger filled me with guilt and dread. First the killer had wounded Enzo, and now he...or she...had brutally killed Jacques.

I could practically feel their cold breath on the back of my neck, and I shivered, breaking out in a rash of goosebumps. A war was brewing, and I was caught square in the middle of the crossfire. I had to do something to stop it, but what could I do against such a ruthless and determined enemy?

Detective DuPont! Maybe he could help me. If I could get word to him, perhaps he could track down whoever was attacking Angelo's men in an attempt to get to me. He could also get me out of this den of vipers.

Poor Elena had fallen asleep with her head on the table, and her soft snores filled the room.

Enzo slid into a chair next to me. He picked up my cold shaking hand. "Serenity?" His soft tone wrapped my name in a blanket of concern.

I shifted my worried gaze from the door to Enzo.

"You'll be all right. I promise I won't let anyone hurt you."

My numb mind returned to the grisly scene of poor Jacques' murder. I searched Enzo's eyes, wondering if he would tell me the truth or only give bits and pieces of what I needed to know.

"Enzo...What's a Nephilim?" My voice cracked with fear.

Please not a demon Please not a demon Please not a demon

Enzo's eyebrows shot up and his jaw dropped open in astonishment. "You didn't discover that in any of the books that Angelo let you read?" His tone said he couldn't believe I was so naïve.

I sighed, thinking of the information I had uncovered. Information I never wanted to know. "They talked of fallen angels..."

Enzo's face softened. "Fallen angels are demons. They were once angels, but they were cast out of from Heaven."

I took a deep breath, bracing myself for the answer to my next question. "Is that what a Nephilim is?"

Enzo hesitated, as if struggling between telling me the truth and protecting me from it. But I needed to know, for my own safety and sanity.

Gianna's gaze bored into mine, her words coming fast and sharp like arrows aimed directly at the heart of the truth. "Nephilim are born from the union between an angel and a human."

The heavy dread on my chest felt heavier with every word. "But some are...?" I trailed off, needing to confirm my suspicions yet terrified to hear the answer.

"Yes," Enzo confirmed solemnly. "Some Nephilim are born from fallen angels."

"You mean demons," I whispered. That meant my father could be buddies with Satan himself. It seemed likely, since he had left my mom and me high and dry. That didn't seem like something an angel would do, but based on what I had read, demons wouldn't think twice about abandoning their young.

Gianna flashed Enzo a frown. "Not all of them, Serenity. Your father could be an Archangel for all we know."

"And if my father was an Archangel, he would be good?" I glanced at their faces.

Enzo grimaced. "Not necessarily."

Gianna glared daggers at Enzo. "We don't know what your father was, Serenity, so don't panic. Not yet anyway."

My heart plummeted as my mind connected the dots, hurtling toward a sinister truth. The pieces of this twisted puzzle came together in slow motion, each one bringing me more dread and fear. I couldn't shake off the memory of the dream where my mother had desperately tried to warn me about something. Or stop thinking about all the times she'd evaded my questions as a child. Well, of course. She didn't want to tell me she'd slept with a fallen angel! It wasn't exactly something to be proud of. And now, between my newfound healing powers and Jacques' brutal murder, it all made sense.

I gasped as my vision blurred and my fingers turned numb—the blood draining from my face. I looked at Enzo then at Gianna. "That message written in blood...about the Nephilim...they were talking about me, weren't they? I am the Nephilim." Desperation crept into my voice.

Enzo's expression darkened and he muttered under his breath. "Shit, Angelo's probably going to kill me for this." Then he met my gaze and nodded. "Yes, you're a Nephilim. That's why the others want you."

My head spun as I tried to wrap my brain around his words. My brows crunched into a deep scowl. "And which supernatural do you think murdered Jacques?"

Enzo shrugged. "I don't know. It could have been anybody." His words settled on my shoulders like a heavy cloak, filling me with fear and uncertainty.

"They want to kill me, don't they? Because my father's a demon."

"We don't know that for sure," Enzo warned.

Gianna got out of her chair and clasped my hand. "What we do know is that you're safe here, Serenity. My brother would never let anyone hurt you." She wasn't fooling me. I could hear the troubled note in her voice.

Silence swept around us, stilling my breathing. My lungs seemed to be frozen in time. I couldn't remember how to inhale or exhale. It was as if the knowledge had flown out of my brain.

Enzo shifted in his chair, and it snapped me back to attention. I finally remembered how to breathe and greedily sucked in a gulp of air.

He put his hand on my shoulder. "You look like you could use a drink."

I met his gaze, my heart heavy with the weight of the night's events. "I feel like I've aged a decade in the past few hours. Yes, that might help, thank you."

It was probably stupid to have a drink around vampires and when something was after me, but right now, I needed something to distract me from everything that was going on. Normally, I would work out or go for a run, but that was out of the question right now.

Gianna sat next to me and smiled wryly. "I don't know about her, but I definitely could."

Drinking after getting bad news was following Freddie's example, but honestly, right now, I didn't care. I needed to chase away the shock of finding out my father could be a demon. That was a million times worse than having Freddie as a stepfather.

Enzo walked over to the bar, moving silently in a way that only a vampire could. He picked up a bottle of red wine and filled three large, ornate goblets, then handed one each to me and Gianna. I swirled the deep crimson liquid around, its rich aroma wafting up to my nostrils.

I hesitated for a brief moment, wondering if it was wise

to accept a drink from a vampire, but the temptation was too strong to resist. I finally found my tiny voice. "If they caught me, do you think they would kill me like they did Jacques?"

He sat beside me again. "Absolutely not. You're too valuable. They need your power. They're desperate for it."

"Great, so they want to unleash a power that never should be released," I murmured bitterly. Demonic powers wouldn't make anyone a superhero.

Gianna looked down at my shaking hand as I kept swirling the wine in my glass, then at my face full of fear and dread. "Drink, Serenity. The wine will calm you."

I numbly did as she asked, unsure if I was doing it on my own volition or if she was compelling me. The minute the wine crossed my pinched lips, it was as if a great thirst came over me. I wanted to forget everything I had learned. Forget I had a price on my head. Forget my dad wasn't just a deadbeat dad, but a fucking demon deadbeat dad.

I downed the glass and handed it back to him. "Another one."

He cocked his eyebrow but didn't argue.

The second glass went down even faster than the first. Usually I drank wine slowly since it went straight to my head, but not tonight.

He pointed to my empty glass. "You're going to get sloshed if you keep drinking like that."

I laughed softly. "That's the idea. I don't want to remember anything. I want another one, right now."

He took the goblet from my shaking hand. "I don't think that's a good idea."

I lifted my chin defiantly. "Do it, or I'll tell Angelo you touched me."

Gianna laughed and held up her own glass in a toast. "I like her. I like her a lot."

Enzo's face paled, his hands gripping the edge of the table as he stared at me in disbelief. His jaw clenched, and for a moment, I thought he might physically lash out at me. But instead, he stood up abruptly and stormed into the kitchen, returning with another glass of wine which he thrust into my hand.

He glared at Gianna. "You compelled her to drink, didn't you?"

Gianna shrugged. "She needs to forget, Enzo."

"Angelo will not like this," he growled.

I should have been furious at Gianna, making me drink when normally I wouldn't, but she was right. Forgetfulness was a gift right now. I smiled smugly at him, then quickly drained the glass just like the previous two. Too quickly. The room spun, and my eyes went in and out of focus. I stood up, knocking over my chair in the process.

"I wanna go t'my room," I slurred.

Enzo clasped my arm. "If he catches me touching her, it's your fucking fault, Gianna."

Gianna took another sip. "Don't worry, enforcer. Your secret's safe with me."

He grabbed my arm and yanked me out of the dining room, sending me stumbling into the hallway. The next thing I knew, I was being dragged down the hall and into my bedroom. My feet barely touched the ground as he threw me onto my bed with a swift, supernatural speed.

I collapsed onto my bed, and Enzo covered me with a blanket. I shut my eyes, trying to block out the spinning room, Jacques' murder, the fact that I was a fucking Nephilim, and most of all that my dad the angel had given me this gift—or maybe it was curse—and now I was on every supernatural's most wanted list.

As I passed out, the last thought I had was that I had to protect myself or I would never survive...

Joy parked the car in front of my house. "Are you going to be okay? You can spend the night at my house again if you want."

I sighed and laid my head against the back of the seat, staring at the small house. "Thanks, but I can't leave Sammie alone with him."

Mom had gotten the yellow lab for me when I was three. He was the sweetest dog, but he was ten years old now and not doing well. He couldn't get up the stairs and peed when he was scared these days, which, with Freddie around, was all the time. Freddie was less than kind to my buddy. Another reason why I hated the man.

"Look, if you're going to stay in this hellhole, Steve gave me something to pass along to you."

Steve was her older half brother, and he was in a street gang. Ever since he found out that DuPont wasn't actually his father, he'd been on a rebellious kick, lashing out at the world in his efforts to find a sense of identity and belonging. The betrayal had driven him to find a new family, one that accepted him without question, even if it meant living a life of crime. He'd taught me how to fight with a knife, insisting that

I needed to know how to defend myself in a world that was full of lies and deception.

Joy reached over and opened the glove box. "Here." She pulled out a six-inch switchblade and handed it to me.

I frowned. "Joy, seriously? Won't your father be mad?"

She scoffed. "Since when has Dad approved of anything Steve's doing these days or the company he keeps?" Her sarcastic laughter died away, and she nudged me in the ribs. "You don't want to piss Steve off, do you? Take it."

I almost argued that I knew Steve would never hurt me. He thought of me as another kid sister.

But things with Freddie had been getting worse...

I took the switchblade and hefted it. It felt right in my hand. "Tell Steve thanks. Even though I don't really think I'll have to use it."

She gave me a doubtful look. "I hope you're right."

I slipped the blade into the pocket of my school uniform. "I know I'm right."

I got out of the car and headed toward the darkened house. Freddie must be out drinking and gambling again. I opened the door, excitedly listening for Sammie clicking his nails across the hardwood floor to welcome me home, wagging his tail.

I was greeted with silence.

That wasn't like him.

I clapped my hands. "Sammie? Sammie? Come here, boy."

The lights whipped on, and I saw Freddie standing in the middle of the living room holding a bottle of tequila. His long hair was pulled back into a greasy ponytail. When he first met

Mom, he'd been handsome, but now…now he was the type of guy you'd cross the street to avoid.

He cast his lecherous gaze over me and sneered. "Y' smell like burg'rs an' onions." He was slurring his words so badly I could barely understand him.

I wrinkled my nose. He stunk like four days' worth of barf. I headed toward the back door to let poor Sammie in.

He snagged my arm. "Yer mangy dog ain' here. Had 'im put down after 'e pissed all over the kitchen floor agin."

His words hit me like a punch in the gut. I couldn't move, couldn't even breathe as the reality of what he'd done sank in.

His disgusting mouth came crashing down on mine, his stale breath making me gag. I turned my head desperately, trying to break away from his unwanted kiss, but he grabbed my chin roughly, forcing me to face him. His grip bruised my flesh as his fingers dug into me.

With a brutal shove, he slammed me up against the wall, knocking the wind out of me. Pain exploded through the back of my head and stars danced in my vision. He pinned my body with his own, his weight crushing me, making it hard to breathe. I could feel his arousal pressing against me, and revulsion churned in my stomach.

I struggled against him, trying to push him away, but he was too strong. His hands roamed all over my body, groping and pawing at me, his touch making my skin crawl. Tears stung my eyes as panic and disgust overwhelmed me. I wanted to scream, but fear had my voice trapped in my throat.

He leaned in closer, his hot, rancid breath washing over my face as he whispered disgusting things in my ear. I closed my eyes, trying to block out the horror of what was happening, praying for someone, anyone, to save me from this nightmare.

Suddenly, I remembered what Joy had taught me and kneed Freddie as hard as I could in the nuts.

He swore, stumbled, and loosened his grip long enough for me to break away. I grabbed the blade and flicked it open.

I gritted my teeth and, holding the blade how Steve had taught me—firmly but not too tight—I took a balanced stance. "Stay away from me, you fucker."

And then Freddie lunged...

Chapter Seventeen

Angelo

As I approached Serenity and Freddie's house, the horrible stench of neglect and decay assaulted my nostrils. The two-story structure was more of a hovel, with patches of dirt instead of grass and the shriveled remains of rose bushes standing sentry by the front door. The peeling, faded pink paint revealed rotting wood, and one splintered shutter hung askew, threatening to fall off its rusted hinges at any moment.

The sight of the home of the man who had dared to hurt Serenity filled me with rage, and I looked forward to teaching him the consequences of his actions. I cracked my neck, my muscles coiled like a snake ready to strike. Before I attacked an enemy, I was always completely calm—a lesson I had learned from Dracula himself.

"Keep your emotions in check," he'd always said. "Rashness leads to death. Assess your surroundings and always remain in control."

My fangs itched to sink into Freddie's flesh, to taste his blood and watch the light fade from his eyes. But I had to be patient.

I couldn't tell if anyone was home as I headed toward the front door. I sniffed the air and detected the scent of humans, but that could have been Freddie's neighbors.

I twisted the rusty doorknob, breaking it, then kicked the weakened door in. The stench of stale alcohol and grease hit me as I entered the trashed living room. Potato chip crumbs crunched under my boots as I navigated a labyrinth of empty beer cans and dirty dishes left haphazardly on coffee tables and couches. A half-eaten steak and baked potato sat abandoned on an end table, surrounded by candy wrappers and more chip remnants. The one smell I wasn't getting was human blood.

Petar and some of my other men arrived, shaking their heads.

Damn. The rat had disappeared. Would Simon have warned him I was coming? No. He'd practically pissed his pants when I confronted him. Maybe someone else had tipped him off.

Nothing annoyed me more than when I had to hunt down my prey when I was eager to strike.

My hands shook with anger as I pulled out my phone, my heart racing as I dialed Keir's number. He picked up on the first ring, his voice tense and hurried. "You need to give me more time—"

I got straight to the point. "Do you know anything about a Freddie Evans?"

"Evans...Evans..." Keir paused, thinking. "Yeah, I remember him. Used to be a big shot around here, always strutting around like he owned the place, bragging about his gambling skills."

"But not anymore?"

Keir let out a mirthless chuckle. "Word on the street is, he's been on a bad losing streak. Owes a lot of people money and can't pay them back."

"Any idea where I can find him?"

"I think he's been holed up with some woman over on Magnolia Crescent Way. Belinda...Stone, I think her name is. She's living at Madame Charlotte's House." A hint of disdain crept into Keir's voice. "She was a dancer at one of Maximo's strip clubs before."

My eyes narrowed. The fact that he knew so much about Belinda Stone and her connection to Freddie suggested he had been keeping tabs on Serenity and investigating her background, but I could tell he was holding something more back. "How do you know all this?"

Keir hesitated before answering. "Let's just say Belinda and some of my men have crossed paths before."

Bingo. "Later, Keir. Thanks."

He quickly added, "Still looking into our agreement about the murdered girls."

"Good." I hung up the phone and turned to my men. "We need to go to Magnolia Crescent Way."

I darted out of the dilapidated shack and transformed into a bat, my leathery wings carrying me toward the seedier part of New Orleans. The streets here were lined with dimly lit bars and strip joints, the acrid smells of urine and cheap beer filling the air.

Hovering above Sweet Babes, one of Maximo's infamous girlie clubs, I could hear blaring jazz music pouring out of its doors. The place was notorious for working their girls until they were worn out and broken.

I landed on the rooftop of Madame Charlotte's House next door and wasted no time in breaking in. I quickly picked the lock with my sharp vampire claws and kicked open the door, sending it crashing against the wall.

As I descended the creaky stairs at lightning speed, my heart was racing with adrenaline. I barged into a ground floor room, finding a bald man shrinking against the wall, his face a mask of horror. I grabbed his collar and yanked him up off the ground, his hands frantically gripping my wrist.

"Please—don't hurt me."

I shook him hard, my grip tightening on his collar until my knuckles turned white. "Where's Belinda Stone's apartment?" My words were laced with venom, every muscle in my body coiled and ready to strike if he didn't answer.

"Number thirteen," the man sputtered, spraying spit into my face.

I dropped him onto the worn green carpet, the smell of mold and mildew hitting me like a punch to the face. I raced down the hallway, past peeling wallpaper and flickering lights, until I reached number thirteen at the end. The stench here was even worse, with only a small window providing a sliver of fresh air.

I kicked open the door and stormed into the apartment,

my rage barely contained as my men began trashing the place. Then I saw her: a startled older woman with bleached blonde hair. Heavy layers of makeup caked her face, but it couldn't hide the sadness in her eyes. I charged toward her, my eyes blazing with a fury that could no longer be restrained. A beaten-up recliner stood in my way, but I simply kicked it aside, sending it crashing into the wall with a satisfying thud.

The woman stumbled backward, tripping over the scattered beer cans that littered the floor. Her face paled, but her obvious fear did nothing to quell the inferno of wrath that consumed me. I loomed over her, my fists clenched so tightly that my knuckles turned white.

"Where's Freddie?" I demanded, my teeth clenched and menace radiating from every fiber of my being. The two words were laced with a fury that promised retribution, a barely contained violence that threatened to explode at any moment.

Her lower lip trembled. "I...I..."

A blood-curdling scream echoed through the hallway just as a tall, thin man careened into the wall in a desperate attempt to escape. Somehow, he almost managed to crawl up the vertical surface like a frantic cockroach, his limbs flailing as he sought an exit. Then, realizing the futility of his efforts, he turned around and stumbled toward the doorway, his movements clumsy and disoriented.

Seeing he was about to flee, I swiftly closed the distance between us with purposeful strides. Just as he reached the threshold, I lunged forward and grabbed him by the collar, my vampire strength allowing me to lift him effortlessly off the floor. His feet kicked at the air, and he struggled in my unyielding grip, but I held him fast, determined to prevent his escape.

As I tightened my grip on his throat, the man's face drained of color, his pupils dilating as he trembled in my grasp. "So, you're Freddie," I snarled.

His eyes got three sizes too big. "I know you. You're... you're Angelo...Santi."

I gave him a smile full of fangs. "Yes. And your worst nightmare. You're the piece of shit who sold Serenity Bryce to Simon Cartier, right?"

I drew on my powers of compulsion and stared into his terrified gaze. "Tell me everything you did to her."

Tears glistened in the corners of his eyes as he struggled to keep his composure. Then the words could not be held in any longer—they tumbled out in jumbled, fragmented sentences as he told me everything. He confessed how he had cruelly beaten Serenity when she was just a child, leaving permanent scars on her back. How he had lusted over her for years as she grew older, waiting until her mother's passing to make his move. As he recounted what he had forced Serenity to endure, my fury reached new heights. The thought of him attacking her, forcing himself upon her, made my blood boil with a rage I had never known before. But when he revealed his ultimate cruelty—that he had killed her beloved dog, Sammie—something inside me snapped.

A roar of pure, unadulterated fury tore from my throat, and I slammed my fist into the wall behind his head so hard that it left a gaping hole in the plaster. The pain in my hand was nothing compared to the agony that twisted in my heart.

Freddie had not only violated Serenity's body, but he had also crushed her soul by taking away the creature that had brought her happiness.

He kicked and squirmed, his hands slapping at my wrists. "I...I needed the money. The Fae...They were going to kill me..."

I gritted my teeth, squeezing my fingers tighter around his scrawny throat. I could feel his pulse thudding under my grip, the frantic heartbeat of a man who knew his end was near. Freddie's face turned purple and red as he gasped for air. The sight of his suffering only fueled the dark satisfaction that coursed through my veins even more.

"P-please," he choked out, his voice barely a whisper. "I-I'm sorry..."

His pathetic words meant nothing to me. All I could think about was the pain he had inflicted upon Serenity, the scars he had left on both her body and soul. I wanted him to feel that pain, to understand the depths of my fury.

"Like I care that the Fae were going to stomp on a cockroach," I snarled, tightening my grip even more. The smell of his fear filled my nostrils, a sickly-sweet aroma that only served to intoxicate me. I could see the terror in his eyes, the realization that there would be no mercy, no escape from the hell I had in store for him.

In that moment, I knew that I would not stop until he had paid for his sins in blood and agony. Torturing him wasn't enough.

I needed more information about who kept setting me and Serenity up.

"Do you owe King Rankin and the dark Fae Mafia money?"

He sputtered. "Yes." So that's why Keir made it a point to know so much about Freddie.

I shook him harder. "Well, lucky you, Simon said you found a way to clear your debt. On that note—what do you know of angels?"

He looked around wildly, as if searching for a way out. "If I tell you...he'll kill me." The dark Fae were quite inventive in their torture. It was usually slow and always painful. No humans ever survived it. I should be handing this bastard over to Keir, but the prospect of killing him myself was giving me great pleasure.

I flashed my fangs. "And I'll kill you if you don't." I was going to kill him anyway, but the dirty little rat didn't need to know that.

"No...I'm begging you..." His sniveling voice just made me want to rip out his vocal cords. He didn't think once of Serenity's well-being, only his own skin.

My fingers tingled as I focused on him, trying to use compulsion to get what I wanted. Surprisingly, instead of his mind bending to my will, it was like my mind hit a solid wall. My body jerked back as if pushed by an invisible force, and I released him. He landed on the floor with a splat, moaning, groaning, and sputtering.

Confusion and fear flooded through me—why wasn't my compulsion working? This had never happened to me before.

As I stood there, trying to shake off the mysterious spell that had rendered me powerless, my mind raced through the list of vampires who could possibly be behind it. There weren't many that were strong enough—The *Fondatori* Kings, Dracula of course, maybe Anton Lange from Legacy Academy. But this felt different, more like dark magic than another vampire.

My thoughts turned to Simon's witch, Marsha, when I noticed her distinct scent of herbs and incense lingering in the air, making my nose twitch in disgust. Where had she been when we attacked Ravenwood Estates? Had she cast a spell on me without me realizing it?

Chapter Eighteen

Angelo

Something in this disgusting apartment was preventing me from using my power. I clenched my fists in frustration.

Killing Freddie in this crappy apartment wasn't how I wanted to end this bastard's life. Someone might try to stop me. Nothing was going to prevent me from taking my full revenge out on Freddie, and for that, I needed to get him someplace where his screams wouldn't be heard. Somewhere like Crimson Stakes.

Petar crept toward the terrified woman who was still cringing against the kitchen sink with no chance of escape.

"Don't even think it, Petar," I growled. The last thing I wanted was Costin shoving a stick up my ass if another drained woman showed up.

As I tore out of the crappy apartment, fast as an angry

wind, my men followed me like good soldiers. The only thing I could hear, which continued driving me on, were Freddie's screams as I dragged him behind me. I lead my men out into the crowded New Orleans streets, knocking over people and leaving them unable to figure out what had hit them.

I arrived at Crimson Stakes and quickly made my way inside. I pushed through the double doors, ignoring the bewildered looks from other patrons. In a matter of seconds, I had taken Freddie into a large room hidden behind the cashier's counter. This was my secret chamber, reserved for those who were unfortunate or foolish enough to cross me. Ornate sconces adorned the walls, each one cradling a thick, ivory candle. Their flickering light cast a warm, golden glow over the swords, daggers, and instruments of torture mounted on the walls. Not one prisoner had ever left this room alive.

I tossed Freddie into the middle of the room where there was a chair with chains. "Dimitri, bind him."

Faster than the blink of an eye, Dimitri had fastened Freddie's wrists and ankles to the chair.

Freddie squirmed and wriggled in the chair. "Let me go." His voice was almost a high-pitched screech.

I circled Freddie like a predator, my anger simmering just beneath the surface. "I asked Simon, and now I'm asking you. You'd better hope you have a better answer than he did. Who ordered the hit on Crescent Manor?" I kept my eyes locked on his, my fists clenching and unclenching at my sides, the tension in my body conveying my unspoken threat.

"Noooo," Freddie wailed, shaking his head frantically. "I can't tell you."

"Wrong fucking answer." I grabbed his hair and yanked his head back, exposing the tender flesh of his throat.

"Please...Let me go." Not once did he apologize for hurting Serenity. If he had done so, I might have killed him quickly and painlessly.

But he didn't.

So tonight, he would suffer like Serenity had suffered.

With a feral snarl, I sank my fangs deep into his neck, tearing messily through skin and muscle with a sickening ease.

Freddie's scream of agony echoed off the walls, a high-pitched, desperate wail that only fueled the dark hunger within me. The coppery taste of his blood flooded into my mouth, thick and tainted with the essence of his foulness. It was like swallowing pure corruption, a vile poison that burned my veins like acid.

Even as I recoiled from the taste, I could feel the savage pleasure of the beast spread through me, a pleasure that reveled in the violence and the suffering of my prey. I tore into Freddie's flesh with a renewed ferocity, my fangs ripping and shredding like the claws of a wild animal.

Freddie's body convulsed beneath me, his struggles growing weaker as I drained his precious life force from him. The sound of my own greedy gulps and feral growls filled my ears, a twisted symphony of rage and hatred.

Finally, I wrenched myself away from his ravaged throat, my breath coming in ragged gasps as I struggled to regain control. Freddie slumped against the chair, his face ashen and his eyes glazed over with pain and terror.

Even as I looked upon his broken, pitiful form, I felt no mercy, nor one hint of remorse for the suffering I had inflicted. Rather, his tainted blood stoked the fire of my hatred, his foulness a reminder of all the pain and misery he had brought into Serenity's life.

He'd shown no mercy to her. He hadn't stopped hurting her even when she'd begged him to. The idea haunted me. Time for him to experience the same pain and horror Serenity endured all these years living with him.

I turned to my men, my eyes blazing with wild intensity. "He's all yours," I said, my breath coming in heaving, ragged gasps, my body still trembling in the aftermath of my own savage feeding. "Make him suffer, as he has made others suffer. Show him the true meaning of pain and despair."

As my men fell upon Freddie like a pack of starving wolves, I watched with a grim satisfaction. His agony had only just begun. This was the price of betrayal, the consequence of daring to cross the vampire king and those I held dear.

As Freddie's screams echoed through the chamber, I knew that I would stop at nothing to protect what was mine, to keep Serenity safe from all the monsters that lurked in the shadows of our dark and twisted world.

"Stop! Enough for now!" I yelled authoritatively as my power surged through the chamber, causing the air to crackle with a supernatural energy, the ground to tremble beneath my feet, and the candles to flicker until the shadows danced along the walls.

My men snapped their heads to me, their red-rimmed eyes wide with surprise and a hint of fear. They knew the extent of my power and the consequences of defying me. Reluctantly, they moved away from Freddie, their fangs still bared and glistening with his blood.

Freddie's head lolled forward, his breathing shallow. Blood oozed from countless puncture wounds on his neck, shoulders, and arms, staining his tattered shirt a deep crimson. The bite marks on his face and throat were ragged and vicious, a testament to the savage feeding frenzy he had endured. The coppery scent of his blood hung heavy in the air, mingling with the musty odor of the dank chamber.

Thick chains still bound his wrists and ankles to the chair, cutting into his flesh as he weakly struggled against the restraints. I approached slowly, my gaze locked on the broken man before me. His heartbeat was faint and erratic, fluttering like a caged bird within his chest. I knew I had precious little time to intervene before he succumbed to his wounds or was drained completely by my men.

Draining him was too easy a death.

Freddie raised his head, tears rushing down his bloody face. "Stop...please...have mercy..."

"I'm the Angel of Death. Mercy isn't an option." I snapped my fingers. "Dimitri."

My brother-in-law grabbed a blade off the wall and handed it to me.

Freddies' eyes pleaded with me as I stood over him, my finger running slowly over the blade. "Was it King Rankin that you owed money to?"

I studied his face, watching for a tremor or a glance that would betray him.

Freddie shook his head wildly. "I can't tell you." He seemed to be more afraid of someone else. Someone scarier than me. Laughable! My reputation was enough to have people cower in front of me.

An unamused smile curled the corner of my mouth. "Keeping information from me also isn't an option." I grabbed his pinky and calmly sliced it off.

Freddie screamed and cursed as blood poured out of the stump. I licked my finger delicately where his blood had stained it.

I thought about it for a minute. "Is there another party involved besides Kings Keir and Trystan?"

Freddie strained against his manacles. "Please, you don't understand—"

I sliced again, cutting off his ring finger.

He spasmed and screamed. "No. Please, stop." Not happening. He had hurt Serenity, and he would pay for it.

As I pulled back his middle finger, breaking it slowly, segment by segment, Freddie's eyes bulged in agony. A fresh scream tore from his throat, his face contorted in a mask of pure anguish. He writhed beneath me, his body jerking with each sickening crack of bone.

"Please, stop!" he begged, tears streaming down his face. "I'm sorry, I'm so very sorry!"

His pleas fell on deaf ears. All I could think about was how Serenity must have cried and begged for mercy when he hurt her, receiving none. The thought of her pain fueled my rage, and I tightened my grip on his finger, bending it back further.

"You showed Serenity no mercy," I snarled, my voice cold and unforgiving. "Now, you shall receive none from me." I leaned closer. "Tell me who ordered the hit on Crescent Manor."

"Noooo," he wailed, shaking his head.

"You're a stubborn one." I broke the last knuckle of his finger with a final snap and then sliced it off, ignoring his anguished shrieks. I was getting tired of this game and tried once again to bring up my power of compulsion. "Tell me the truth."

As I delved into Freddie's mind, his eyes turned dull, and drool began to drip from his mouth, the usual signs of the power taking hold. But despite being within the walls of Crimson Stakes, where my abilities were normally amplified, I found myself unable to penetrate Freddie's thoughts fully.

I pushed harder, focusing all my power on breaking through the barrier that blocked me from accessing the information I sought, yet Freddie's mind remained stubbornly closed off to me.

Frustration and anger welled up inside me as I slowly realized that someone had managed to place a powerful psychic shield in Freddie's mind, one strong enough to withstand even the enhanced abilities normally granted to me by Crimson Stakes' dark essence. It was something I had never encountered before, and the idea that someone was able to hide the truth from me, in this place of my supreme power no less, sent a chill down my spine.

I redoubled my efforts, pouring every ounce of my power into breaking through the barrier, but it held fast, unyielding. The complete picture remained tantalizingly out of reach, taunting me. Whoever had done this possessed a level of skill and knowledge far beyond anything I had ever encountered, and the realization left me both enraged and unnerved.

"Who has done this to you?" I snapped, the words coming out like the crack of a whip. Rage surged through my body, a white-hot fury that threatened to consume me from the inside out. "Who's trying to keep me from seeing the full picture?"

I stalked closer to Freddie, my every step fueled by the anger coursing through my veins. But he remained unresponsive, his vacant eyes staring past me, the barrier in his mind an impenetrable fortress. I slammed my fist against the wall, the pain barely registering as I grappled with the knowledge that I had been outmaneuvered. Whoever had done this, they were clever, and they had just made a powerful enemy.

Not many people had magic this powerful. I didn't think Marsha did, but maybe I underestimated her. Or it could be someone entirely different. Someone who might conceivably also be responsible for the murders.

"Please, have mercy," he begged. "He wanted—"

His pleas briefly interrupted my thoughts, but then images of Freddie's cruelty flashed through my mind—Serenity's beloved dog taken away from her, and her delicate flesh bruised and battered from his relentless beatings. It was the sick, twisted desires lurking in his depraved mind, however, that pushed me over the edge. I had seen the perverted acts he longed to inflict upon her, the fantasies that consumed his every waking moment.

And now, one of my own had fallen victim to his darkness and corruption. I didn't think Freddie killed Jacques, but he knew who did, and he was denying me my revenge by keeping it from me. The bonds of loyalty that tied my men to me were sacred, the very foundation of my power. And now the respect I commanded as king had been shaken by his actions.

I couldn't let this stand. To allow such a transgression to go unpunished would be to invite chaos and rebellion into my kingdom. I had to send a message, to make an example of this traitorous filth for all to see.

My grip tightened on the handle of the blade, the metal cool and unyielding against my palm. I pictured Serenity's face, the terror and pain in her eyes that had haunted her for too long. I thought of my fallen comrade.

A cold, terrible calm settled over me as I raised the knife high overhead. This was vampire justice—swift, brutal, and irrevocable. With a single, powerful stroke, I brought the blade down, driving it deep into Freddie's soft, vulnerable flesh.

His agonized scream rang off the walls, and I watched dispassionately as he writhed in his bonds, his face contorted with shock and horror. Good. Let him suffer, as Serenity had suffered. Let him feel the depths of my wrath and pay the price for crossing the vampire king.

As his blood pooled on the floor, something dark and primal unfurled within my chest. In one last vicious act, I bit him once more, tasting the coppery liquid that gushed down my chin, draining him until he grew limp in the chair. As his life force left him, power flooded into me, making me stronger.

I released him and wiped my mouth with the back of my arm. Then I met Dimitri's eyes. "Get rid of the body. Dump it in the Mississippi."

Dimitri's eyebrows shot up, a mix of surprise and impressed amusement dancing in his eyes. "Wow, remind me never to get on your bad side. I'd say 'you missed a spot,'" he gestured to his own chin with a smirk, "but honestly, the whole blood-drenched look really works for you. Very 'vampire chic.'" His tone sobered slightly, though the corner of his mouth still twitched. "I'll take care of it. Want me to gift-wrap him for the gators, or is this more of a catch-and-release situation?"

I turned without answering him and left Dimitri and the others to carry out my orders.

Chapter Nineteen

Serenity

The stench of Freddie's sweat mixed with his alcohol-laced breath assaulted my nostrils as he lunged at me, his eyes wild with fury. His meaty hand reached for the blade, but I twisted away, feeling the cold steel slice through his wrist and arm. He let out an agonized scream and fell to his knees, blood splattering the dirty wooden floor.

"You bitch," he spat, his voice dripping with venom. "I'll take you fast and hard for that. You'll be begging me to stop before I'm done with you."

His words made the bile churn in my stomach. The thought of his filthy hands on my body, his weight pressing me down, made my skin crawl. I refused to lose my virginity to such a horrible, disgusting man. He'd steal my innocence and shatter my soul.

I backed up slowly, my heart pounding in my ears, until I felt the rough grain of the door against my sweat-soaked shirt. My hand felt around behind me, fumbling for the handle as Freddie staggered to his feet. The coppery scent of blood, mingled with the musty odor of the room, made my head spin.

"You ain't goin' nowhere, girl," Freddie growled, his good hand making a fist. "You're mine now."

I swallowed hard, my mouth suddenly dry. My fingers finally found the cool metal of the door handle, and I turned it, praying it was unlocked. The door creaked open behind me, and I stumbled backward into the unknown, desperate to escape the nightmare that threatened to consume me...

I jerked awake. The nightmare was already fading, but adrenaline still surged through my body, setting every nerve on fire. Someone was brushing the hair off my forehead, and a fresh jolt of pure terror shot through me. My eyes snapped open, but I couldn't seem to focus, my mind still trapped in the lingering tendrils of the dream. It had felt so real, like Freddie was actually here in the room with me.

I thrashed my head back and forth, my arms and legs flailing. "Get off me!" I screamed at my unknown attacker, my voice raw and desperate. "Get off!"

Strong hands clamped down on my wrists, holding me steady. "Serenity, shh. It's me. It's Angelo."

At the sound of his voice, the fog of fear began to dissipate. I blinked rapidly, my chest heaving as I sucked in deep, ragged breaths. Angelo's handsome face swam into focus above me, his dark eyes filled with concern.

For a fleeting moment, a wave of relief washed over me. Angelo's presence felt like a lifeline, anchoring me to reality and chasing away the lingering shadows of the nightmare. But as my adrenaline faded and my mind cleared, confusion and unease crept in.

Why was he here, in my room? The question swirled in my mind. The part of me that yearned for comfort and safety wanted to lean into his touch, to let him chase away the demons that haunted me. But another part, the part that remembered the cold reality of our situation, recoiled from his proximity.

I was his prisoner. No matter how gentle his hands or how concerned his gaze, I couldn't forget that. He had bought me, refused to set me free, ripped me away from the people I loved. The nightmare might have been a product of my own mind, but the waking world held its own horrors, and Angelo was the architect of them.

A dull ache pulsed at the base of my skull, and I winced, remembering all the wine I'd drunk the night before. Clearly, I'd overindulged, and now I was paying the price by having vivid nightmares about Freddie.

"Angelo?" I croaked, my throat dry and tight. "What are you doing here?" I shifted my weight on the luxurious bed. Angelo released my wrists and leaned back, allowing me to sit up. As I massaged the knot in my neck, I couldn't help but notice the intricate thorny tattoo that snaked down his neck and over his chest, exposed by the completely unbuttoned white shirt he wore. His long, curly hair was pulled up into a man bun, a style that somehow managed to look both effortless and very deliberate, and his dark green eyes glinted in the sunlight streaming through the window.

"I came to check on you," Angelo said softly. "I heard you screaming." His scowl deepened as he noticed my discomfort. "What's wrong?"

I dragged my fingers through my hair. "It's nothing. Too much wine last night."

He stiffened. "Enzo shouldn't have given you so much to drink."

I sighed heavily, then dropped my arm. "He didn't have a choice."

His eyebrows raised in confusion. "Excuse me?"

I met his gaze head-on. "I told him if he didn't, I would tell you that he touched me."

He threw his head back and an enormous guffaw burst out of him as his eyes sparkled with amusement. "Well, aren't you the little minx."

His laughter caught me off guard. It was rich and warm, filled with genuine amusement, and for a moment, I forgot myself. I forgot the fear, the anger, the confusion that had been my constant companions since he'd taken me, and a smile danced over the corners of my mouth.

But the moment was fleeting. As quickly as it had come, it was gone again as reality crashed back in, and the smile died on my lips. I couldn't let myself be swayed by a charming laugh or a playful nickname. This man was my captor, not my friend.

And so I schooled my features into a neutral expression, trying to ignore the way my heart had leaped at the sound of his amusement. "I'm glad you approve," I said in an even voice, "but don't let it go to your head. I'm not here to entertain you." The words were a reminder for myself as much as they were for him.

Angelo's eyes narrowed slightly, and for a moment, I thought I saw something flicker in their depths. Disappointment? Frustration? I couldn't be sure. But just as quickly, it was gone, replaced by the same amused sparkle as before.

"Oh, of course not," he said, his voice still tinged with laughter even as he tried to be stern. "But there's no harm in enjoying yourself a little, is there? After all, we're going to be spending a lot of time together."

As much as I didn't want to give into the feeling, his words made me want him to hold me. Maybe he was using some kind of compulsion on me? Or was it something deep inside me that yearned for someone to take care of me?

He inclined his head and his eyes traced over my body, sending a shiver down my spine. He gently brushed a stray strand of hair out of my eyes and whispered, "You look absolutely breathtaking in the morning, Serenity. I could wake up to this every day."

My chest tightened as sudden fear coursed through me. I edged away from him. "Are you going to feed on me?" My voice trembled.

He immediately snatched away his hand and a sorrowful look flashed in his eyes. "No, little one, I'm not. I would never hurt you. You're mine to protect."

"Why do you keep saying that? Unless you mean you're just protecting your investment."

He smiled again. "You're much more than an investment."

"If there are bad guys out there ready to snatch me up, then I need to protect myself. I know how to fight with a knife. Can I get either a switchblade or a blade?"

He slowly lifted his eyebrows. "Do you really think either of those will kill a vampire?"

I searched his eyes, trying to gauge his sincerity. Was he mocking me, or was he genuinely trying to help? I couldn't be sure, but if I was going to survive in this world, I needed to understand the rules of engagement.

"So...I need a stake?" I asked, hating the uncertainty in my voice.

Angelo shook his head, a hint of a smile playing around the edges of his mouth. "Stakes are a myth. Truthfully, you need a sword. You saw how poor Jacques was killed. You need to cut a vampire's head off to kill them. If you shoot us or stab us, it's like a bee sting. All you'll do is piss us off."

I swallowed hard, the image of Jacques' decapitated body flashing through my mind. The utter brutality of it, the finality, made my stomach churn. But beneath the revulsion, there was something else: a tiny spark of hope. If Angelo was telling me this, if he was telling me how to defend myself, maybe he wasn't entirely the monster I'd thought him to be.

"Why are you helping me like this?" I asked, my voice barely above a whisper.

Angelo's gaze locked on mine, and for a moment, I felt like I could drown in the depths of his eyes. "Because I want you to survive," he said, his voice low and intense. "I see something in you, Serenity, something special. And I'll be damned if I let anyone, human or vampire, snuff that out."

His words sent a shiver down my spine, and I couldn't

look away. There was a sincerity in his voice, a raw honesty I couldn't ignore. But there was also a fierce possessiveness. I didn't know how to feel about that, just as I didn't know how to reconcile the warring emotions that swirled within me. But one thing was clear: if I was going to make it out of this alive, I needed to learn how to navigate this world, and Angelo, for better or worse, was my guide.

He blinked. "Wait. You said you knew how to handle a switchblade or a knife? How did you learn how to fight?"

"Joy's older brother, Steven. He taught me after Freddie came after me one night. I managed to get away…" I hung my head and took a shaky, shuddering breath. "But it was too close."

He scowled. "Steven as in Detective DuPont's boy? He taught you how to fight?"

"Yes and no. Steven found out DuPont wasn't his real father and it sent him down a rebellious path, joining a street gang. Last I heard, he was in with the mob. But yes, he's the one who taught me."

Angelo narrowed his eyes. "Which family?"

"The Barones." My heart lurched. "Wait, are they—"

"Human. If that's what you're asking."

Something in his eyes said this worried him.

"You need to learn how to kill a supernatural, Serenity. I will teach you."

"You're going to teach me how to kill a vampire?" I asked, my voice trembling slightly. "Why would you do that?"

Angelo leaned back, his gaze still locked on mine. "Because knowledge is power, Serenity. And in the vampire world, power is everything. If you're going to survive, you need to know what you're up against. You'll need to know how to fight back, for your own sake."

His words sent a mixture of fear and exhilaration through me. The thought of learning how to kill a vampire, of having that kind of knowledge, was both terrifying and thrilling. But it was also a stark reminder of the danger I was in, that I was trapped in a world where such knowledge was necessary in the first place.

"Won't that put you at risk?" I pressed, unable to keep the concern from my voice. "If I know how to kill vampires, doesn't that make me a direct threat to you?"

Angelo smiled, a slow, sultry curve of his lips that made my heart skip a beat. "Oh, Serenity," he murmured, "you're already a threat to me. But not in the way you think."

He reached out, his fingers brushing against my cheek in a featherlight caress. I shivered, my skin tingling at his touch. "You see," he continued, his voice low and tender, "the greatest danger you pose to me isn't physical. It's emotional. You make me feel things, Serenity. Things I haven't felt in a long, long time. And that scares me more than any weapon ever could."

I didn't know what to say to that, but I could feel the truth of his words, could sense the depth of sincere emotion behind them.

In that moment, I realized my fate was now inextricably linked with his. For better or worse, we were in this together. And if I was going to survive, I needed to learn to trust him, even as I learned to fight against everything he represented.

Chapter Twenty

Serenity

Angelo's soft words stirred something in me again. It scared me. The touch of his fingers on my skin sent a shiver down my spine and sent my heart racing in my chest. I wanted to lean into him, to feel his strong arms around me and his lips pressed against mine. The memory of our last kiss danced in my memory—the taste of him, the way his mouth had moved against mine with such passion and hunger.

But even as these heady thoughts flooded my mind, I couldn't shake the fear that this might all just be compulsion. How could I be experiencing these feelings for not only a vampire, but also the very man who had taken me captive? It made no sense.

And yet, even as I tried to convince myself that it was all just a magician's trick, a callous manipulation of my mind and heart, I knew deep down that I was lying to myself. The attraction I felt for Angelo, the desire that now coursed through my veins whenever he was near, was real. It was terrifying and exhilarating all at once, and I didn't know how to reconcile it with the reality of my situation.

I needed to change the subject before I lost myself completely in the depths of his eyes and the magical intensity of his touch. There was too much at stake, too much I still didn't understand about this world and my place in it.

I cleared my throat. "Did you find out who killed Jacques?"

He held my gaze, his eyes cold and unflinching. "Yes, I did. Or at least, I should say I found out who plotted it, even if he did not strike the blow. The bastard refused to spill the truth on that, even when I had him at my mercy."

My stomach twisted into knots at the hardness in his voice, the barely restrained fury simmering beneath the surface.

Angelo's jaw clenched, and he looked away for a moment, as if gathering his thoughts. When he spoke again, his voice was low and unhurried. "No one has ever ordered a hit on Crimson Manor. But I have reason to believe that Freddie was involved, or at least had knowledge of the plan."

I staggered back a step, my breath catching in my throat as the implications hit me like a baseball bat, stunning me. "Freddie? But how? And why?" I felt like the ground had been yanked out from under me, leaving me disoriented and struggling to regain my balance. My thoughts raced, trying to make sense of this new information, but it was like trying to put together a puzzle with half the pieces missing.

Angelo sighed, his shoulders sagging slightly. "Freddie had connections, Serenity. He was a lowlife scum, but he was a lowlife scum with his ears to the ground."

What did that even mean? The last thing I wanted to do was run into him. I looked around wildly, expecting Freddie to pop out like the boogeyman at any second. "Is Freddie here? I mean...I won't run into him, will I?" Fear was in my every word.

"You never have to worry about Freddie again," he said softly as he gently rubbed my back.

I jerked my head up, my heart pounding in my chest as I processed this. "What?" The words came out in a hoarse whisper, barely audible over the pounding of my heart. I broke out in a cold sweat, my knees buckled, and I had to reach out to steady myself against the nearest available surface as the earth tilted beneath my feet. It was as if the very foundation of my world had been shaken, leaving me scrambling to find solid ground amid the chaos. I pulled back slightly, searching Angelo's eyes for any hint of deception or uncertainty, but found only solemn sincerity there.

My hands began to tremble, and I clenched them into fists to steady myself. "Did you..." I swallowed hard, almost afraid to ask. "Did you kill him?"

Not even a flinch crossed his face as he spoke. "That man sold you to Simon. Not only that, he tortured and killed your dog, Sammie. For hurting you, he paid with his life." His voice lowered, almost gentle. "It was ugly. You don't need to know the details."

I stared at Angelo as the words pierced my stunned mind, my hands trembling and my skin prickling with a cold sweat as I fought to make sense of the bombshell he had just dropped. Freddie was dead. The monster who had tormented me, who had haunted my every waking moment, was gone. I should have felt relief, but instead, a cold numbness settled over me like a shroud.

"He...he killed Sammie?" I whispered, my voice cracking. "And sold me to Simon?" The words felt foreign on my tongue, too horrible to comprehend.

A sob tore from my throat, raw and ragged. Grief and betrayal warred within me, a tempest of emotions that threatened to sweep me away. How could Freddie have done something so cruel and unforgivable? The memory of Sammie's warm, wriggling body brushing against me, of his joyful barks and enthusiastic, sloppy kisses, twisted like a knife in my chest.

And the knowledge that Freddie had sold me...traded me like a piece of property to satisfy his own greed...It destroyed my last shred of trust in the world. The betrayal cut deep, reopening wounds I thought had long since healed over.

Even as the anger and pain surged through me, I couldn't ignore the small, insistent voice whispering in the back of my mind. Did I really want to know the "ugly" details of Freddie's death? Did I want to bear the burden of that knowledge, to picture the violence and suffering he had endured at Angelo's hands?

Part of me yearned for the truth, for the closure that came with understanding. But another part, the part that had seen too much darkness already, shied away from the gruesome realities of Angelo's world.

I took a deep breath, trying to calm the storm of

emotions raging inside me. "No, I don't know that I want to know the details," I said quietly, my voice trembling slightly. "I just...I need a moment to process all of this, please."

A tidal wave of rage and anguish crashed over me, threatening to drag me under. My hands shook, and I felt like I couldn't breathe, like the walls of the room were closing in on me.

Angelo gathered me into his arms, his strong embrace an anchor in the storm of my pain. I buried my face in his shoulder, my tears soaking into his shirt. Part of me recoiled from the thought of him taking a life, even Freddie's. But another part whispered that this was just the way of his world—a world of blood and shadows, where the strong protected what was theirs.

As he held me, murmuring soft words of comfort, I clung to him like a lifeline. In that moment, the numbness began to ebb away, replaced by a flicker of something else—a fragile spark of hope, and the knowledge that I wasn't alone in the darkness.

As I wept in Angelo's arms, I felt his hand come up to cradle my face, his thumb gently wiping away a tear. I lifted my eyes to his, and in their depths, I saw a flicker of tenderness and a silent understanding of the pain that gripped my heart.

Slowly, hesitantly, he lowered his head until his forehead rested against mine. His breath ghosted across my lips, so cool and comforting. "I'm here, Serenity," he whispered. "You're not alone."

Then, with a gentleness that made my heart melt, he pressed his lips to mine. It was a soft, chaste kiss, a touch of warmth amid the coldness that had seeped into my bones. For a moment, the entire world fell away—all the grief, all the betrayal, all the fear—and there was only the two of us, our hearts beating as one.

When he pulled back, I saw a glimmer of uncertainty in his eyes, as if he was worried he had overstepped. But I reached up, my fingers tracing the line of his jaw. "Thank you," I murmured, my voice thick with emotion. "For being here. For...for everything."

"Always," he vowed—and in that moment, I believed him.

Someone tapped on the door softly. "Angelo?"

He glanced over his shoulder. "What is it, Dimitri?" Instantly, he was back to being the head of the Santi family.

"We've prepared Jacques' body for burial. We're just waiting for you." His low voice hinted at the sadness of losing a brother-in-arms.

"I'll be there shortly," Angelo said, staring into my eyes.

"Very well," Dimitri said on the other side of the door.

"You don't have to—"

I wiped away my tears. "No. I want to be there."

Angelo's brow crinkled and he brushed the hair out of my face. "Really? Why?"

I took a sobering breath and exhaled shakily. "Because Jacques was kind to me? Because he was killed because of me?"

Angelo's eyes searched mine, a mixture of concern and admiration flickering in their depths. "Serenity, don't think like that," he said softly, his hand still caressing my face.

"Jacques' death is not your fault. The blame lies solely with Freddie and his friends."

I leaned into his touch, drawing strength from the contact. "I know," I whispered, my voice trembling slightly. "But still. Jacques showed me kindness when I was at my lowest. He always treated me well, even though he didn't have to. I owe it to him to pay my last respects."

A sad smile tugged at Angelo's lips. "You have a good heart, Serenity. I know Jacques saw that in you too." He paused, his thumb brushing gently across my cheekbone one last time. "Well, if you truly wish to attend, I won't stop you. Though I must warn you—we burn the body on a pyre at a vampire funeral."

I couldn't imagine the smell, but it wouldn't change my decision. Jacques died because of me, and he deserved to have me pay homage.

"I still want to go."

Angelo released a soft breath. "You don't have to be strong all the time, you know. It's okay to grieve, to let yourself feel pain."

I nodded, swallowing past the lump in my throat. "Yes, I know. But I think...if I go and see him laid to rest...it might help me find some closure. Some peace."

Angelo's gaze softened. "Then we'll go, and we'll face this together," he murmured, pressing a gentle kiss to my forehead. "You're not alone, Serenity. Not anymore."

He sat back, his hand falling from my face even as the warmth of his touch lingered. With a deep breath, he straightened his shoulders, the mantle of leadership settling over him once more. He slid off the bed and stood. "Come," he said, offering me his hand. "Let's go honor our fallen brother."

I looked down at my crumpled clothes. "Wait, let me just change quickly."

"Of course. I'll wait for you outside."

I grabbed a black dress with cap sleeves out of the closet. In the bathroom, I pulled my hair into a soft bun and quickly put on the dress. I washed my tearstained face and applied some mascara and red lipstick that Gianna had given me. I thought it made me look more presentable for a vampire's funeral.

I opened the door and Angelo flashed his gaze over me in appreciation.

"You look beautiful, Serenity. And you did all that in less than five minutes. I'm impressed."

He smiled and stretched out his hand. As I placed my hand in his, feeling the strength and support that radiated from him, I knew that whatever challenges lay ahead, I wouldn't be facing them alone. In this world of shadows and sorrow, I had found an unexpected light—a beacon of hope in the form of a vampire king.

Chapter Twenty-One

Angelo

As I walked with Serenity down the hallway, holding her hand, I ventured a sideways glance at her. Her beauty stole the breath from my lungs. She was a vision of tasteful elegance, in a simple black dress that hugged her curves. Her shimmering blond hair was pulled into a soft bun, displaying the graceful curve of her neck. The red of her lips stood out in striking contrast to her pale skin, a touch of color in a sea of mourning.

But it was the look in her eyes that truly captivated me. Despite the sadness that lingered there, a quiet strength shone through—a clear determination to face the challenges ahead with grace and resilience. In that moment, I knew Serenity was a force to be reckoned with, a beacon of hope in the darkness. My darkness.

"You look beautiful." I leaned closer to her. I was almost four hundred years old, and this woman made me tongue-tied. No woman had ever done that to me, not even when I was still human.

She blushed under my gaze. It only made her look even more radiant.

"Take my arm," I said.

As she placed her hand in the crook of my elbow, I felt a surge of protectiveness wash over me. I silently vowed to stand by her side, to shield her from any storms that might be looming on the horizon.

Together, we made our way through the mansion, the somber silence broken only by the soft rustle of her skirts. As we stepped out into the night, the air cool against our skin, I marveled at the strange twists of fate that had brought us, a vampire king and a Nephilim, together.

In this moment, as we walked toward the gathering in the courtyard to honor our fallen brother, I knew that no matter how shrouded in mystery the path ahead was, one thing was certain—Serenity had become a part of my world, and I would move mountains to keep her safe.

Moonlight lit up the solemn sight. A black drape covered the iron gates, keeping curious onlookers at bay. My men had built a wooden pyre, and Jacques' body was already laid out on top of it. Torches surrounded the courtyard. Dimitri hadn't hoisted up the wooden spikes yet and they rested against one wall. Freddie escaped this death, but he wasn't the one who had murdered Jacques. The murderer was still on the loose. Once he was in my grasp, the stakes would be for him and his friends.

I would find him, and heaven help him when I did. But this was a time for sorrow, not revenge.

Serenity gazed at Jacques' body without flinching. Pride swelled in my chest at her bravery. Dimitri and Gianna held hands. Enzo looped his arm through Elena's; she was holding a handkerchief to her nose. Her eyes were bright red and tearstained. Petar and my other men stood at solemn attention.

On a table there were unlit torches, one for everyone at the ceremony.

All eyes were on me as their leader and their king. I reluctantly released Serenity's hand and stood in front of my family.

I cleared my throat. "We are gathered here to honor our fallen brother, Jacques Girard. For centuries he stood by our side, a loyal friend and a fierce warrior. His bravery and dedication to this family knew no bounds, and his presence brought light to even the darkest of nights."

I cast my gaze over the assembled crowd, their faces etched with grief and sorrow. In a single, synchronized movement, they all bowed their heads, even Serenity. The sight of her, an outsider, willingly participating in our ancient rituals, sparked something deep within me—a flicker of hope in the darkness.

"Jacques was more than just a soldier; he was a true member of our family. His laughter filled our halls, his wisdom guided our decisions, and although his heart may have ceased to beat, it was always full of love and compassion for each and every one of us."

With a heavy heart, I gestured to the pyre.

"Now, it is time to bid him a final farewell and send him to the great beyond. Though he may not find the same afterlife as humans, may his spirit find peace in the eternal embrace of the vampire realm, knowing that his memory will live on in our hearts and minds."

Someone sniffed. I realized it was Serenity. She wiped a tear off her cheek. My sister rested her head on Dimitri's shoulder, and, in the moonlight, I could see she was crying too.

My chest tightened and a lump formed in the back of my throat as I gazed at the pyre. "Jacques, our brother, our friend...We will miss you more than words can express." I paused, swallowing hard as memories of our time together flooded into my mind. "Your sacrifice will not be forgotten, and your legacy will endure through the ages. Rest now, dear friend, knowing that we will carry on the fight in your honor." My voice cracked and I coughed, trying to mask the grief that was threatening to burst through. As the vampire king, I had to be strong for my people. I clenched my fists, feeling a flash of anger begin to stir beneath the sadness.

I took a deep breath, my shoulders squaring and my posture growing more resolute as I continued. "To those responsible for his untimely demise, know this: our grief may stay our hand today, but it will not forever quell the fire that now burns within us." My jaw clenched, and my hands trembled, a physical manifestation of the unwavering resolve that coursed through my veins. My voice grew to a crescendo, echoing across the gathered mourners. "Your actions have awakened a sleeping giant, and you will soon feel the full force of our wrath."

Anger surged through my body, causing my hands to ball into fists at my sides, my fingernails digging into my palms. I trembled with barely contained rage, every muscle in my body drawn taut like a bowstring ready to be released.

"The fury of the Santi family will rain down upon you, and you will pay the ultimate price for the blood you have spilled. There will be no place to hide, no mercy to be found. We will hunt you down like the vermin that you are and make you suffer as we have suffered."

I bowed my head, struggling to push down my anger. Silence gripped the courtyard. I took several deep breaths, then raised my head. "But for now, my friends, let us celebrate the life of Jacques Girard, a true son of the night. May his soul find eternal rest."

I headed over to the table with the unlit torches and picked one up. The torches had been soaked in kerosene, and as I touched the oil-soaked cloth to a flame, it sparked to life, casting a warm glow across my face.

Turning to face my family, I held the torch aloft. "Each of you will take a torch and light it from mine, representing the way Jacques touched each of our lives and the way his spirit ignited our own. Then, you will place your torch on the pyre, aiding his transition from this world to the next. In this way, we will honor his memory and guide him on his final journey."

With somber nods, the mourners began to approach me one by one. Dimitri was first, his eyes glistening with unshed tears as he lit his torch from mine. He placed a hand on my shoulder in a silent gesture of support and shared grief before moving to the pyre and nestling his torch among the kindling.

My sister, Gianna, was next, her movements graceful even in sorrow. Then came Elena, Enzo, Petar, and the others, each taking a moment to light their torch and pay their respects to our fallen brother.

Finally, Serenity stepped forward, her face illuminated by the dancing flames. As she lit her torch from mine, our eyes met, and in that moment a glimpse of understanding passed between us—a recognition of the significance of this moment and the bond we now shared.

Together, we watched as the pyre blazed to life, the fire consuming Jacques' body. I put my hand on her lower back, and we moved slightly away from the others to watch the pyre burn in silence. The crackle of the fire mingled with the soft murmurs of my family, their voices raised in an ancient hymn of farewell. As the smoke drifted toward the heavens, I hoped that wherever Jacques was now, he knew the depth of our love and felt the honor we bestowed upon him.

Serenity slipped her shaking hand into mine, and I met her sorrowful gaze. Tears stained her long dark eyelashes, and she leaned close to me. "Your heartfelt speech...it touched me. You truly cared about him, didn't you?" There was a hint of surprise in her tone.

I gave her a curious gaze. "Jacques had been with me since the beginning. He was more than a soldier or a friend —he was like a brother."

A tremor rippled through my body, threatening to shatter my composure. My breath came in short, shaky gasps and my heart pounded against my ribcage, the force of my emotions nearly overwhelming me.

"Your many faces constantly surprise me, Angelo," she murmured, her voice low and filled with wonder.

The space between us seemed to crackle with electricity, the air heavy with unspoken desires. I reached out, my hand cupping her cheek as I drew her closer.

"You have no idea the surprises I can show you," I whispered, my thumb tracing the delicate line of her jaw. "You need only open your heart to me."

I watched as a delightful blush bloomed on her cheeks, making her look like a pink rose in the moonlight. But there was a flash of unease in her eyes that didn't escape my notice, and a pang of worry shot through me. Had I pushed too far, too fast? The last thing I wanted was to frighten her or make her feel pressured.

As the silence stretched out between us, I cursed myself inwardly. I already knew the intensity of my feelings for her, but I had to remember that this was all new to Serenity. She doubtless needed time to come to terms with the growing connection between us.

Gently, I lifted her chin, seeking her gaze. "I will never do anything against your will, Serenity," I said softly, pouring all the sincerity and reassurance I could into my voice. "And I will never allow anyone to hurt you. On that, you have my word."

I held her gaze, willing her to see the truth in my eyes. I needed her to understand that my desire for her wasn't just about physical attraction or her healing abilities, but a deep, abiding need to protect and cherish her. She was a precious new light in my dark world, and I would do everything in my power to keep that light safe and shining brightly.

She put her slender hand on my chest and her eyes widened in surprise. "You have a heart?"

I clasped her hand and kissed her wrist, rolling my tongue over her skin, feeling her rapid pulse. "You didn't think I would?"

"I don't know...I guess." Her voice was soft, almost a whisper, as she held my gaze. In the dim light of the room, I could see the delicate blush on her cheeks spread down her neck like a trail of rose petals. She bit her lower lip, a gesture that was both innocent and alluring, and my heart skipped a beat. "I think I want you to show me. I'm yours, Angelo."

Chapter Twenty-Two

Serenity

As the funeral pyre began to burn lower and the mourners started to disperse, Angelo left my side to talk quietly with some of the others. I let my gaze wander over the vampires that remained, their faces etched with a grief that mirrored my own. The deep sadness reflected in their eyes transported me back to the day of my mother's funeral—the somber faces of the attendees, the suffocating weight of my black dress, the scent of lilies that seemed to cling to everything. I remembered how lost I felt, how utterly alone in a world that seemed determined to break me.

Jacques's funeral had been a revelation for me, the depth of emotion on display hinting at a world I had never before imagined, a world where the boundaries between life and death were not as clear-cut as I had always believed. As the smoke climbed higher into the night sky, I felt a sense of kinship with these supernatural beings. They, too, knew the pain of loss, the ache of a void that could never be filled.

Here, among the vampires, I saw a simple kinship. They had each other, their bonds forged over centuries of shared experiences and loyalties. And in this moment, as the embers drifted upward like so many tiny stars, I realized that I longed for that same connection. I wanted to belong, to be part of something greater than myself. I was tired of doing everything alone.

Angelo's deep care for someone who was technically almost an underling stirred something within me. This display of emotion served as a poignant reminder that even the most powerful and intimidating figures could experience pain and loss. Witnessing this unexpected vulnerability in Angelo made him appear more human, more relatable. His raw emotion drew me to him in an unanticipated way, forging a connection that ran deeper than I had ever imagined possible.

Angelo turned, catching my gaze. For a moment, our eyes locked, and a spark of connection passed between us before he made his way through the crowd, coming to stand beside me. "Walk with me?" His voice was still tinged with grief.

I nodded, falling into step beside him as he led me through the sprawling halls of the manor. The silence between us was as thick as early morning fog hanging over the Mississippi, but it wasn't uncomfortable—it was as if we both understood the pain the other was feeling so well that we didn't need to discuss it. Finally, we reached a set of ornate double doors, and Angelo pushed them open to reveal a glimpse of a grand bedroom overlooking the glittering tapestry of New Orleans' nightscape below.

I hesitated, not sure if I should enter. I had never been inside a guy's bedroom before, not even Steven's. There was something very intimate about crossing the threshold into Angelo's room. If I entered, something would change forever between us.

Angelo stretched out his hand. "Please, Serenity. You're quite safe."

There was something in his eyes that made my heart quicken and my breath catch in my throat. His eyes promised something that was forbidden, but also something that I wanted. I could easily turn tail and run back to my room. But would Angelo allow me to? And the bigger question was, did I actually want to? The daring part of me wanted to bite into the forbidden fruit and accept what he was offering.

For several long breaths I stood there debating what to do. In the end, I put my trembling hand in his and allowed him to pull me into his bedchamber.

As I stepped into the room, I was struck by its grandeur. The space was expansive, with high ceilings and elegant, dark wood furnishings. The walls were adorned with intricate tapestries and centuries-old paintings, their gold frames glinting in the soft light cast by the crystal chandelier overhead. A large, four-poster bed dominated the center of the room, its rich, crimson bedding plush and inviting.

Floor-to-ceiling windows dominated the far wall, offering a breathtaking view of the city skyline. Below us,

New Orleans' vibrant cityscape stretched out, a patchwork of warm gold punctuated by Bourbon Street's neon signs. Distant jazz music and raucous laughter drifted up from the streets, carried on a balmy breeze that whispered through the open windows. Savory aromas of Cajun spices tinged the air, a tantalizing blend of paprika, cayenne, and thyme. In the distance, the mighty Mississippi River snaked its way through the city's heart, its dark waters reflecting the luminous moon and countless stars dotting the inky sky above. This panorama captured the very essence of New Orleans.

But what caught my attention the most was the wall of bookshelves that lined another side of the room. They were filled with ancient tomes and leather-bound volumes, their spines bearing titles in languages and sometimes even alphabets that were unfamiliar to me. It was a collection that hinted at centuries of knowledge and wisdom, and I longed to run my fingers along their worn covers and peek inside them.

Angelo's words drew my attention. "This is my private sanctuary," he revealed. "The place where I come to find peace and solitude."

I moved to the window, gazing out at the city skyline. The French Quarter stretched out beneath me, a vibrant tapestry of history and culture. The streets below were lined with colorful buildings, their wrought-iron balconies and ornate facades speaking to the city's rich past.

I shifted my gaze to the Mississippi River, winding its way through the city like a dark ribbon. I could just make out the shapes of riverboats and barges, their silhouettes cutting through the inky blackness of the water like ghostly apparitions. The deep, mournful sound of a foghorn echoed across the water, a haunting melody that suggested countless stories and secrets hidden beneath the murky depths. The air was heavy with the scent of brackish water and the faint aroma of diesel fuel, a reminder of the ceaseless activity that continued even in the darkest hours of the night. As I watched, a lone tugboat chugged steadily upstream with quiet, unwavering determination, its powerful engine thrumming like a beating heart.

Beyond the river, the city stretched on further, a sea of twinkling lights and shadowy streets. It was a view that took my breath away, reminding me of the magic and mystery that permeated every corner of this old city.

As I stood there, I felt a sense of awe and wonder. It was as if I was seeing New Orleans through new eyes, a city of endless possibilities and untold secrets.

"It's beautiful," I breathed, feeling a sense of calm wash over me for the first time in days. All the chaos and heartache of the past week melted away as I lost myself in the city below. The distant note of a saxophone drifted up again from the streets, its soulful melody mixing with the laughter and chatter of the crowds. I took a deep breath, inhaling the heady scent of magnolias, honeysuckle, and spices carried in on the warm breeze. I closed my eyes and inhaled deeply again, letting the unique essence of New Orleans fill my lungs and soothe my troubled soul as it wrapped me in a comforting embrace.

The city's vibrant energy pulsed through the air like a living, breathing entity, a constant reminder that life goes on, even in the face of tragedy and upheaval. Angelo moved to stand beside me, his presence both comforting and energizing. I could feel the warmth emanating from his body, the light brush of his arm against mine igniting a tingling sensation that coursed through me. It was as if every nerve ending in my body was attuned to him, every sense heightened by his nearness.

"Yes," he agreed softly, his voice a low murmur that resonated through me. "Very beautiful."

When I turned to look at him, I realized that he wasn't gazing at the cityscape. His eyes were instead fixed on me, their depths filled with an intensity that took my breath away. Slowly, almost reverently, he reached out and clasped my chin, his touch gentle but insistent as he turned my face toward his.

"But it pales in comparison to your beauty," he whispered, his breath warm against my skin. "You are a true marvel, Serenity. A treasure beyond all compare."

My heart raced at his words, a crimson glow emanating from my cheeks. No one had ever spoken to me like this before, with such raw honesty and admiration in their voice.

Angelo's gaze dropped to my lips, his own parting slightly. He looked up again at me briefly and there was a question in his eyes, a silent request for permission. In answer, I tilted my face to his, my eyes falling closed in anticipation.

His kiss was soft at first, the gentlest brush of his lips against mine. But as I leaned into him, my hands coming up to rest on his chest, the kiss deepened. His tongue traced over the seam of my lips, seeking entrance, and I granted it willingly. His taste and smell were intoxicating, a heady mix of wine and spice that left me wanting more.

He wrapped his arms around me, crushing me to his chest. His kiss turned passionate, possessive, powerful. I melted into him, my body molding to his as if it had been made purely for this moment. Every touch, every taste, sent waves of pleasure coursing through me, igniting a fire in my veins that threatened to consume me.

Even as I lost myself in the dizzying sensations, a small voice in the back of my mind whispered doubtfully. Was this real? Was this truly what I wanted, or was I being caught up in some supernatural force beyond my control? Angelo was a vampire, a creature of immense power. Was it possible that he was influencing my emotions, compelling me to feel this way?

Or was this really my own wicked desire, a hunger that had been hiding within me all along, waiting for the right moment to be set free? I wasn't sure, and in the fervor of the moment, I didn't care. All that mattered was the feel of his body against mine, the taste of his lips, the promise of pleasure that hung heavy in the air between us.

He planted kisses down my throat then whispered in my ear. "Surrender to me, Serenity. Let me show you a night of passion."

My breath caught in my throat, desire warring with uncertainty in my mind. I wanted this, wanted him, with an intensity that frightened me. But there was also a smaller part of me that hesitated, unsure if I was ready to take this step.

"Angelo, I…" My voice trembled slightly. "I've never…I mean, I'm…"

I trailed off, a flush of embarrassment blazing across my face. How could I tell him that I was a virgin with no experience of men? Would he think any less of me, or would it inflame his desire further?

Angelo drew back slightly, seeing my hesitation, his hand coming up to cup my cheek. "Serenity," he murmured, his eyes searching mine. "We don't have to do anything you're not ready for. I want you—more than I've ever wanted anyone—but I would never pressure you."

His words of gentle understanding eased some of the tension in my body.

I leaned into his touch, drawing strength from his presence. "It's not that I don't want to," I whispered. "I do. It's just…I've never done anything like this before. I'm a virgin."

"I know." He brushed a stray hair off my face. "Remember the auction? Simon said as much." He broke out in a small smile. There was no judgment in his gaze, only a fierce possessiveness that sent a shiver down my spine. "Allow me to be your first. Not just your first—your only," he breathed, his voice low and rough.

He leaned in closer, his lips brushing against the shell of my ear as he spoke. "I want to be the only one ever to touch you like this, Serenity. The only one to bring you pleasure, to worship your body in the way it deserves. I want to claim you, to make you mine in every way possible."

I never thought a man would say anything like this to me. All the guys I had ever gone out with had only ever thought of themselves. This was someone who had killed for me, and as horrible as the thought might be, he had gotten rid of the man who had haunted me my entire life, making each day a living nightmare.

His words and the raw desire in his voice ignited a fire deep within me. I knew that if I gave myself to him, there would be no going back. He would consume me body and soul, and I would be forever changed.

He slipped his hand through my hair. "Any man who dares to lay a hand on you from this day forward will answer to me," he growled, his grip on my waist tightening. "I will destroy anyone who tries to take you from me, who tries to touch what is mine."

I should say no. Tell him that I wasn't ready. But I was tired of always doing the right thing, always being the good girl. For once, I wanted to tiptoe into danger and taste the forbidden.

I placed my hands on his rugged cheeks and nodded. "Yes. Yours."

Chapter Twenty-Three

Serenity

Angelo ran the back of his knuckles down my cheek, his touch gentle and cool against my flushed skin. "Are you sure, my Nephilim?" His voice was soft, barely a whisper, but filled with a deep longing that resonated within me.

He wasn't using compulsion on me. He was allowing me to make the decision myself, giving me the power to choose. I knew I was free to say no, and if I did, he would respect my choice. A warmth blossomed in my chest, spreading through my body. Surely that was the greatest gift he could give me— the freedom to decide for myself.

My heart raced, and a shiver ran down my spine as I considered this monumental crossroads in my life. I took a deep breath, feeling the certainty settle in my bones. I squared my shoulders, meeting his gaze with unwavering determination. "Yes. I want this. I want you."

I reached up, holding his strong jaw in my hands, feeling the smooth, cool texture of his skin beneath my fingertips. Then the world fell away, and all that existed was the space between us, charged with anticipation and desire. I leaned in closer, my lips parting slightly, inviting him to seal our destiny.

He lifted me into his strong arms, and I wound my arms around the back of his neck, nestling my face into the crook of his shoulder. My fingers tugged at his man bun, setting his hair cascading down. His scent, a mix of spice and something uniquely him, surrounded me, making me feel safe and cherished.

He carried me over to the bed, his strides confident and purposeful. My heart pounded in excitement, and my chest tightened with anticipation. He kicked back the comforter and lowered me down gently, his eyes never leaving mine. The silk sheets were cool against my hot skin.

The candlelight cast a warm glow over his features, highlighting the chiseled planes of his face and the depth of emotion in his gaze. I reached up to trace my fingers along his jawline, marveling at the strength and tenderness I found there. His long hair brushed over my fingers, and I was surprised at how soft and silky it was. I threaded my hand through his hair as goosebumps broke out over my arm.

"I want to see you," he whispered, his voice rough with desire. "All of you."

He knelt down beside the bed, his hands skimming over my sides and leaving two paths of fiery desire in their wake.

Slowly, reverently, he lifted the hem of my black dress, his fingers brushing against my skin and sending fresh shivers down my spine. I raised my arms, allowing him to slip the garment over my head and toss it aside.

I lay before him clad only in a simple black bra and panties, feeling more exposed and vulnerable than I ever had in my life. I folded my arms over my chest and crossed my legs, trying to cover myself. Such a stupid virgin move.

Angelo gently lifted my arms, his touch warm and reassuring against my skin. He met my embarrassed gaze steadily, his eyes filled with understanding and affection. "Never hide what is mine from me," he murmured, his voice low and soothing. "You're beautiful, Serenity, inside and out. I want to see all of you, to cherish every part of you."

A wave of heat surged over my face, and I lowered my gaze, suddenly feeling even more exposed and vulnerable. "I'm just nervous," I confessed, my voice barely above a whisper. "I've never...I've never been with anyone like this before. I'm afraid I won't be enough."

My hands trembled slightly, and I clasped them together in a vain effort to steady myself. Memories of my stepfather Freddie's unwanted advances flickered through my mind, sending a chill down my spine. I took a shaky breath, trying to push away the haunting images and focus instead on the present moment with Angelo.

I yearned for his touch, for the comfort and safety of his embrace. Yet I also feared that my past trauma and inexperience would somehow taint this beautiful connection we shared. Tears pricked at the corners of my eyes, but I blinked them away, not wanting to let my insecurities win.

I forced myself to look up at Angelo, searching his face. Instead of disappointment or rejection, I saw only understanding, patience, and a desire so profound that it took my breath away. His gaze held a promise of sanctuary, a vow to cherish and protect me always, no matter what.

Angelo cupped my face between his hands, his thumb brushing gently over my cheekbone. "You are more than enough," he assured me, his gaze fiercely sincere. "You are exquisite. Through all the centuries I lived, I've never encountered a woman like you, Serenity. You've touched me in a way that no other woman has. Your vulnerability, your trust...they are precious gifts that I will treasure forever." His husky tone sent a thrilling tingle down my spine, as if he'd run his fingernails down my back.

He was a centuries-old vampire who had, I am sure, been with countless women, but had he ever known love? The thought lingered in my mind as I searched his eyes for answers. Could a being who had lived through so much, seen so many lives come and go, truly open his heart to someone like me, a fleeting spark in the vast expanse of his existence?

Yet there was something in the way he held me, the way his words caressed my soul, that made me want to take the leap. Could I fall in love with a ruthless vampire, the king of the Santi family? What kind of love could even flourish between us? He was immortal, and I was mortal. He was a king, and I was a poor college student. He was darkness to my light. We were no different from Romeo and Juliet. Like theirs, our story could only end in tragedy.

All my muscles tightened up as I inhaled a sharp breath

and clenched my legs together. I didn't know if I could do this after all.

"You're tensing. I promise we'll go slow. I'm not going to make you do anything you don't want to do. If you say stop, we'll stop."

My doubts and thoughts faded as he leaned down, pressing a soft kiss to my forehead. His lips moved against my skin. "I mean it. If it gets too much for you, say stop."

He had no idea how much those words meant to me.

I took a quivering breath and a sense of relief rolled over me. Then I gave him a shy smile as I stared into his eyes. "I will. But I really do want to do this."

He lifted my chin. "I'll cherish every moment, every discovery. I'll show you how much you mean to me, how deeply I care for you."

His soft words, his gentle touches, and the depth of emotion in his eyes melted away any lingering fears and insecurities. But how many times had he said these very words to other women over the centuries? I was probably just one conquest among many. At the same time, no one had ever said such romantic words to me, and I fell under his spell, wanting to feel him inside me. As I lost myself in his eyes, a radiant sense of being treasured and revered blossomed within my heart, like a flower blooming under the gentle caress of the sun. I reached up, winding my arms around his neck and pulling him closer.

"Yes, show me," I whispered, my nervousness giving way to a growing sense of anticipation and desire. "I want to feel everything with you. I want to be yours in every way."

Angelo smiled tenderly and lovingly, making my heart

skip a beat. "You already are," he murmured, before capturing my lips in a kiss that sealed our connection and ignited the passion between us.

He took my breast in his hand, molding his fingers to my flesh and squeezing gently. The intimate contact made me gasp, and a surge of electricity shot through my body. It was a sensation unlike anything I had ever experienced, a potent mixture of pleasure and vulnerability that left me trembling.

My nipple hardened beneath his touch, and I instinctively arched into his palm, craving more of this exquisite feeling. Sparks of electricity danced along my skin, igniting a fire deep within me that threatened to consume me entirely. A soft moan escaped my lips, and I felt a shuddering flush of embarrassment roll over me.

I bit my lower lip, trying to stifle any further noises that might betray the depth of my desire. What if he thought I was too eager, too wanton? The worry nagged at the back of my mind, even as my body yearned for his touch.

"Angelo..." I breathed, my voice barely recognizable to my own ears. It was both a plea and a prayer, a desperate invitation for him to continue his exploration of my body. At the same time, I felt self-conscious about the breathy, urgent quality to my voice, wondering if it sounded as needy to him as it did to me.

I forced myself to meet his gaze, searching for any hint of judgment, of disapproval. Instead, I found only adoration and a hunger that matched my own.

He murmured, "It's okay, my sweet. Let yourself go. You're safe with me."

And so I allowed myself to sink further into the sensations, letting the sounds of my pleasure fall freely from my lips. The whispers of doubt began to fade, replaced by a growing confidence in the beauty of our connection.

Every touch, every kiss, stoked the flames of my desire, building toward a crescendo that threatened to shatter me. Yet even as I teetered on the edge of blissful oblivion, a flicker of nervousness curled in the pit of my stomach again. This was uncharted territory for me.

Angelo must have sensed my slight hesitation, for he paused and met my gaze with a look of tender understanding. "I can feel you tensing again. We'll go at your pace, my sweet Nephilim," he murmured, his thumb caressing my cheek. "Tonight is all about your pleasure and your comfort. If, at any point, you want to slow down or stop, just say the word."

The tenderness in his voice and the sincerity in his eyes soothed my nerves and reignited the flames of my desire. I trusted him implicitly, knowing that he would guide me through this new experience with the utmost care and devotion. With a shy smile I nodded, silently granting him permission to continue his sensual explorations.

As Angelo's hands and lips resumed their worship of my body, I surrendered myself to the overwhelming sensations, my nervousness giving way to pure, unadulterated bliss, knowing I was safe and cherished in Angelo's arms, ready to discover the heights of passion that awaited us both.

Chapter Twenty-Four

Serenity

Angelo's touch grew bolder and more purposeful, as if he was mapping out every single curve and contour of my form and committing each detail to memory. His fingers skimmed along the sides of my breasts, tracing delicate patterns that left me burning for more. I pressed into his touch, a silent plea for him to go further, to claim me as his own.

He met my gaze, his eyes dark with desire, and I saw my own hunger reflected back at me. "I want to touch every part of you," he murmured, his thumb brushing over the sensitive peak of my nipple. "I want to make you feel cherished, worshipped, loved...alive."

I thought he would remove my bra, but instead, his mouth fastened over my nipple, sucking hard through the lacy material. The sudden sensation consumed me, my body surrendering to the overwhelmingly intense pleasure as I cried out, my back arcing off the bed. The contrast of the rough lace against my sensitive skin and the hot, wet pull of his mouth was exquisite torture, driving me to the brink of madness.

He slipped his hand down to my panties, his fingers stroking the delicate material, teasing the flesh underneath. His touch was hot through the thin fabric, and my hips instinctively lifted, seeking more contact. It was a maddening, delicious tease, a promise of the pleasure to come.

I was about to demand that he shed his clothing too and join me in this vulnerable state, but before I could do so, he slid his hand across my back, deftly unbuttoning my bra and rendering me speechless. The garment hung loosely below my breasts, and he greedily gazed down at my exposed flesh, his eyes darkening with desire.

"Aren't you going to remove your clothes too?" I panted, my shaky hands tugging at his shirt, desperate to feel his bare skin against mine.

"After I pleasure you, beautiful." He looked up from my breast, passion and mischief filling his green eyes, the intensity of his gaze making my heart race.

"You are exquisite," he murmured reverently. "A work of art, created by the very gods themselves."

He lowered his head, placing his hot mouth on my other nipple. He sucked and licked, his tongue swirling around the hardened peak, sending fresh waves of pleasure crashing through my body. I writhed beneath him, my hands fisting the sheets, anchoring myself against the onslaught of new sensations.

Then, without warning, he nipped me, his teeth grazing the sensitive bud. I jerked up, a sudden fear cutting through the haze of passion. I remembered with sudden, abundant clarity that I was with a vampire.

"Are you going to suck my blood?" I asked, terror edging into my voice where moments before there had been only passion. My heart pounded in my chest, and I pictured his fangs sinking into my flesh, draining me of life.

Angelo raised his head, his expression softening when he saw the naked fear in my eyes. He cupped my cheek, his thumb brushing gently over my trembling lips.

"No, my sweet Nephilim." His voice was gentle but firm, his eyes holding mine with an intensity that stole my breath. "Not tonight. I will never harm you like that. Never again take blood from you without your consent. Your trust and your safety are everything to me."

He traced a finger down my nipple, circling the sensitive peak until I shivered, not from being cold, but from the desire his words and touch ignited within me. "Someday," he continued, his voice low and tender, "you'll learn that when you reach your peak in orgasm, while pleasure is consuming you entirely, that being bitten will take you to even greater heights, to a place of ecstasy you've never known or even dreamed of before."

The thought of his fangs sinking into my flesh in the throes of passion sent a thrill of both excitement and trepidation through me. It was a reminder of his otherworldly nature, of the dark and seductive power that lurked beneath his gentle touch.

"But that is for another time, when you are ready,

and when you crave it as much as I do." He cupped my face in his hands, his thumbs brushing over my cheekbones with a tenderness that made my heart ache. "Right now, I crave only your heart and soul, and I want you to crave mine. I want to know every part of you, to cherish and revere you as you deserve to be. I want to be yours and for you to be mine in every way that matters."

Tears stung my eyes at his words, at the depth of emotion and sincerity they conveyed. I had never experienced a connection so profound and all-encompassing like this. It was both terrifying and exhilarating—a leap into the unknown that I knew, with sudden certainty, I was ready to take.

"I do crave you," I whispered, my voice trembling. "Heart, soul, and body. I'm all yours, Angelo."

At least, for now, I was. The future was uncertain, but I wanted to experience the pleasure only he could give.

"Music to my ears," he murmured, a smile playing at the corners of his mouth. His eyes shone with a mix of adoration and desire as he held my gaze, his hands skimming down my sides, leaving trails of fire in their wake.

Slowly, teasingly, sensually, he slipped his thumbs into the waistband of my lacy panties, nudging them down my trembling thighs. The cool air kissed my feverish skin, and I shivered.

He lowered his head, pressing fervent kisses between my breasts, his lips lingering on the soft swells of flesh. Then he began to trail a path of kisses down my torso, his mouth hot and wet against my skin. He paused at my stomach, swirling his tongue around my belly button, then dipping in and out of it with a playful, erotic rhythm.

My toes curled and my thighs quivered, my entire being laser focused on the exquisite sensations radiating from every point where our heated skin touched. The sensation of his silky hair falling across my skin, tickling and teasing, only heightened the pleasure coursing through me. The longing was delightful, anguish, a passion I could no longer deny.

"Angelo," I breathed, my voice a plea and a prayer. "Please..."

He chuckled, a low, seductive rumble that vibrated against my skin. "Patience, my sweet Nephilim," he whispered, his breath hot on my hipbone. "I want to savor every moment of this and every inch of you. I want to bring you to heights you've never known before."

His words, his touch, the intensity of his gaze...they were my undoing.

He placed his mouth onto my secret curls, his hot breath teasing over my sensitive flesh. Then, with a hunger that took my breath away, he kissed and sucked me, his tongue delving deep into my core. He lapped up my essence, savoring it, his moans of pleasure vibrating against my most intimate place.

I sucked in a breath, my eyes squeezing tightly shut as wave after wave of ecstasy crashed over me. My hands twisted the comforter into knots, my knuckles turning white as I tried to withstand the onslaught of sensations. It was almost too much; the pleasure was so intense it bordered on pain, but I never wanted it to end.

"Angelo," I gasped, my voice a breathless plea. "Don't

stop...please, don't ever stop."

He responded with renewed fervor, his tongue swirling and thrusting, his fingers joining in the delicious torment as he stroked and teased my sensitive bud. I could feel the spring coiling tighter and tighter within me, my body trembling on the brink of a precipice I'd never fallen over before.

As the waves of pleasure crested within me, I gasped, my fingers digging into Angelo's thick hair. The sensations were so intense and all-consuming that I feared I might lose myself entirely. Desperately seeking an anchor, I focused on one of the flickering candles scattered around the room, one directly in my field of vision, its soft light providing a soothing contrast to the fiery passion engulfing my body.

Just as I reached the pinnacle of my climax, the flames of the nearby candles responded in kind, flaring upward like miniature flame throwers. Each surge emitted a hissing sound, filling the room with bursts of light and noise, casting our shadows in sharp relief against the walls.

I struggled to catch my breath, my thoughts scattered like leaves in a gale, torn between the lingering aftershocks of pure bliss and the bewildering display put on by the candles. "Angelo," I gasped, my voice barely above a whisper, as if speaking too loudly might disrupt the delicate balance between the physical and the mystical.

Was this a common occurrence during the mating of vampires, or was there something more profound at play? Could our passion, our connection, somehow be intertwined with the elemental forces that governed the world around us? The questions swirled in my head, even as my body hummed with the echoes of our shared ecstasy.

"That's what I want to hear, you crying out my name." He kissed my thigh, and I panted hard.

I propped myself up on my elbows, breathless, staring at the candles that had now returned to normal. They flickered innocently, as if they hadn't just moments ago blazed with an unnatural intensity. "Did you see that? The candles?" I asked, my voice tinged with a mix of wonder and confusion.

He cocked his eyebrow and followed my gaze. "See what?"

My cheeks grew hot, and I felt a twinge of self-doubt. "Nothing. I guess." Maybe I had imagined it, my mind playing tricks on me in the throes of ecstasy. But deep down, I couldn't shake the feeling that something extraordinary had just happened, something that went beyond the normal realm of physical pleasure.

I was about to voice my thoughts when Angelo ran his hand down my shaking thigh, his touch sending electric sparks through my body and effectively derailing my train of thought. "Now I'm going to claim you," he declared, his voice low and filled with promise.

My mouth went dry at his words, my mind too focused on the anticipation of what was to come to dwell on the mystery of the blazing candles. As Angelo's hands and lips began to work their magic once more, I surrendered myself to the sensations, pushing the strange occurrence to the back of my mind. But even as I lost myself in the pleasure of his touch, I couldn't help but wonder if this was just the beginning of something much larger and more profound than I had ever imagined.

Chapter Twenty-Five

Angelo slowly climbed off the bed as he kissed, licked, and scraped his fangs down my trembling leg, his touch leaving a trail of fire on my electrified skin. He stood by the edge of the bed, his eyes locked with mine as he stripped so fast, I barely saw him move. When my gaze finally landed on him, I was left breathless.

I had never seen a naked man before, and Angelo's gloriously bare form sent a sharp rush of heat to my cheeks, spreading down my neck and all across my chest. My breath caught in my throat, my heart pounding so loudly I was sure he could hear it. I felt torn between the instinct to avert my gaze out of modesty and the overwhelming desire to memorize every detail of his sculpted physique.

Adonis himself could not have been more beautiful,

each muscle and sinew a testament to Angelo's raw masculine perfection. A mixture of curiosity, desire, and trepidation coursed through me as I realized this magnificent male specimen, this Herculean figure, was about to become my lover.

I swallowed hard, my mouth suddenly dry as a fresh wave of nervousness washed over me. How could I possibly compare to the perfection that stood before me? But then Angelo's gaze softened, a gentle smile playing on his lips, and I saw the adoration and reassurance in his eyes, and any concerns were swept away. He would guide me, cherish me, and worship me, just as he had promised.

As my gaze traveled over the contours of his body, I found myself transfixed by the tattoo that adorned his neck. I had noticed it before, but hadn't realized it swirled down his body, winding its way across his muscular chest and toned abdomen. As my gaze followed the intricate, swirling lines, I swear it looked almost alive, the inked design seeming to dance and shimmer on his skin with each breath he took.

The tattoo featured blood droplets and red roses, blending seamlessly into a vine that appeared to pulse with an otherworldly energy. The colors were so vivid and the lines so crisp, I couldn't help but wonder whether the tattoo had been inked by human hands or by some supernatural force.

The vine of blood droplets and red roses snaked its way down his neck, curling and twisting like a living entity. It continued its path along his chest, the thorny stems and delicate petals standing out in sharp contrast against his pale skin. Lower and lower the vine snaked, until it finally came to a stop just above his navel. There, the blood droplets seemed to pool, forming a small, glistening reservoir that somehow caught the light and drew the eye inexorably toward it.

I swallowed hard, my mouth suddenly dry as I studied the tattoo and contemplated the meaning behind it. Was it a symbol of his vampiric nature, a reminder of the blood that sustained him? Or did it hold another, more personal significance, a story waiting to be unraveled?

As if sensing my intense scrutiny, the tattoo seemed to shimmer and dance, the vines undulating softly on his skin. I blinked, unsure if it was a trick of the light or if the tattoo truly possessed a life of its own. A shiver ran down my spine, and I tore my gaze away from the ink, both thrilled and unnerved to take in his entire physique again.

He was a vision of masculine perfection, his body chiseled and defined as if sculpted by Michelangelo himself. Every muscle was honed to perfection, from the broad expanse of his shoulders to the taut planes of his abdomen to strong, powerful thighs. He was a living, breathing embodiment of strength and beauty.

His cock was erect and huge, jutting out proudly from his chiseled hips. I swallowed hard, shock shooting through me as I took in the impressive size of his manhood. A mixture of desire and apprehension swirled within me. How would that possibly fit inside my untried body?

But it was more than just his physical appearance that took my breath away. It was the way he looked at me, his eyes filled with a mixture of desire, adoration, and vulnerability. In that moment, I felt that he was baring much more than just his body to me—he was revealing his soul, his very essence.

Angelo clearly sensed my nervousness, for he took a step closer, his hand cupping my cheek with a soft tenderness that belied the raw passion burning in his eyes. "We'll take it slow, beautiful," he murmured soothingly. "I would never harm you. Yes, it will hurt briefly, but then you'll experience pleasure. Trust me to guide you and to show you the heights of pleasure we can reach together."

My heart swelled with jumbled feelings so profound that they almost brought tears to my eyes. I couldn't identify them, but no other man had ever touched that part deep within me that I kept hidden. He spread my trembling thighs apart, his hands gentle but firm, as if he had every right to be there, to claim me as his own. As I lay there, exposed and open for him, I felt a heady cocktail of exhilaration and nervousness coursing through my veins. Slowly, he climbed back up on the bed, his body a solid, comforting presence as he wedged his hips between mine.

I sucked in my breath and braced myself, my heart pounding wildly in my chest. The rigid length of his cock pushed against my inner thigh, a tantalizing promise of what was to come. I tried to quell the panic swelling inside me, focusing instead on how much I trusted Angelo.

"Serenity," he rasped, his voice rough with emotion. "My little Nephilim. Look at me."

I met his gaze, seeing in his eyes a reflection of my own desire, tempered by a profound tenderness and understanding. He brushed his thumb across my cheek gently, wiping away a tear that lingered there.

"I've got you," he murmured, his forehead resting against mine. "I'll always be here for you, to protect you, to cherish you. You'll be safe with me, now and forever."

He raised his hips and slowly pushed into me, breaking down the last barrier I possessed. I tensed and sucked in a sharp breath, my eyes squeezing shut as a searing pain shot through me, momentarily overshadowing everything else. My body stretched wide, straining to accommodate his substantial size, the sudden discomfort causing me to dig my fingers into his shoulders.

Angelo instantly stilled, his breath hot on my neck as he whispered soothing words of encouragement. "Breathe, my little Nephilim. The pain will pass, I promise."

As I forced myself to take slow, deep breaths, the pain did gradually begin to subside, replaced by a satisfying sense of fullness and connection. The discomfort melted away, giving way to a blossoming pleasure that started at my core and radiated outward, spreading warmth and tingling sensations to every part of my being.

I tentatively rocked my hips against his, marveling at the exquisite friction where our bodies joined. Angelo groaned, his eyes dark with desire as he matched my movements, slowly at first, then with increasing intensity. Each new thrust sent fresh waves of ecstasy crashing over me, drowning out any lingering traces of pain and leaving only pure, unadulterated bliss in its wake.

I opened my eyes and stared into Angelo's handsome face. His gaze was filled with tenderness and understanding even as he took what he wanted from me. Ultimately, he was putting my well-being above his own desire. I hadn't expected that. A surge of feelings swelled inside me, feelings I couldn't name...or was too afraid to name.

"I'm okay," I managed, my voice trembling slightly. "It's...intense. But I like it. I want this, Angelo. I want you, all of you."

He leaned down, pressing a gentle kiss to my forehead. "And you shall have it, Serenity. You will experience pleasure such that only I can give you." He began to move within me, slowly and gently, allowing my body to adjust to his presence. With each tender thrust, the discomfort faded more, replaced by an ever-growing sense of pleasure and connection. I clung to him, my hands roaming over the sculpted planes of his back, marveling at the strength and beauty of the body joined with mine.

Each time he thrust inside me, he did so harder and faster. The feeling intensified, surging within me like a rising tide until it crested, threatening to engulf me. A thousand questions pumped through my mind, but I didn't know how to give voice to them.

"I claim you as mine, now and forever." He thrust harder and harder, then finally buried his seed deep within me. "Call out my name, Nephilim."

"Angelo," I whined, terror and pleasure twisted together in one single word. As his fangs grazed my skin, a blast of energy coursed through me, igniting every cell in my body. The air around us crackled with electricity, and suddenly, the objects in the room began to tremble and vibrate, as if resonating with the energy emanating from our connected bodies. One by one, they levitated, swirling around us in a dizzying dance that defied gravity.

The bed beneath us shuddered, and then, astonishingly, began to rise too, hovering inches above the floor as if suspended by an unseen force.

Around us, books, pens, and various other trinkets swirled erratically in the air. They whizzed past our heads, sometimes only narrowly missing us as they danced to an invisible, chaotic rhythm. The room was pulsing with an unseen energy, the very air crackling with a power I couldn't comprehend.

My heart raced, fear mingling with the pleasurable sensations flooding my body. A small, terrified part of me wondered if we had unleashed something beyond our control, perhaps something malevolent. A cold sweat broke out across my skin, and I shivered involuntarily, goosebumps rising on my flesh as if in response to the unseen. Did this mean I was evil? That my dad was a fallen angel? My stomach churned as blood pounded in my ears, nearly drowning out the sound of my own ragged breathing.

The room seemed to spin around me, the swirling objects blurring into a dizzying kaleidoscope of colors and shapes, and for a moment, I thought I might pass out from the sheer intensity of it all.

I clung to Angelo as if my life depended on it, my fingers digging into his skin hard enough to leave bruises, wanting his solid presence to act as an anchor for me amid all the chaos. "Angelo," I gasped, my voice trembling, "what's happening? Is this...normal?"

His eyes met mine, a flicker of surprise and confusion passing over his features before being replaced by a look of protectiveness. "I don't know. I've never experienced anything like this before," he murmured, his voice tinged with a mixture of awe and apprehension. "I think our connection has unleashed some kind of primal energy, something ancient and powerful beyond measure."

His words sent a fresh wave of fear cascading through me, and I could feel my heart hammering against my ribcage, each beat a deafening roar in the eerie silence that had fallen over the room, broken only by the soft tinkling of the levitating objects.

Then, as we lay there together, our breathing gradually returning to normal, something extraordinary began to happen. At first, it was just a faint shimmer, a barely perceptible glow that seemed to emanate from our entwined bodies. As the seconds ticked by, the light grew stronger and brighter, until it had enveloped us completely in a shimmering cocoon of silver.

I gasped as I watched the aura dance around us, casting shifting patterns of light and shadow across our skin. It was like nothing I had ever seen, a manifestation of pure energy that pulsed and swelled with each beat of our hearts.

At the same time, the air around us hummed with a strange, ethereal vibration, as if the very molecules were resonating with the power that flowed between us. I could feel it tingling along my every nerve ending, a warm, electric sensation that made my skin prickle and my breath catch in my throat.

"What's happening to me?" I whispered, my voice trembling with a mix of fear and excitement.

Angelo's expression was one of wonder and adoration, tinged with a hint of satisfaction. It was as if he had been expecting this, waiting for me to unlock the secrets of my true nature. "You're amazing," he murmured, his eyes full of appreciation and reassurance. "You've unleashed the power inside you."

I hesitated, holding my breath, then closed my eyes. "But is my power demonic...or angelic?"

He stroked my cheek. "Based on the silver aura—definitely angelic."

I opened my eyes and exhaled a sigh of relief, but a flicker of doubt still remained. "So, does that mean my father was a heavenly angel?" I pressed, my voice quaking slightly. "All this time, I've been so unsure, so afraid of what his true nature might have been."

Angelo's expression softened and he reached out to take my hands in his. "The nature of your power is a reflection of your own heart, Serenity," he said gently. "It doesn't necessarily reveal the truth about your father."

I nodded slowly, still not quite understanding. "But if my power is angelic, surely that means he must have been a heavenly angel too...?"

"Not necessarily," Angelo replied, his brow furrowing slightly. "The path your father took, whether he was a fallen angel or a heavenly one, was his own. Your power, your destiny, is shaped by your own choices and the purity of your intentions."

A warmth spread through my chest at his words, a sense of hope and determination that I had never known before. "So I'm not bound by his legacy," I murmured, more to myself than to Angelo. "I can forge my own path, form my own goals."

He kissed me on the lips. "Exactly," he said, squeezing my hands gently. "You are your own person, Serenity, with your own strengths, your own dreams, and your own destiny to fulfill. Always remember that."

His words filled me with hope. I wasn't evil.

"Your power created an unbreakable bond between us," he murmured, his voice low and thrumming with intensity. "And that connection we shared was manifested in the physical world."

"Unbreakable bond?" My brows drew into a deep frown. "What does that mean?"

Don't say it Don't say it Don't say it

He placed his finger on my lips. "I've claimed you. You're mine forever. No one else's."

I clasped his finger. "So I can't be with anyone but you?"

He gave me a hard stare, then his lips turned up into a smirk. "What do you think?"

I matched his mischievous look. "Does that also mean you can't be with anyone but me?"

I held my breath, waiting for his response, wondering if I'd been too cheeky.

He leaned in close, his lips brushing against mine in a searing kiss that stole the air from my lungs. When he pulled back, his eyes locked with mine, intense and unwavering. "Why would I ever want to? No other woman compares to you."

Chapter Twenty-Six

Angelo

Serenity looked up at me, her eyes shimmering with a complex mix of emotions—remnants of anger, sweet vulnerability, and a newfound sense of connection. I was still deep inside her, my cock pulsing with the aftershocks of our intense lovemaking.

As I gazed down at her, I was hit by a wave of sensations unlike anything I had ever experienced before. My heart raced, pounding in my ribcage with a ferocity that took my breath away. It was as if our joining had awakened a dormant part of my soul, revealing a hidden well of emotions I had never tapped into or even known existed.

Tenderly, I brushed a strand of her blonde hair away from her face, my fingers trembling slightly as they lingered on her cheek. I struggled to keep my composure, to prevent the overwhelming feelings from surging forth and spilling out in words I wasn't yet ready to say.

"Talk to me, Serenity. What are you feeling?" I finally managed, my voice rough with the effort of restraint.

She leaned into my touch, her initial frown softening as she searched for the right words. "This was...so intense, so intimate. I wasn't prepared for how much it would affect me and how much it would change everything between us."

I nodded slowly, swallowing hard against the lump that had formed in my throat. If only she knew the depths of what I was feeling, the way our connection had shaken me to my very foundations! But I couldn't burden her with that, not right now. She needed me to be strong, to guide us through this uncharted territory.

"I know. It was powerful for me too." The understatement of a millennium, but it was all I could give her in that moment.

She sighed and looked up at me with lovely, beautiful eyes. "What do we do now?"

"One thing's for sure, I don't want to sleep apart from you anymore."

She cocked her eyebrow and pursed her lips. "Are you asking me, or telling me?"

Normally, I would demand, not request, but in this, I wanted her to give herself freely to me. If she said no, it would shatter me, but I'd respect her wishes and do everything in my power to win her heart eventually.

"I'm asking. If you say no, you may return to your room as always. I won't force myself on you." My breath caught in my throat, waiting for her to respond.

Her brow furrowed as she considered the question. Each second that she didn't answer put a crack in my heart. Then she smiled, a radiant, genuine smile that lit up her entire face. "I accept your offer, my vampire king. And I'm eager to see where this journey takes us together."

I exhaled my pent-up relief and gathered her closer, burying my face in the crook of her neck as I fought to steady my racing heart. She had no idea what this meant to me. To have someone else hold my life in their hands was new to me; frankly, it scared the hell out of me. This slip of a girl could bring me to my knees.

I breathed in her intoxicating scent, letting it ground me in the present and in the reality of what we had just shared. Even though I couldn't yet put a name to the emotions swirling within me, I knew one thing with absolute, crystal-clear certainty: my life would never be the same again.

I rested my forehead on hers. "Serenity...my sweet Nephilim."

There was no doubt that she had the power to restore the Aeternum Stone. I was so close to saving my people and to victory, I could almost taste it. Finally, my people would be safe from Dracula.

In that moment, everything else faded away—the troubles with the other Mafia kings...DuPont's investigation...the murdered women...all that mattered was the undeniable fact that Serenity possessed the power to replenish the Aeternum Stone, the magical artifact that held the key to my people's salvation.

I could feel the weight of all the years of struggle and sacrifice lifting, the countless lives lost and the endless nights spent searching for a way to protect my kind from the ever-present threat of Dracula's punishment. Now, with Serenity, I finally allowed myself to believe victory was within reach.

My mind raced, considering the alliances that would need to be forged and the battles that would need to be fought. But through it all, one thought remained constant. With Serenity at my side, anything was possible.

I wanted to tell her about the stone, about the ancient power it held and the grave responsibilities that came with possessing it. I longed to share the burden that weighed heavily on my shoulders, to confide in her all the secrets I had kept for so long. But as I looked into her eyes, still hazy with the afterglow of our lovemaking, I couldn't bring myself to shatter the fragile beauty of the moment.

The mounting dangers surrounding us loomed like gathering storm clouds on the horizon, threatening to overtake the brief respite we had found in each other's arms. I knew I would have to face them soon, to confront the enemies that sought to destroy everything I held so dear. But for now, I wanted to shelter Serenity from the harsh realities of our world, to allow her a few more precious moments of peace and contentment.

There would be time for truth and revelations later, when we were both better prepared to handle the consequences. For now, I needed to keep her safe, to fortify the bonds between us so that we could weather the coming tempest together.

The time would come when I would lay bare all my secrets, when I would trust her completely with the truth of who I was and the destiny that awaited me. But that time was not now, not when the wounds of her past were still so fresh and the scars on her soul still so raw.

Instead, I leaned in and captured her lips in a searing kiss, pouring all the unspoken emotion that churned within me into that one passionate gesture. When we finally broke apart, both of us panting feverishly, I rested my forehead against hers. "Tonight," I whispered. "You move into my quarters tonight."

It was a declaration, a promise, and a vow all rolled into one. By bringing her into my private space, I was offering her more than just physical proximity. I was inviting her into my life and into my heart in a way I had never done with anyone else before. It was a step toward the future together I envisioned for us, a future where we would face our challenges and our enemies side by side, bound together by a love that could overcome any obstacle.

I just wished I could tell her how I felt.

Serenity's eyes widened at my words. Then she nodded slowly, a soft smile playing around the corners of her mouth. "Yes, I'd like that," she murmured, her voice filled with a quiet contentment that mirrored my own.

And as I gathered her close once more, I silently vowed to do whatever it took to keep her safe, to protect the precious bond we had forged in the heat of our passion.

Chapter Twenty-Seven

Angelo

Two hours later, Serenity lay next to me, still fast asleep, in the very bed that had unleashed her powers. I wouldn't make love to her again, though, not unless she wanted it.

The moonlight shone on her angelic face, revealing cheeks wet with tears.

I raised my hand to touch her, wanting to tell her that our bonding had changed me too, but I couldn't find the words and lowered my hand again.

In all my centuries as a vampire, I had never experienced a connection so profound, so deep, so all-consuming. Love had escaped me ever since Vlad had turned me. But her trust, her surrender, and her unwavering devotion had touched something deep within me and reawakened a part of my soul I had thought was long dead.

I lay back on my pillow and stared up at the ceiling. The raw power that had surged through her during our mating had truly shocked me—the electric current that had passed between us in the moment my fangs grazed her skin, unleashing a force that seemed to come from the very essence of her being. When the room had come alive with swirling objects and crackling energy, I knew I was witnessing the awakening of her true potential, the full manifestation of her Nephilim heritage.

I knew Serenity was special the first time I touched her, but to feel the sheer magnitude of her power intertwined with my own, to experience it firsthand, had been glorious. She had shared something special with me and sparked something in me, and it had knocked down the walls I had kept around me for so long.

I got out of bed and grabbed my robe off a chair, moving slowly so as not to disturb her. I retrieved a bottle of red wine from the bar and poured myself a drink, then stepped out onto my balcony. Dawn wasn't too far away, but the night's energy still pulsed in the streets below.

Bourbon Street was alive with activity, even at this late hour. Neon signs flickered and buzzed, casting a kaleidoscope of colors over the faces of the revelers who crowded the sidewalks. Music spilled from the open doors of bars and clubs, a cacophony of jazz, blues, and rock that blended together in a chaotic melody.

Groups of drunken friends stumbled along, their laughter and chatter rising above the din, while street performers entertained the masses with their talents. A man juggled flaming batons, his deft movements drawing cheers and applause from the assembled crowd. Further down the street, a woman's voice soared above the sound of a saxophone, her soulful lyrics telling of love and heartbreak.

The air hung heavy with the scent of alcohol, cigarette smoke, and the spicy aroma of Cajun cuisine wafting from the restaurants that lined the street. Despite the lateness of the hour, vendors still hawked their wares, offering everything from colorful beads to voodoo dolls to gator-tooth necklaces.

As I sipped my wine, I felt a certain sense of kinship with these night owls of Bourbon Street. Like them, I was a creature of the darkness, thriving in the shadows and the secrets they held. I was old enough and powerful enough that the impending dawn held no sway over me, and I relished the knowledge that I could linger here and watch the world pass by long after the sun had risen and the humans had retreated to their beds.

For now, I was content to simply observe, to let the energy of the street wash over me as I drank in the sights, sounds, and sensations of this vibrant, pulsing corner of the city. It was a reminder of the life that still went on beyond the walls of my own existence, a connection to the mortal world I had left behind so long ago.

Someone knocked on my door, the sharp, rapid sound echoing through the room and piercing the tranquil silence. Anger surged through me at the thought of them waking Serenity and disrupting her peace. Using vampire speed, I sped through my bedroom, my bare feet barely touching the cold hardwood floor as I whipped open the door.

Dimitri stood on the other side, a smirk playing on his

lips despite the urgency in his eyes. "Well, don't you look cozy. Nice pajamas, by the way. Very... regal."

I took a menacing step toward him, my jaw clenched with barely contained rage. "Then why did you?!" The words tore from my throat as I took a step forward, my hands curled into fists.

His smirk widened. "Oh, I'm sorry. Did I interrupt your nightly brooding session? Because we've got a slight apocalypse brewing downstairs, but if you'd rather stay here and perfect your scowl..."

I gritted my teeth. "Don't try my patience, Dimitri. Spit it out."

Dimitri's eyes sparked with a mix of amusement and urgency. "So, good news and bad news. Which do you want first? Oh, who am I kidding - you'll love both."

I raised an eyebrow. "Surprise me."

"Alright. Crimson Stakes decided to spice things up with a kitchen explosion. Don't worry, Enzo played firefighter and saved the day. No crispy vampires on the menu tonight."

"And the bad news?"

Dimitri's smirk widened. "Oh, that was the good news. The bad? We've got a father-son cop duo downstairs. Detective DuPont and his mini-me are demanding an audience with His Royal Vampireness. That's you, by the way."

I sighed. "Fantastic. Another woman murdered?"

"No idea. But I'm betting it's about Joy DuPont. They're getting a bit... testy down there. Might want to hurry before they start flashing their badges at the furniture."

A cold dread settled in the pit of my stomach, mingling

with the hot anger that still coursed through my veins. Had she been murdered, with all the clues pointing once again to me and my family? The last thing I needed was a couple of hotheaded humans causing a scene in my home.

I closed my eyes for a moment, trying to calm myself. "Tell them I'll be right down."

"Oh sure, I'll just tell the angry cops to sit tight while you finish your beauty routine. Want me to offer them some AB negative while they wait? Maybe a game of charades?"

I opened my eyes and growled.

Dimitri raised his hands in mock surrender, his smirk never faltering. "Alright, alright. I'll tell them you're coming. But if they start a stake-whittling contest in the foyer, that's on you."

He turned and hurried back down the hallway. I closed the door, leaning against it for a moment as I tried to gather my thoughts. I really didn't want to deal with the detective and his son right now, but I knew I couldn't ignore their presence.

With a heavy sigh, I turned back toward the bedroom, my mind already racing with the possible reason for their visit. I could only hope that whatever they wanted, it wouldn't bring more danger or sorrow into Serenity's life. She had already been through so much.

I got dressed in my usual three-piece dark suit with a crisp blue shirt faster than the human eye could blink. During that time, Serenity slept peacefully in our bed. I liked the sound of that—"our bed." Nothing would make me happier than slipping in beside her again, but business came first.

As I headed downstairs to the living room, a sense of unease settled in the pit of my stomach. I had no idea what Detective DuPont and his son wanted, but their unexpected visit at this hour could only mean trouble.

Dimitri was waiting by the double doors to the living room. As I approached, he leaned in with a smirk. "Ready for the Dupont family reunion? I hear they're dying to see you. Well, not literally... yet."

I shot him a warning glare, but he just shrugged and opened the doors for me.

The living room was dimly lit, with only a few lamps casting a muted glow over the plush furniture and elegant décor. The heavy curtains were drawn, blocking out the first hints of dawn that would break over the horizon any minute.

Detective DuPont and the young man with him were pacing back and forth like caged tigers. I had never met the detective's son, but the first thing that struck me was that the young man didn't look anything like DuPont. He was taller, more muscular. He had dark amber-red hair and fierce blue eyes. The look he gave me was one of pure malice, as if he wanted to slit my throat right then and there.

I forced a false smile to my lips. "Detective DuPont, to what do I owe the pleasure of this early morning visit?" I kept my voice calm.

DuPont gritted his teeth. "Where's my daughter, you bastard?"

I studied the two men, taking in the desperation etched into their faces. DuPont's eyes were bloodshot, his hair disheveled as if he'd been running his hands through it repeatedly. The younger man had a determined set to his jaw, and I could see the hatred rolling off him like fiery smoke.

"I don't have your daughter," I said, keeping my tone measured. "And I don't appreciate you coming into my home and slinging around baseless accusations."

DuPont's hand went to his gun. "Baseless? Baseless?! Witnesses saw your enforcer stalking her just before she vanished. You expect me to believe that's a fucking coincidence?"

I resisted the urge to bare my fangs. As much as I wanted to put these insignificant humans in their place, I couldn't afford to escalate the situation.

"No, I expect you to use your head, Detective," I said coolly. "If I had taken your daughter, do you really think I would have left witnesses? And what possible motive could I have for abducting her, anyway?"

DuPont gritted his teeth. "I'm not here as a cop, Santi. I'm here as a father. I'll put a bullet through your heart unless you tell me where she is right now. Did you sell her?"

I squared my shoulders. "You know my lines of business, DuPont. Human trafficking is not one of them."

Steven looked at me frostily. "Not that we know of. But Barone says you were at Simon's and you bought Serenity. Maybe you've discovered that trafficking put lots of cash in your pockets. Or maybe you're looking for leverage against the cops and the other families."

My blood ran cold at the mention of Barone's name, a bitter taste flooding my mouth. I clenched my jaw, my eyes hardening into icy shards of green as the realization of the betrayal sank in. Barone had sold me out. He'd gone to the police with information that could have them descending onto Crescent Manor any moment and taking Serenity from me.

Searing rage exploded through my veins like molten lava. The vein in my temple throbbed, pulsing in time with the furious beat of my heart.

I refused to admit I had Serenity. Instead, my focus shifted to Steven's insidious accusation. With menacing steps, I closed the distance between us until mere inches remained. "I am not a trafficker," came my snarl through clenched teeth, jaw muscles twitching as barely contained rage threatened to spill over. Drawing myself up to full height, I towered over him, daring defiance. "Nor do I have any need for petty leverage. My power is absolute."

Steven opened his mouth to retort, but I cut him off. "Enough. You're not here to debate my family's business practices. You're here to find Joy. And I find it very interesting that you're so quick to point fingers, young man, considering the recent troubles at Crimson Stakes. Tell me, what does your boss know about tonight's fire?"

DuPont winced. Obviously, it pained him greatly to think that his son was a member of the Barone family syndicate.

Steven lifted his chin high, a good soldier defending his commander. "We didn't have anything to do with that."

"Tell me...boy." I drawled out the last word. "Are you in Barone's inner circle?"

"I'm his driver."

I chuckled. "That doesn't exactly make you important,

boy. Unless Maximo Barone is in the habit of telling his chauffeur his business."

I ignored the fact that my brother-in-law was my chauffeur and he knew most of my business. That was different.

I watched Steven closely. Hesitation flashed in his eyes, but he kept his jaw clamped tightly shut. I'd definitely hit a nerve though. If the Barone family was behind the attack on my casino, there would be hell to pay.

Even as I considered the possibility of human treachery, a nagging doubt chewed at my mind. The wolves had been my prime suspects, but could I have been wrong all along? Could the humans be playing a longer game than I realized? That didn't feel right, but suddenly I wasn't sure.

"Look, Santi," DuPont said, his voice laced with rage. "I don't care what's going on between you and the Barone family. All I want is my daughter back."

I held DuPont's gaze, letting a hint of my power bleed into my words. "I give you my word, I do not have Joy. But I will find out what Enzo was doing following her."

I wasn't about to tell them Enzo was following Joy under my own orders.

My gaze still focused on them, I tilted my head toward the door. "Dimitri."

Dimitri raced inside. His sudden actions caught even me off guard. In a blur of motion, he disarmed both DuPont and Steven, sending their guns clattering to the floor. The two men stared at their empty hands in shocked disbelief, their faces paling as they realized how easily they'd been overpowered.

Dimitri stepped back, a smirk playing on his lips as he

twirled one of the confiscated guns around his finger. "Gentlemen, I hate to break it to you, but you brought guns to a vampire fight. Next time, try holy water. Or better yet, an invitation."

I ran a cool eye over the two men. "And now, I'll use my powers of compulsion on you."

DuPont blinked. "Compulsion? What do you mean?"

I drew on my power, my heart quickening, never taking my gaze off them as I spoke. "You will both sit down on the couches quietly. You will only answer questions when I ask them. You will not remember anything that happened here and will leave no longer believing that I'm responsible for Joy's disappearance."

DuPont and his son's eyes glassed over as they sat on the couch, staring straight ahead.

"Did you have something to do with Joy's disappearance?" a soft female voice asked from behind me.

I turned around to find Serenity standing in the doorway, her delicate face lined with suspicion and concern. The white robe she wore over her nightgown accentuated her ethereal beauty. Her blonde hair was disheveled, making her look even more beautiful. But it was the look in her blue eyes that stopped my heart. She had already convicted me of the crime.

Chapter Twenty-Eight

Angelo

This night was going from bad to worse. "Serenity, what are you doing down here? I thought you were asleep."

Ignoring me, Serenity hurried over to the couch and waved her palm in front of DuPont's and Steven's faces. Neither of them blinked. She turned to me, her posture tense and her eyes flashing with accusation. "What did you do to them, Angelo? Why are they just sitting there like that?"

I held up my hands in a placating gesture. "Serenity, please, let me explain—"

"Explain what?" she cut me off, her voice rising. "That you used your powers on them? That you're manipulating them? Maybe you manipulated me too!"

Her words cut me to the quick, but I forced myself to

remain composed. "Serenity, I didn't manipulate you. I would never do that. I only used compulsion on them to keep the situation from getting out of hand."

She folded her arms across her chest. "Like you did on me so I would be your little plaything?"

I flinched as if she'd struck me even as fury rattled through me at her sharp tone. No one had spoken to me like that in centuries—not unless they wanted to be a corpse.

Tears blurred her eyes, but she blinked them away. I went to comfort her, but she clearly wouldn't hear of it. She turned her head away from me, leaving an emptiness in my chest.

I cursed myself inwardly. If she stayed angry with me, she might not help me rejuvenate the Aeternum Stone, leaving my family vulnerable. Forcing her wasn't an option; a Nephilim had to give their power freely. I had just fucked this up, big-time.

Dimitri cleared his throat, a smirk playing on his lips despite the tension in the room. "Well, this is awkward. Should I start taking bets on who wins this lover's quarrel? My money's on the angry angel, by the way."

I shot him a glare that would have made a lesser vampire spontaneously combust. "Dimitri, fetch Enzo," I gritted out, trying to remain in control of the maelstrom of emotions swirling within me.

Dimitri raised an eyebrow, his smirk widening. "Fetch? What am I, a vampire or a golden retriever?" He sighed dramatically. "Fine, I'll go get the brooding brother. Try not to start the apocalypse while I'm gone, okay?"

With a mock salute, he disappeared through the doors, leaving us alone with the two humans.

I took a measured step toward her, my hands held out in a gesture of appeal. "Serenity, I never used any compulsion on you to get you into my bed. What happened between us...it was real, it was genuine."

She flinched as I approached, her eyes glistening with unshed tears. "How can I be sure, Angelo?" She nodded her chin at DuPont and Steven. "How can I trust anything you say when I've seen what you're capable of?"

The pain and uncertainty in her voice tore at my heart, and I had to fight the urge to take her in my arms. "You know me, Serenity. You've seen who I am beneath the monster; know that I would do anything to keep you safe and make you happy."

She scoffed and curled her lip into a snarl. "Happy? You bought me, Angelo. I'm a prisoner in your home. Everyone in this house is able to come and go as they please except for me...and maybe Gianna."

I held her gaze, pouring every ounce of sincerity I possessed into my words. "I'm not perfect, Serenity, and I'll admit I've made mistakes. But I have never once lied to you, and I never will. What I feel for you...it's the most real and honest thing in my life."

I was surprised at the words spilling out of my mouth. I'd never said anything like that to a woman.

Serenity's lower lip trembled, and for a moment, I thought she would cry. But then, she drew in a shuddering breath, squaring her shoulders as if steeling herself against the entire world. "Prove it, then. Find Joy. Bring her home safe. Show me you're not a monster…that you won't kill the people I love." She put her hand on DuPont's shoulder as her voice trailed off into a sob.

I nodded, my resolve hardening into an unbreakable vow. "I promise you, I will move heaven and earth to find out what happened to Joy."

We stood there, the silence broken only by the soft hitch of her breathing, and I knew that this was a turning point, a moment that would define the course of our future together. I was determined to seize it with both hands and never let go.

Heavy footsteps echoed in the living room, announcing the arrival of Dimitri, who had brought not only Enzo but also Gianna. I shot him a cold stare, my displeasure at my sister's unexpected presence evident.

Dimitri, far from blushing or looking uncomfortable, met my gaze with a trademark smirk. "What? You said 'fetch Enzo.' You didn't specify the 'no tagalongs' rule. Besides, I thought we could use a family reunion to liven things up."

Gianna, ignoring our exchange, stepped forward. "Don't blame Dimitri. I insisted on coming."

She ran over to Serenity, her arms outstretched in a gesture of comfort. Serenity stepped back from her, anger still flashing in her eyes.

Dimitri leaned against the doorframe, crossing his arms. "Well, isn't this cozy? Nothing says 'family bonding' quite like tension thick enough to stake a vampire with."

"Serenity, please. Tell me what happened." At the sound of the softness in my sister's voice, the stiffness in Serenity's shoulders fell away and she ran into my sister's outstretched arms. I winced. I should be the one comforting her, not my sister.

Gianna hugged Serenity and stroked her hair as Serenity bit back a sob. "What have you done this time, dear brother?" The icy condemnation in her tone pricked the frustration simmering beneath my skin.

I gritted my teeth, trying to keep my anger under control. I had no time to get into a debate with Gianna, not when my priority was proving to Serenity that I had nothing to do with Joy's kidnapping—and, furthermore, helping to find her.

I turned my attention to Enzo and fixed him with a piercing stare as I leaned forward, getting right into his personal space. "Tell me what happened at Crimson Stakes and with Joy DuPont." I kept my gaze locked on his, my body tense and poised like a coiled snake ready to strike.

Serenity wiggled free from Gianna's embrace, putting distance between herself and the vampires in the room. Her eyes were hard as she focused on my enforcer. "Enzo? What did you do to Joy?" The accusation in her voice was unmistakable, and Enzo bristled under the weight of her suspicion.

"I didn't kill her, if that's what you mean." Enzo's words were brittle, his tone laced with anger and frustration. I could tell there was more to the story and that getting the truth out of him would require a delicate touch.

I poured myself a glass of wine, the rich, crimson liquid swirling in the crystal glass. I took a moment to collect my thoughts, to choose the right approach. "Tell me what happened, Enzo," I said, struggling to remain calm. "Leave nothing out."

As I waited for Enzo to speak, I could feel the weight of Serenity's gaze on me, all her questions and doubts hanging heavy in the air. I knew that the truth, whatever it might prove to be, would either vindicate me in her eyes or shatter forever the fragile trust between us. The stakes had never been higher, and I could only hope Enzo's words would be the key to unlocking the truth and winning Serenity back.

Enzo's jaw clenched. "Joy was passing out those damn flyers again on Bourbon Street, bothering people."

Serenity's brow furrowed, a look of dread spreading over her face. "Flyers?" She placed a hand on her chest, her voice trembling slightly. "You mean of...me?"

Enzo nodded grimly. "Yes. She was bothering the wrong people, if you get my meaning." He glanced at me and shook his head, a mixture of frustration and concern etched into his features. "Foolish girl."

Dread crept through my veins, and I stiffened before tossing the wine back. "What people?"

Enzo met my gaze, his eyes dark and serious. "Our people."

The implications of his words sent a cold silence creeping into the room. Serenity's face drained of color, her eyes widening with fear. "You mean the Mafia?"

Dimitri, who had been uncharacteristically quiet, finally chimed in with a sardonic smirk. "No, sweetie, he means the local knitting circle. They're vicious with those needles." His eyes glinted with dark humor as he turned to Enzo. "I guess Joy missed the 'Don't feed flyers to vampires' memo. Paper cuts are a real pain, you know."

Gianna scowled. "Dimitri." Her tone less than pleased.

He flashed her a debonair smile and shrugged but bit back on another retort.

Enzo didn't answer, his focus remaining all on me. He took a deep breath before continuing, his voice low and urgent. "Joy was a block away from Crimson Stakes when the explosion happened." He gestured toward Steven. "He was with her. I'm not sure if he played a part in the explosion since I couldn't hear what they were saying, but they seemed to be arguing."

Enzo cursed under his breath, then scrubbed his face. "I ran inside. I assumed the bastard would protect his sister. People were streaming out of the casino, pushing and screaming. It was pandemonium."

A wave of unease washed over me, quickly replaced by a simmering anger that threatened to boil over. If Steven was involved in the explosion, it wasn't something I could let go unpunished. Joy's brother or not, he would suffer consequences for participating in a hit on Crimson Stakes.

I clenched my jaw, my fingers tightening around the glass in my hand so hard it was a miracle I didn't break it. I would get to the bottom of this, no matter what it took. If Steven was guilty, he would suffer my full wrath.

Serenity had locked her gaze on me as if she were reading my thoughts. She would consider me punishing Steven another betrayal, I was sure, but at the same time, I couldn't show weakness when it came to the Santi family.

I turned away from her, picturing the awful scene—the smoke, the flames, the terror on the faces of the patrons as they fled for their lives. My mind raced, trying to figure out who had started this, but I kept my jaw set tight, not giving any thoughts away.

Enzo would never have abandoned Joy. Maybe the Barone family knew he was watching Joy, and the explosion had all been a ploy to distract him so they could snatch her.

"We have to find her," I said, my voice low and intense. "And when we do, the Barone family will pay for what they've done."

Enzo nodded, his eyes hardening with determination. "But are we sure it's the Barone family? It could easily be the wolves or the dark Fae."

"That's what we have to find out," I grumbled.

Serenity stepped forward, her eyes wide with concern. "But what about Joy, Enzo? Did you see what happened to her?"

Enzo hesitated, his gaze flickering to the floor before meeting Serenity's eyes. "No. I lost sight of her in the chaos. By the time I made it back outside, she and Steven were gone."

Serenity gazed at me, the unspoken question in her eyes —did I order Joy to be taken because she was handing out those flyers?

I put my wine glass down. "Steven must know something."

Serenity looked between me and him. "What are you going to do?" I could hear the panic in her voice.

"Get the truth."

She rushed over to me and put her hand on my arm. "Please, don't kill him."

I met her gaze. "You're going to have choose between

them, Serenity. Steven works for the Barone family. They may have Joy, and the Barone family is neck deep in human trafficking."

She shook her head. "No, Steven...he wouldn't...he couldn't...his own sister?"

I looked down at her. "I can find out the truth right now if you let me. If you don't, and we waste time investigating, she'll probably vanish, and we'll never pick up her trail again."

Beads of sweat broke out across Serenity's forehead, glistening in the dim light of the room. She stared at Steven as if seeing him for the first time, her eyes wide with a mixture of fear and disbelief.

Gianna stepped forward and wrapped a comforting arm around her slender shoulders. "Serenity, compulsion won't hurt Steven physically. You want to find out what happened, don't you?" Her voice was soft and reassuring, but there was an underlying urgency to her words.

Silent tears welled up in Serenity's eyes, spilling down her cheeks in rivulets. She nodded numbly, her body sagging against Gianna's. My sister gently guided her to a nearby chair, easing her down into the plush cushions.

Taking a deep breath, I focused my mind and drew upon the ancient power of compulsion that coursed through my veins. Earlier I had just wanted them to sit on the couch, but for this, I drew on every ounce of compulsion I could muster. I felt the power surging through my body, pulsing in my temples and crackling at my fingertips.

I sat down on the coffee table directly in front of Steven, my gaze boring into his. Beads of sweat formed on my brow as I channeled the immense energy, directing it like a laser beam into Steven's mind. "Steven, tell me what happened to Joy earlier tonight when she disappeared." My voice was low and commanding, infused with the irresistible force of my will.

As I pushed my power toward him, I felt an invisible barrier push back against me, resisting any intrusion. It was the same strange sensation I had encountered when I tried to compel information out of Freddie, but this time it was even stronger and more malevolent. A cold, evil presence emanated from Steven's mind, chilling me to the bone as if I had plunged my brain into a vat of liquid nitrogen.

Steven's mouth fell wide open, and his face contorted in pain, the veins in his neck bulging. Then, without warning, he let out a blood-curdling scream that echoed throughout the room. I flinched. Out of the corner of my eye, I caught Serenity's stricken face, and guilt gnawed at my insides, but if I didn't get at the truth, Joy was a dead woman.

"You will tell me what happened to Joy," I commanded, pushing harder against the unseen force that blocked my path. I could feel the power surging through me, my determination fueling my strength.

"You're hurting him!" Serenity's anguished cry cut through the air. "Gianna said it wouldn't hurt! Please, stop!"

I glanced over my shoulder, my heart twisting at the sight of Serenity's tearstained face. "It's not me," I admitted, the words tumbling out before I could stop them. "Something is preventing him from speaking."

Enzo, Dimitri, and Gianna all gaped at me, their eyes wide with disbelief. "But how can that be, brother?" Gianna's voice trembled, fear and confusion in her voice. "You're more powerful than any of us."

Dimitri, never one to let a moment of tension pass without comment, chimed in with his trademark smirk. "Well, well. Looks like our big bad vampire just hit the supernatural equivalent of a 'No Entry' sign. Should we try knocking? Or maybe slide a note under the invisible door?" His eyes glinted with a mix of amusement and concern. "I'd offer to give it a try myself, but I prefer my mind games without the actual mind-bending, thanks."

"I don't know what's happening." I turned back to Steven, my mind racing as I tried to make sense of the impossible. What could possibly be strong enough to resist the compulsion of an ancient vampire as old and powerful as myself? And how was it connected to Joy's disappearance?

As I stared into Steven's eyes, I saw a flicker of something dark and malevolent there, an ancient presence that mocked me from the depths of his soul. In that moment, I knew we were dealing with something far more dangerous than anything we had ever faced before.

Chapter Twenty-Nine

Serenity

The atmosphere in the room was so thick that I felt like I was drowning, and the tension was so heavy, it was almost a physical presence, pressing down on me from all sides until I could barely breathe. Even worse than the suffocating pressure was the overwhelming sense of fear that radiated off everyone surrounding me.

It was like a living thing...a dark, insidious entity that crept into my mind and wrapped its icy fingers around my heart. I could feel it emanating from Enzo, Dimitri, and Gianna, could practically taste their sharp, acrid terror on the back of my tongue. I'd never been able to sense anyone's feelings before like this. Did it have to do with the bonding between Angelo and me?

Only Louis DuPont sat motionless, his eyes still glazed

over and vacant, as if he had been transformed into a wax dummy. The compulsion that Angelo had used on him had him in its thrall, rendering him oblivious to the growing horror that threatened to engulf us all.

I watched as Angelo turned back to Steven, his jaw set with grim determination. The air around him crackled with barely contained power, a tangible force that made the hairs on the back of my neck stand on end. Because, beneath the surface, I could sense his fear and uncertainty in the face of this new and terrifying threat.

I thought about Angelo killing Freddie. He'd said it was ugly. I couldn't bear the thought of him killing Steven too. My chest tightened, and I could barely breathe as I pleaded with Angelo. "Please don't hurt Steven. He's always been like a brother to me."

Angelo ignored my plea and turned to Louis, his eyes intense and focused. "I need to see if he is possessed by this presence as well. Tell me everything you know, Detective."

Louis struggled against the compulsion, his face contorting in agony. "I...can't." He began to drool, his body convulsing violently. A blood-curdling scream tore from his throat before his eyes fluttered shut and he slumped over, unconscious.

"Damn it," Angelo growled, frustration and anger flowing from him in waves. "His mind is blocked from me too."

Enzo rubbed his chin thoughtfully, his brow furrowed. "Angelo, do you think Marsha might be behind this? Perhaps she conjured up some kind of spell."

Angelo shook his head, his expression grim. "It doesn't

feel like witchcraft. I've sensed her magic before, and this is different, much more powerful."

Goosebumps broke out all over my arms. The mention of her name brought a flood of vivid, visceral memories—the suffocating fear, the helplessness, the searing pain of her cruel spells. My stomach churned, and I could almost feel the phantom ache of invisible bonds tightening around my limbs, a ghostly echo of the magical restraints she'd used at Simon's auction.

A cold, creeping dread settled into the pit of my stomach, and I could feel the pressure of the situation pushing down on me. I turned to Angelo, my voice trembling. "So... Joy...do you think Simon has her?"

He rubbed his forehead wearily. "Possibly." His gaze shifted to Enzo, and he spoke with authority, his face hardening with resolve. "Lock these two up in the dungeon, and then take your men and go to Simon's Ravenwood. Report back to me."

Fear pulsed through my veins, and I could feel my heart pounding in my chest. "Dungeon?" I whispered. "How can you have a basement? We live in New Orleans."

"The dungeon isn't in a basement. It's in a secure room." He held up his palm, his eyes flickering with a hint of warning. "Don't worry, I'm not going to torture them." Yet I could hear it in his voice. If Angelo didn't get what he wanted, he would use force.

God, this was beyond awful. If Angelo didn't kill them, whatever dark force was controlling their minds certainly would. Worse, I was powerless to help them.

"Where's this secure room?"

My question was met with silence.

Enzo focused on Angelo, his posture tense and alert. "Dimitri, Petar, and I will go to Ravenwood Estates. Are you going to contact Keir?"

Dimitri's eyebrows shot up, a sardonic smirk playing on his lips. "Oh joy, a field trip to Simon's house of overpriced knick-knacks. Just what I always wanted." He glanced at Angelo, his eyes glinting with a mix of humor and wariness. "You sure you want to bring Papa Keir into this? Last I checked, his idea of 'helping' usually involves blood, mayhem, and a body count that would make the Grim Reaper blush."

Angelo sighed heavily, slumping his shoulders. "Looks like I don't have a choice." He glanced at Gianna, his voice firm as it echoed off the high ceilings. "Stay with Serenity." It was an order, not a request.

To my surprise, Gianna nodded, her expression completely solemn for once. "I will protect her." I couldn't tell if her agreement stemmed from a genuine affection for me, or from fear of the unknown force that threatened us all.

His face dark and troubled, Angelo began to leave the living room, his footsteps heavy on the polished wooden floor. I ran after him, my hand grasping his arm desperately, the fabric of his shirt rough beneath my fingers. "Wait! You don't even know what this power is, what you're up against."

He turned to face me, his hands gripping my shoulders tightly, the scorching intensity of his touch branding me through my robe and nightgown. "Stay with Gianna."

Determination surged through me, and I straightened

my spine, meeting his gaze head-on. I refused to be a helpless victim. I knew Angelo would never let me leave the house with Joy missing, but I had to do something. "I want to go to your library. Maybe there's something you overlooked. Maybe Gianna and I can find it together?"

I looked at Gianna questioningly, hoping she would back me up.

To my relief, she smiled and nodded.

"Please, Angelo. I need to do something. Louis, Steven, and Joy are my family. Think about how important your family is to you. I can't just sit around and do nothing." My voice cracked, and tears pricked at the corners of my eyes, blurring my vision.

"All right. You may go to the library." He raised his finger, his tone brooking no argument. "But only the library."

I looked over to Gianna, my resolve strengthening. "I understand."

Angelo headed for the door, his footsteps echoing in the cavernous foyer. "I'll have Elena prepare coffee for you to have in there."

I clasped his rough hand. "Thank you."

He pulled me against him, his strong arms encircling my waist, and kissed me hard. His lips were demanding and urgent as he poured all his frustration, fear, and desire into that one searing moment of contact. I knew I should push him away—this wasn't the time or the place for such intimacy, not with everyone watching us, but his kiss was too intoxicating, and I found myself melting into his embrace.

The world around us faded away as I lost myself in the

sensation of his mouth moving against mine, his tongue teasing the seam of my lips, seeking entrance. I parted them with a soft gasp, and he deepened the kiss, exploring my mouth in a way that made my knees weak and my heart race.

His hands roamed over my back, pulling me closer. The searing touch of his skin through my flimsy robe and night-gown was like a brand, marking me with its intensity—

Someone cleared their throat significantly, and I pushed on his broad chest.

He reluctantly released me. What was wrong with me? One minute, I vowed not to let him touch me, then the next I wanted his lips and hands all over me. He claimed never to have used compulsion on me, but sometimes I wasn't so sure. Or was it that my traitorous body simply craved a vampire's touch?

Gianna escorted me out of the living room while the men left to fulfill Angelo's orders. I hoped that there wasn't a second ambush; the thought of it made my stomach churn with dread. The memory of Enzo's close call was still fresh in my mind, and the idea of any of these men—especially Angelo—facing a similar fate filled me with a sickening sense of fear and helplessness.

My mind was suddenly filled with lurid images of Angelo lying in a pool of his own blood, his lifeless eyes staring up at me in silent accusation. I rubbed my slick fore-head and felt a sudden, desperate need to find a way to protect him, to watch his back and ensure his safety.

My hands clenched into fists at my sides, and I had to take a deep, steadying breath to calm the frantic pounding of my heart. I knew I couldn't be in two places at once, but the urge to protect him, to shield him from the dangers that lurked in the shadows, was overwhelming.

For now, at least, Angelo was staying within these walls, but I knew it wouldn't be for long. He was the Angel of Death, and he would soon be tearing this town apart, looking for what he wanted.

"Do you mind if I go change?" I picked at the folds of my robe, feeling exposed and vulnerable. "I'm really self-conscious walking around like this."

Gianna's lips quirked up in a sympathetic smile. "Why not," she said, her tone understanding. "I don't want to walk around in my nightgown all day either."

We made our way upstairs to our respective rooms, the silence between us comfortable despite the doom and gloom of the situation. It felt strange going to Angelo's bedroom, but this was where all my clothes were now, whether I liked it or not. I slipped into a pair of jeans and a soft, oversized T-shirt, the familiar garments helping to ground me and ease some of the anxiety buzzing just underneath my skin.

As we headed back down to the library, Gianna glanced at me curiously. "What are we looking for anyway?"

I shrugged, biting my lip, considering the question. "I don't know, but I have a feeling we must have missed something earlier."

She frowned. "Like what?"

I thought about Steven and Louis. "Maybe there's something on what kind of creature could block Angelo's power of compulsion? Or something on witchcraft or ancient curses that could resist a vampire's influence?"

"Whatever it is, it would have to be super powerful to

overcome Angelo." The nervousness in Gianna's voice made me tense up.

Elena passed us on the stairs. Her hair was pulled back into a loose bun today, softening the lines of her face.

She bowed her head slightly and gave us a slight smile. "*Bonjour, Mesdemoiselles.* So, you are going to the library this morning? *Monsieur* Angelo told me to bring you coffee there."

Elena really was like the grandmother I never had.

"Yes, thank you," Gianna said. "Could you bring us some breakfast too?"

"*Oui, bien sûr.* I'm fetching the newspaper, and I'll bring it all on a tray."

"Thank you," I said.

We went our separate ways, and Gianna and I had just reached the library when a high-pierced shriek almost made my bones leap out of my skin.

"Come on." Gianna jumped up, knocking her chair over. "That was Elena."

I ran after her, hoping Elena had just seen a mouse or a big hairy spider. We found her at the front door. Angelo had gotten there first and had his arms around her. She was sobbing, clinging to him.

The sound of heavy footsteps echoed through the hallways of Crescent Manor as Angelo's men converged on us, their faces grim and determined. Among them, I recognized Lorenzo, one of Angelo's most trusted guards.

"Search the grounds," Angelo barked, his voice cutting through the chaos like a knife. "Look for any signs of an intruder, anything that might give us a clue as to what happened here."

The men nodded as they fanned out, moving with practiced efficiency. Lorenzo paused for a moment, his gaze meeting Angelo's in a silent question.

Angelo gave him a curt nod in reply. Lorenzo's jaw tightened, and he turned to follow the others, his hand bringing out his gun as he disappeared into the gloom.

Angelo turned his head. "Gianna, keep her back." His hard voice echoed like thunder.

Keep me back? Why? I dodged around Gianna as she reached out to me. Then my gaze fell upon the figure lying face down at the front door, and my heart stopped.

The woman's long, black hair, the same shade as Joy's, spilled across the porch like a river of ink. A pool of blood bloomed out from her head, staining the wood beneath her in a grotesque imitation of a red sunflower, its petals reaching out in a silent cry for help.

The world around me fell away, replaced by a suffocating darkness that threatened to engulf me. Joy, my sister in all but blood, who had been there for me through every trial and triumph, lay motionless on the ground. The sight hit me like a physical blow, knocking the air from my lungs and sending me to my knees.

Anger, grief, and shock swirled within me, building into a raging tempest that consumed every fiber of my being. I threw my head back, a scream tearing from my throat with the force of a thousand anguished souls. The sound echoed through the foyer, shattering the windows and sending shards of glass flying like lethal daggers.

Objects leaped from their perches, caught up in the maelstrom of my turmoil. Vases...books...furniture...they all spun through the air, their paths erratic and dangerous, but I barely registered their presence. All I could see was Joy's lifeless form, her blood staining the ground in a silent accusation.

Angelo had promised to find her, to bring her back from wherever she'd been taken. But he had failed, and now my best friend lay dead on his doorstep.

Distantly, I heard Gianna cry out behind me, her voice laced with fear and confusion. Then strong arms encircled me, pulling me up from the ground and into a solid embrace.

Elena screamed and fell to the ground, covering her head.

"Serenity, stop." Angelo's usually commanding voice reached my ears, but it sounded muffled, as if coming from underwater. For once his voice was unable to penetrate the haze of pain and soothe the anguish that consumed me.

He shook me, his grip tightening as he tried to break through the walls of my grief. "Serenity! Listen to me."

I was beyond listening, beyond reason. All the dark emotions that had bubbled within me for so long finally burst free, erupting out of me in a torrent of uncontrollable power. The very foundations of the manor shook, the walls cracking and groaning under the onslaught of my anguish.

Nothing mattered anymore. Not Angelo's pleas. Not the destruction I was causing. Not even my own safety. All that mattered was the gaping wound in my heart where Joy had once been, a wound that could never be healed.

I surrendered to the darkness, allowing it to consume me in the hopes it would take away the pain and the grief and the unbearable weight of my loss. In that moment, I wished for nothing more than to join Joy in the oblivion of death, to escape the reality of a world without her in it.

Yet even as I sank into the abyss, I felt Angelo's presence beside me, his arms holding me tightly, anchoring me to the world of the living. And deep down, beneath all the layers of despair and rage, a tiny spark of hope flickered within me, a reminder that even in the darkest of times, love could still light the way.

Chapter Thirty

Angelo

I knelt in the shattered remains of the foyer of Crescent Manor, my arms still wrapped around Serenity's trembling body. My eyes swept over the devastation that surrounded me. It was hard to comprehend the sheer magnitude of the damage Serenity had caused in her grief-stricken rage. Clearly, her abilities were far stronger than I had ever imagined.

Shards of glass littered the floor, glittering like fallen stars in the dim light. Some had briefly embedded themselves in the walls before ricocheting out again, leaving behind jagged holes that gaped like open wounds. The once-pristine hallway floors were now marred by deep cracks that split the planks, as if a giant's fingernail had scratched through the very foundations of the manor.

The furniture lay scattered and broken, a testament to the violence of Serenity's outburst. Coffee tables, end tables, and bookshelves had all been upended, their contents strewn across the floor. Some pieces had survived the onslaught, while others lay shattered beyond repair, their fragmented ruins mixing with the glass and debris.

As I took in the chaotic scene of destruction, my heart tightened with a mixture of sorrow and fear. Sorrow for Serenity's pain, for the loss that had provoked such an extreme reaction. And fear for what this display of power could mean, not just for her, but for the delicate balance that existed between the supernatural factions in New Orleans.

If word got out about the raw, untamed power that coursed through Serenity's veins, I knew she would be hunted for that power—just as I knew, with a fierce certainty, that I would do whatever it took to protect her, even if it meant going to war with the entire city.

Gianna sank down next to me, and fear settled in her eyes as she looked at Serenity. My Nephilim's sobs were heartbreaking as they echoed throughout my home.

Elena was still on the floor, her hands covering her face, crying softly.

"Stay with her, Gianna." I carefully unwound my arms from around Serenity.

Gianna nodded silently, cradling Serenity's head against her shoulder, stroking her hair.

I shook with rage, my fangs lengthening as the primal urge to hunt and to kill surged through my veins. Whoever had done this to Joy, and thereby shattered Serenity's heart into a million pieces, would pay with their life. I would track them down and make them suffer for every single shred of pain they had inflicted.

They would learn the true meaning of terror, the agony of having their still-beating heart ripped from their chest even as they watched. I would paint the streets of New Orleans red with their blood and send a message to anyone who dared to cross the Santi family and harm those under my protection.

I strode over grimly to Joy's motionless body, my hand reaching out to turn her over. When I caught sight of her face, I hissed in surprise, yanking my hand back as if I had been burned. It wasn't Joy lying there, her eyes wide and staring in frozen horror. It was Emily Bastion.

As I stared down at her lifeless body, a sense of dread settled over me like a heavy shroud. This was the fourth woman murdered in the French Quarter, her blood drained and her eyes wide with the horror of her final moments. And once again, the implication was that I was behind it.

I whirled around, my hands grabbing Serenity's shoulders as I shook her hard, trying to break through the haze of grief and shock that consumed her. "Hush, Serenity," I said, my fingers digging into her skin, my brow furrowed in intense concentration and my chest pressing against my pounding heart as I gazed at her, willing her to look at me. "It's not Joy."

Serenity choked back her sobs, confusion swirling in her lovely blue eyes. Her lower lip trembled, and she squeezed my forearm desperately, as if she were trying to anchor herself to reality. "It's not?" she asked, her voice raspy and raw with emotion.

I shook my head, my sense of relief warring with the growing unease in the pit of my stomach. "No."

Gianna gasped, her hand flying to her mouth. "Oh!"

Serenity stared at the lifeless body of the girl in shock and confusion, her eyes wide. She was transfixed by the gruesome sight, unable to tear her gaze away. "Then...who is it?"

"A girl I knew," I said grimly. "Her name is...was...Emily Bastion."

Lorenzo came rushing down the hallway toward us, his face pale and his eyes wide. "Angelo, what's all this...?" he began, his voice trailing off as he took in the destruction that surrounded us.

"We'll talk later," I said, my tone clipped and harsh. "More importantly, did you find any evidence of who did this?"

Lorenzo shook his head, his expression grim. "Do you know who the girl is, at least?"

"Emily Bastion," I replied shortly, my mind already racing with the implications of this new development.

Serenity looked around, her eyes filling with horror as she truly took in for the first time the shambles that had once been Crescent Manor. The evidence of what she had done, of the power she had unleashed in her grief, hit her like a physical blow.

"Did I...did I do this?" she whispered, her voice trembling with a mixture of awe and fear.

"I said later," I snapped, my voice coming out harsher than I intended.

Serenity flinched, cowering as if I had struck her. I felt a pang of guilt, but this was no time for comfort or softness. I had to act fast and contain the situation before it spiraled out of control.

I grabbed Lorenzo by the neck, my fingers tightening around his throat as I pulled him close. "You'll tell no one of this," I growled, my eyes boring into his.

Lorenzo nodded, his face turning purple as he struggled to breathe. "No, sir," he choked out. "Of course not."

I released him abruptly, watching as he staggered back, rubbing his bruised throat. "If you do," I warned, my anger flowing through me like a raging river, "you'll sign your own death warrant."

Serenity had wrapped her arms around her knees and was rocking back and forth, gripped by the shock of what she had done. I didn't have time to comfort her, as much as it killed me. My family's world was falling apart.

Lorenzo cleared his throat, his voice hesitant. "What should we do with the body—"

Before he could finish his question, sirens began to wail in the distance, growing louder with each passing second. Someone had alerted the authorities about Emily's murder, and I was certain the killer had a hand in it. Word would spread like wildfire throughout the French Quarter, and while I wasn't worried about the police, the thought of King Nico and Costin Tarus finding out sent a chill down my spine. They had made it all too clear what would happen if these murders continued, and I knew that they would stop at nothing to see me and the Santi family brought to our knees.

"You will do nothing with it. I will return momentarily."

Without waiting for a response, I grabbed Serenity's wrist, my grip firm but gentle.

Gianna's hand shot out, grabbing my arm. "Angelo, what are you doing?" Her voice was filled with dread.

I broke free of her grasp, my eyes locking with hers. "Saving our family," I said simply.

I lifted Serenity into my arms, cradling her close to my chest as I carried her to my office. She clung tightly to me, her face tucked into my shoulder, and I could feel the rapid flutter of her heartbeat against my skin.

"Angelo, I'm sorry for what I did to Crescent Manor," she whispered, her voice muffled. "I didn't mean to. I...I lost control. I don't know how to handle my power yet." She pulled back, her eyes shimmering with unshed tears. "I promise I'll find a way to fix this place...if I can."

I set her down gently, my hands coming up to cup her face, my thumbs gently brushing away the tears that had begun to fall. I leaned in close, my forehead nearly touching hers, our breath mingling in the space between us. "You can, I know it," I whispered, hoping my words and my gentle touch reassured her in her moment of vulnerability.

I turned away from her, moving to the desk where the Aeternum Stone sat. The sight of it, now almost completely dark, sent a wave of dread washing through me. With its power fading, Dracula, King Nico, and Costin would easily be able to overpower me and my family. It was a fate I refused to accept, and a reality I would do anything to prevent.

I lifted the glass case, my fingers closing around the

stone. It pulsed in my hand, but it was only a faint flicker of energy that seemed to grow weaker by the second.

Serenity tilted her head, her eyes narrowing on the stone in confusion. "What is that?" she asked, her voice hesitant.

"This is the Aeternum Stone." I held it out for her to see. "The witches enchanted it with healing powers, and for years, it has protected my family from Dracula's wrath."

She stared at the Stone, her expression skeptical. "Enzo told me he was still alive. I still can't believe the guy from Bram Stoker's book is real."

I shook my head, a mirthless smile tugging at the corner of my mouth. "Stoker's book was fiction, but Dracula himself is very real. His true name is Vlad Țepeș, and believe me, he is not someone to be trifled with."

Serenity's face was still etched with doubt. "Why are you telling me all this? And what do you mean, protect your family from Dracula's wrath?"

I sighed, running a hand through my hair. "Some time ago, Vlad imposed a set of rules on all vampires, to be followed without question. He now believes humans should not be drained against their will, and has decreed that all vampires must swear an oath not to do so in a ceremony called the *Obliterictus*."

"And let me guess," Serenity said, her voice tight. "The Santi family hasn't been following these rules."

I met her gaze, my own eyes steely. "We have merely done what we had to do to survive and protect our own. Unfortunately, in doing so, we have made an enemy of Dracula. He sees us as a threat to his power, to the order he has tried to impose on our kind."

Serenity shook her head, confusion and disbelief on her face. "But why? What could he possibly hope to gain by controlling vampires like this?"

"Power," I said simply. "Vlad's laws are not about morality or compassion. Rather, they are about ensuring that all vampires are beholden to him. Those who defy him, who refuse to participate in the *Obliterictus* Ceremony and receive a Rose Unaknium Stone...which is not in fact a stone at all, but a drop of Vlad's blood that has crystallized...are branded as his enemies and hunted down without mercy."

I held up the Aeternum Stone, its surface pulsing weakly in the dim light of the office. "This stone is all that stands between us and Dracula's wrath. Without it, we are vulnerable, exposed. And now, with Emily's murder drawing fresh attention to us, I fear Vlad will not hesitate to strike."

Serenity peered closely at me, her arms crossing defensively over her chest. "Angelo, you still haven't told me why you're sharing all this with me."

I held her gaze, my expression solemn. "Because you have the power to save my family, Serenity. Your healing abilities as a Nephilim are the key to restoring the Aeternum Stone, thus protecting us from Dracula's wrath."

She scoffed, shaking her head in disbelief. "So...what? You're just going to use me to ensure that you can go on killing people without suffering the consequences?"

I bristled at the accusation but tried to keep my tone calm. "We don't follow Dracula's rules, Serenity. Blood is what makes us powerful, what allows us to maintain our position as the Santi Mafia. Without it, we would be vulnerable and weak."

Serenity's eyes flashed with anger, her cheeks flushing with indignation. "So is that why you bought me at the auction? Because you thought I had the power to revitalize this stone, to keep your family's murderous ways going strong?"

I flinched at the venom in her words and the raw hurt that simmered beneath the surface. I wanted to deny it all, to tell her that my feelings for her were real and I would never see her as just a means to an end, but I couldn't lie to her. The truth was, I had been drawn to her power from the moment I first laid eyes on her, had seen in her the potential to change everything.

I stepped toward her, needing her to understand. "Serenity, please. It's not that simple. Yes, your power was what first caught my attention, but that's not the only reason I wanted you at my side."

She backed away from me, her eyes shimmering with unshed tears. "How do I know that, Angelo? How can I trust you, when you've been keeping so much from me? When you've been planning to use me for your own personal gain?"

The words hit me like a speeding train, the truth of them impossible to ignore. I had been so selfish, had put my own needs and desires above hers. And now, with my family's very survival resting on her shoulders, I realized just how much I stood to lose.

"Serenity, I..." I faltered, my breath hitching in my throat as a wave of emotion crashed over me. I took a moment to find the words that were buried deep in my heart. "I never meant to hurt you. I never wanted you to feel like a pawn in some game. But the truth is, I need you. My family needs you. And I honestly don't know what I would do if I lost you."

The admission hung heavy in the air, a fragile bridge between us. Serenity stared at me, her expression unreadable, and for a moment, I feared I had shattered the trust between us beyond repair. I could see it in her eyes. She thought I was a monster.

Serenity's gaze shifted from me to the stone. "And if I don't use my power on the stone...what happens?"

What indeed? I fought to control the surge of emotions that threatened to overwhelm me. I had always prided myself on my strength, on my ability to face any challenge with unwavering, stoic resolve. But in this moment, I felt more vulnerable than I ever had before. My very existence hung in the balance.

I squared my shoulders. "Since I'm the head of the Santi family, Dracula will kill me." The admission felt like sandpaper in my throat, each word scraping against my vocal cords, leaving them raw, and my chest tightened from finally admitting the truth out loud.

I held my breath, waiting for her answer. For centuries, I had held the fate of my family in my hands. Now, it was in hers.

Chapter Thirty-One

Serenity

I stared mutely at the Aeternum Stone, feeling as though I stood at a terrible crossroads, both paths leading to an uncertain and perhaps perilous future. If I refused to use my power, Dracula would undoubtedly come for Angelo, possibly his entire family. Their lives hung in the balance. But if I did heal the stone, thereby restoring its power, then I would be helping the Santi family to continue their murderous reign, to keep taking human lives to sustain their own.

I swallowed hard, my throat tight with emotion. "How many people does your family kill?" My voice trembled but was insistent.

Angelo's expression grew somber, and his eyes flickered with a hint of shame. "Probably not as many as you'd suspect," he said softly. "The older we get, the less blood we need to survive. Sometimes we feed on willing hosts who offer themselves up freely. Others, we kill those who deserve it...people like Freddie."

I flinched slightly when I heard Freddie's name, my stomach churning with revulsion. It was true—he had been a monster, a sadistic creature who delighted in the suffering of others. But did that justify his death? Did that make it right for the Santi family to play judge, jury, and executioner?

If Dracula did come out of the woodwork to kill Angelo —god forbid—then what would happen to me? I already had a target on my back. All the other families wanted me for their own purposes, it seemed. At least here I was protected. I knew Angelo would never allow anyone to hurt me. That might not be true for the other families. The thought turned my blood cold.

Angelo, sensing my inner turmoil, placed the Aeternum Stone on his desk, his movements slow and deliberate. "I'm not going to force you, Serenity," he said, his voice low and earnest. "You gave yourself to me freely, and that was precious to me beyond measure. You're more special to me than any woman I've ever met in all my centuries of existence."

His words washed over me like a balm, soothing the ragged edges of my soul. I wanted to believe him, wanted to trust in the sincerity of his feelings for me. But doubt still gnawed my insides like a hungry rat, sending shooting pains through my gut and stealing the air from my lungs.

I closed my eyes, my mind racing with a thousand

conflicting thoughts and emotions. I had seen the darkness that lurked within the Santi family, their casual disregard for human life. And yet I had also seen the fierce, deep-seated love, loyalty, and devotion that bound them together.

I hadn't experienced an unwavering connection like that since Mom had died. The DuPonts were extremely close, like a surrogate family to me, but I was still always an outsider. Here, I had been cherished and protected. I knew no one within these walls would hurt me.

Could I really condemn them all to death, knowing that my own inaction would be the cause? Could I live with the guilt of knowing I had let Angelo die, that I had stood by and watched as Dracula tore apart the man that had changed my life? My chest ached at the idea of losing him. And if Dracula killed Angelo, how would I even find Joy, never mind save her? I would be at a loss there.

At the same time, could I really condone their actions, could I let them keep killing, keep feeding on the innocent and the guilty alike? Wasn't there a middle ground, a way to save Angelo and his family without compromising my own morals and beliefs?

I didn't know the answer. I didn't know if there even was one. All I knew was that this decision was the most important one I would ever make; the consequences of my choice would change the course of countless lives.

I opened my eyes, my gaze locking with Angelo's. In his eyes, I saw a reflection of my own fear and uncertainty, but also a glimmer of hope.

"I don't know what to do," I whispered, my voice cracking with emotion. "I don't want to lose you, Angelo.

But I don't know if I can be responsible for the deaths of innocent people either."

Angelo reached out, his fingers brushing against my cheek in a featherlight caress. "I know, Serenity." He drew in a deep, shuddering breath. "I am who I am. I'm the head of the Santi family. We're a Mafia family just like any other, except we're also vampires. The same holds true for the wolf and dark Fae Mafia families. We all do what we have to in order to survive."

I looked at him, a mixture of curiosity and apprehension swirling in my gut. "You said you're like the other Mafia families. What exactly does that mean? What are your lines of business, besides the casino?"

"I acquire magical artifacts and sell them on the black market. Some of them I keep for my own purposes."

I bowed my head. "Including me?"

He gave me a hard look. "Yes."

"Have you murdered people for hire?"

He shrugged, lifting his shoulders in a casual way that belied the gravity of the question. "Surely you know my reputation."

I thought about Freddie. How many times had he lied to me? Steven hadn't always told the truth, either, especially when it came to his illegal activities, first in the street gang and now with the Barone family.

The only man I felt had been honest with me had been Louis DuPont. He was a good man and had done the best he could to protect me. I knew Louis would tell me to walk away, to let the Santi family be destroyed.

I hesitated, my heart torn between my feelings for

Angelo and my own moral code. Could I actually walk away, knowing he'd be murdered, maybe even tortured before he died? My heart hurt at the thought and a lump formed in the back of my throat.

And what would Dracula do to Enzo, Gianna, Elena, Dimitri, and even Lorenzo? I doubt that he would spare their lives. Would they end up like Jacques?

Icy fear slipped up my spine as I thought of Jacques's horrible death. "You...you have to behead a vampire to kill them, right? Isn't that what you said?"

"Yes and no. Born vampires, like Dimitri, will someday die of old age, but made vampires are immortal. The only way to kill us is through beheading."

I swallowed hard, my mouth suddenly dry. "So that's what Dracula would do to you?"

"Eventually." The implication made me feel sick. He meant Dracula would torture him.

Angelo left me and walked over to the window to gaze down upon Bourbon Street. He wasn't a hero, not like Captain America. And yet... he wasn't all bad either.

In the end, I knew there was no easy answer. My brain said to walk away, to leave Angelo to his fate and wash my hands of the whole sordid affair.

But my heart...my heart couldn't bear the thought that I would be responsible for his death, that I would have as good as stood by and watched as Dracula tore him apart, along with the others.

With closed eyes, my thoughts drifted. Jacques' brutal, senseless murder filled my mind. The countless other lives lost to the Santi family's thirst came next - their hunger not just for blood, but for power and control. The weight of these deaths pressed heavily upon me.

I also thought about the man standing before me, the man who had shown such depth of feeling for me. He'd demonstrated a devotion I had never known before. My deadbeat supernatural dad couldn't leave Mom and me fast enough. He taught me not to trust men, just as Freddie taught me to fear them. Meanwhile, my own romantic history teetered on the brink of you're-better-off-without-him. I had steered away from men, never wanting to end up like my mom.

But Angelo had changed all of that. He'd shown me something I never dreamed existed, except for in the movies or books.

In that moment, I knew my heart had made its choice. I couldn't walk away from Angelo, couldn't abandon him to a fate worse than death. I cared for him more than any other man in my life, even though I wasn't sure if it was love. I couldn't even bring myself to utter that word to myself, never mind to him.

I reached for the Aeternum Stone with a trembling hand, my fingers closing around its hard, angular surface like a vice. The moment I made contact, a searing pain burst inside my heart, as if a white-hot dagger had been plunged deep into my chest. I gasped, my breath catching in my throat as agony spread through my body like wildfire.

Every muscle in my body tensed up, and I felt as though my entire body was being pulled inside out. My skin prickled with a thousand needles, and a fiery heat coursed through my veins, leaving me breathless and dizzy. I squeezed my eyes shut, but even behind the closed lids, I could see a blinding light emanating from the very core of my being. How was this possible?

I tried to cry out, but no sound escaped my lips. The pain was all-consuming, to the point that I could feel my grip on reality slipping away. The room around me melted into a distant blur, until all that existed was the stone gripped tightly in my hand and the excruciating sensations that wracked my body.

Just as the pain reached such a crescendo that I thought I couldn't bear it any longer, my eyes snapped open and the light that had been building inside me burst forth, bathing the room in an eerie, otherworldly glow. I felt a sudden release, as if something had been unlocked deep within me, and the stone grew warm in my palm, pulsing with strange, ancient power.

My head jerked back, a guttural scream tearing from my throat as the agony began to intensify again, making my muscles spasm uncontrollably.

"Serenity!" Angelo's voice was distant and barely audible over the roaring in my ears.

The Aeternum Stone seemed to come alive, and I could feel the stone's insatiable hunger as it greedily drained every ounce of power from my being, determined to survive at any cost. It latched onto my energy like a parasite, siphoning off my life force with relentless determination. My legs buckled beneath me, and my teeth chattered so violently I feared they might shatter. The pain was all-consuming, a raging inferno that threatened to incinerate me from the inside out.

I cried out in agony, my voice raw and desperate. The

darkness closed in on me as the stone's hunger for me proved too much to bear. My vision faded, the darkness slowly replaced with a dizziness that made my stomach topsy-turvy. With a final, shuddering gasp, I crashed to the floor, my body limp as I felt the energy continue to drain from me.

Chapter Thirty-Two

Angelo

A burst of blinding white light assaulted my eyes, forcing me to shield them with my hand. As the light began to fade, a sudden surge of energy coursed through my body, like an electrical current that set every nerve ending ablaze. It was as if a dam had burst within me, unleashing a river of power that had been held back for far too long.

I gasped as the energy continued to build, filling me with a strength I hadn't felt in decades. My heartbeat thundered in my ears, and my skin tingled with the sheer potency of the magic flowing through my veins. It was exhilarating and overwhelming all at once, a heady rush of renewed vitality that left me breathless.

As the initial shock began to wear off, I could feel my senses becoming keener, my mind becoming clearer and sharper. The world around me seemed to come into better focus—colors were more vivid, sounds crisper. I felt alive in a way I hadn't in a long time, as if a veil had been lifted from my eyes, revealing the true depth and breadth of my power to me.

I clenched my fists, marveling at the raw energy that thrummed just beneath the surface of my skin. It was intoxicating, this feeling of strength and capability. With this renewed power, I knew I could face any challenge that lay ahead.

Even as I reveled in the rush of my restored abilities, a flicker of unease passed through me. Serenity had managed to heal the stone, but not completely. I knew that this was only a fraction of my true potential, and the thought of what I might be capable of at full strength both thrilled and terrified me.

Then I turned, and my world shattered into a million pieces.

I saw Serenity spasming in front of me before she crumpled on the floor, her body going unnaturally still. The realization that I had prioritized restoring the Aeternum Stone's power over her well-being hit me like a sledgehammer and tears welled up in my eyes as I rushed to her side.

Her outstretched hand still clutched the Aeternum Stone in a deathly grip. I gathered her limp form into my arms, cradling her against my chest. "Serenity," I choked out, the word sticking in my throat as a wave of anguish crashed over me, so intense that it stole the breath from my lungs and sent my world spinning off its axis. My body trembled, and a searing pain cut into my chest, as if my heart were being ripped from my ribcage. "Serenity! What have I done?"

Crimson rivulets trickled down her nose, cheeks, and throat, the evidence of my selfishness painting her porcelain skin. For so long, I had only cared about what was best for me and my family.

Until I met her.

I clutched her tighter, my fingers digging into her unmoving flesh as if I could somehow return her to consciousness. "No, no, no," I mumbled, my voice breaking on each word. "Please, Serenity, don't leave me. I'm sorry. I'm so sorry."

My vision blurred as I gently rocked her back and forth, not from tears but from shock. Each shudder that coursed through me was like a silent sob, the gravity of my actions hitting me as harshly as a gale force wind. The stark realization that I had extinguished the one true light in my dark world through my own selfishness was nauseating. She had brought me hope and brightness, and now, all was shadow and guilt, her light snuffed out. And it was all my fault.

I shook her gently, desperately searching for any sign of life. "Can you hear me?" I pleaded, my heart shattering more with each passing second of silence.

Her eyes remained closed, her lashes dark on her too-pale cheeks. With trembling fingers, I pried the stone from her grasp. It pulsed in my palm, alive once more, its power restored just enough to keep my enemies at bay...for now. As I gazed down at Serenity's lifeless form, I realized the price I had paid was far too steep. I had killed the woman who had stolen my heart. The woman I loved.

I blinked at that thought. Love? Did I truly love this woman? I had never known love except for what I felt for my family. This...this was different...more powerful. Yes. I did love her. And my actions had killed her.

Tears stung my eyes. The head of the Santi family was about to break down into sobs. That hadn't happened since the plague years.

Scooping her up in my arms, I kicked open the office door, ready to face whatever lay outside. Voices echoed from downstairs, but I didn't care if they belonged to the police, King Nico, even to Dracula himself. In that moment, Serenity was my sole concern. I bellowed at the top of my lungs, my voice raw with desperation. "Elena!!!"

I carried Serenity's unconscious form to our bed and gently lowered her onto the mattress. With each passing moment, my heart cracked further, until it threatened to shatter into a million pieces.

"Elena," I screamed again, my voice hoarse.

Hurried footsteps echoed down the hallway, growing louder. After what felt like an eternity to me, Elena burst into the room. Her eyes were still red from crying and her face pale from fright. She stumbled into my bedroom and came to an abrupt halt. "Angelo, *mon Dieu*! Whatever has happened?"

Her face was accusatory as her eyes bored into me, as if she believed I had intentionally harmed Serenity.

"She touched..." I paused, fighting past the constriction in my throat. "She touched the Aeternum Stone." My hands curled into fists at my side. "I didn't know...I had no idea it would do this to her."

Elena clasped my arm, offering me momentary comfort before approaching Serenity. She rested her palm on Serenity's sleek forehead, her brow furrowed in deep concentration, and closed her eyes. After a few tense seconds, she opened them again and let out a sigh of relief as she glanced over her shoulder at me. "*Dieu merci*, she's alive."

The words hit me like a thunderbolt, and for a moment, I couldn't breathe. My heart stuttered in my chest, and it felt as if the ground had suddenly shifted beneath my feet as a dizzying rush of emotions—relief, joy, disbelief—surged through me.

"Alive?" I whispered, my voice hoarse and trembling. "Are you sure?"

I stumbled forward, my legs unsteady as I closed the distance between Serenity and myself. I sank to my knees beside her, my hands shaking as I reached toward her face, almost afraid that she would vanish like a mirage if I dared to touch her.

But she was no mirage. She was real, solid and warm beneath my fingertips. I could feel the faintest flutter of a pulse, hear the soft whisper of her breath against my skin. Tears sprang to my eyes as a wave of relief so powerful that it nearly knocked me off my feet crashed over me.

"Serenity," I breathed, my voice cracking with emotion. "You're alive. I thought I'd lost you."

I gathered her into my arms, cradling her against my chest, the most precious thing in the world. The warmth of her body against mine, the steady beat of her heart, were both miracles I hadn't dared to hope for.

I buried my face in her hair, inhaling its sweet scent,

letting it fill my lungs and chase away the lingering shadows of despair. She was alive, and with that knowledge, I felt a flicker of hope reignite within me, a tiny flame that had nearly been extinguished in the depths of my anguish.

In all the time she had known me, Elena had never seen me break down. I had always been the strong one, the pillar of strength that everyone relied upon. Now, as I stood before her, my walls crumbled.

The shock in Elena's eyes as she beheld the raw, unguarded emotion in my features gradually melted away, replaced by a deep, unwavering compassion. "She'll survive, Angelo. I feel it. But she needs time to heal." Her gaze darted toward the door, and she whispered, "You need to go downstairs. The police are here."

I wiped the tears from my face with the back of my hand, struggling to regain my composure. "Forget them," I muttered, the words escaping my lips in a harsh whisper. "I don't care about them." Rage surged through me as I thought about the police taking me away from Serenity just when I'd almost lost her. My hands clenched into fists, and I could feel the tension radiating from my body. I knew that in this state, talking to the police would be a terrible idea.

Elena grasped my arms, her fingers digging into my skin as she tried to ground me. "You are the head of the Santi family, Angelo. It is your duty. Go talk with them." Her gaze softened as she glanced toward Serenity's unconscious form. "I will take care of her. But there's something you should know before you go down there. When she touched the stone, it restored Crescent Manor."

My brows furrowed in confusion. "What?"

"Go and see for yourself, Angelo. Fortunately, it happened before the police arrived, but I fear it may not have escaped prying eyes entirely."

A change in her tone made my blood run cold. "Who else is down there?" I demanded, the words rushing from my lips in a harsh, guttural rasp. My body was tense, every muscle coiled tight like a guitar string ready to snap as I leaned forward, my face mere inches from hers.

Elena hesitated, but the flash of anger in my eyes compelled her to answer. "Costin Tarus and Keir Rankin," she whispered.

I moved swiftly toward the bedroom door, my mind already racing with the possibilities of what might be lying ahead. Serenity was in a weakened state, and I couldn't risk her coming down and losing control of her power again. If she did so, it might be the death of her.

"Lock the door behind me," I instructed, my tone leaving no room for argument. "Don't open it to anyone but me, you understand?"

"*Oui, monsieur,*" Elena replied, watching me go, her voice trembling slightly.

The moment the door was shut and I heard the lock click into place, I bolted down the stairs, my feet carrying me faster than they ever had before as I prepared to face whatever challenges awaited me below.

I slowed my pace again as I approached the main hall, the sound of voices growing louder with each step. One of them belonged to Keir Rankin; I would have to fight the urge to wrap my hands around his throat when I saw him. His presence here felt far too convenient. I also couldn't help but wonder how Costin had found out about the whole situation so quickly.

As I drew closer, I spotted a tall, thin man interviewing my sister and Lorenzo. Before I could take another step, Enzo grabbed my arm, pulling me aside.

His hard gaze bore into mine as he leaned in close, his voice low and urgent. "We've had news from Simon about Joy. It's not good."

I nodded solemnly, my heart sinking. If Joy had been sold or killed, it would devastate Serenity.

Steeling myself, I approached the scene with Enzo at my side.

The tall man turned to face us, and I immediately recognized him as Chester Flanagan, DuPont's partner. "Well, well, the man of the hour himself finally makes an appearance," he drawled, his tone dripping with disdain. "What took you so long, Santi? I thought the death of a girl you once had a relationship with would be more important to you."

"Flanagan." I narrowed my eyes, meeting his gaze with forced politeness. "I came as soon as I heard."

"A likely story," he countered, his lips curling into a sneer. "You sure you haven't been busy covering up evidence while we've been investigating the poor girl's death?"

I didn't bother responding to his ludicrous accusation. Instead, my gaze drifted surreptitiously to Tarus and Rankin, who stood off to the side, their eyes fixed on me. They were dissecting my every move, hunting for cracks in my armor. If what Elena had hinted was true, and they had witnessed the house's restoration, I knew I would have to tread carefully. The pristine windows, unblemished walls, and perfectly arranged furniture would undoubtedly raise questions I was neither prepared for nor able to answer. My chest tightened—a brief but telling fault line in my composure.

Enzo drew the attention from me and onto himself. "How did the girl die?" His tone was a perfect blend of curiosity and concern.

Flanagan's gaze flicked to Enzo, a hint of annoyance flashing in his eyes. "Ah, yes. Santi's right-hand man. I suspect she was drained like the three other girls, but we won't know for sure until the coroner does an autopsy." He turned to both of us and waved his pen over his open notebook. "Tell me, where were you two between three and five this morning?"

I met his eyes, my expression carefully neutral. "I was in bed asleep."

"Do you have any witnesses who can corroborate that?" Flanagan pressed, his eyes glinting.

I gazed at him calmly. The last thing I wanted to do was bring Serenity into this scenario. "No."

Flanagan's attention shifted to Enzo. "I assume you were asleep as well."

Enzo shrugged, a hint of a smirk playing at the corners of his mouth. "Oh, like a baby, officer."

Lorenzo stepped forward, his posture straight and his voice clear. "I was on duty, sir, and I didn't see anyone come onto the grounds with the girl at that time."

"So you *say*," the detective muttered, his skepticism evident. His piercing gaze returned to me, his next words laced with suspicion. "The other issue is that my partner, Detective DuPont, seems to have disappeared. But I take it you wouldn't know anything about that, either."

I could see the gears turning in Flanagan's mind as he fished for information, trying to provoke a reaction that would implicate me or my men. Let him fish. I was too experienced to fall for such tactics, and my men were too well-trained to crack under pressure. We all stood our ground, our expressions revealing nothing.

"No, we don't," I said, my gaze steady as I met the detective's eyes. I stood tall. "Do you honestly believe I would be stupid enough to leave a dead body that I had anything to do with on my own doorstep?" I raised an eyebrow, a hint of a smirk curving the corner of my mouth. "Have you ever known the Santi family to be so careless with evidence?"

"There's always a first time," Flanagan mumbled, sneering. "I don't suppose you'd be willing to allow us to search your home for any evidence related to the case?"

I could feel Costin's gaze boring into me, his eyes practically burning a hole through my skull. Legally, of course, I could refuse until he came back with a warrant; but doing so would only cast more suspicion on me and my family. I was confident they wouldn't be able to find the detective and his son in a million years; the hidden door was so well-concealed that they could stare directly at it without ever realizing its existence.

Serenity's situation was a different matter entirely, but I was sure that Elena would have her in bed resting and out of sight by now. The sooner I could get the police out of here, the better. Dealing with a search warrant and the added scrutiny one entailed would only complicate things.

I spread my hands and forced a smile to my face, meeting the detective's gaze head-on. "By all means, Detective Flanagan. Search my home. I have nothing to hide."

The detective shook his head in disbelief, clearly taken aback by my unexpected cooperation.

I also didn't miss the flash of surprise that crossed Costin's and Rankin's faces, nor the slight widening of Lorenzo's and Enzo's eyes. But there was a method to my madness, a carefully calculated reason behind my apparent compliance. And my men knew better than to doubt Angelo Santi's decisions, even if they didn't fully understand them in the moment.

Chapter Thirty-Three

Angelo

As the coroner prepared to remove the body, Detective Flanagan wasted no time in deploying his men to scour the grounds of the Santi estate. With a series of barked orders, he sent them haring off in all directions, their eyes keen and their movements precise as they began their search for any shred of evidence that might link me to Emily's death. I watched them carefully, a sense of relief washing over me as I noted the glazed look in their eyes—a telltale sign that my earlier compulsion was still firmly in place.

Despite the countless pictures of Serenity they had undoubtedly seen, they would look right at her without a flicker of recognition. It was a necessary precaution, one that would keep her safe from their scrutiny, at least for now. The thought of them recognizing her, of them trying to take her away from me, actually put an icy fear in my heart. I hadn't experienced fear for centuries. She was mine and I would kill anyone who tried to take her from me.

Surprisingly, Flanagan insisted that Tarus and Rankin remain in the foyer. I couldn't help but wonder if they were working with the police and that their true purpose here was to observe my reactions, to catch any tiny flicker of unease or infinitesimal hint of guilt that might cross my features.

As the next couple of hours ticked by, I carefully maintained an air of calm detachment, even as the sound of footsteps and the occasional murmur of voices echoed throughout the halls. The detective's men were very thorough, leaving no room unsearched, no potential hiding place unexplored. They rifled through drawers, peered behind furniture, even tapped on walls, clearly hoping to uncover a hidden compartment or secret passage.

But just as I had anticipated, their painstaking efforts yielded nothing. There was no evidence to be found, no smoking gun that could tie me to the crime. I had been meticulous in all my dealings, always careful to keep my hands squeaky clean and my tracks well covered.

Eventually, their search led them to my bedroom, where Serenity still lay sleeping. I refused to stay back and hovered over them as they entered. Watching her sleep, a momentary calm washed over me—the rage and tension that had been simmering inside me temporarily stilled. Elena had tenderly washed her face, and with her blonde hair fanned out across the pillow, she looked serenely peaceful, like Sleeping Beauty herself.

A fierce protectiveness surged through me, tightening

my jaw and clenching my fists at my sides. I silently vowed that if they dared to disturb her peace, none of them would walk out of that bedroom alive.

Elena glared at the detectives and put her hands on her hips. "What is the meaning of this interruption, *messieurs*? The little *mademoiselle* isn't feeling well and should not be disturbed."

One of the detectives frowned and gestured toward Serenity. "What's wrong with her?"

As the men approached the bed, Elena stepped forward, her posture protective and her voice getting even more firm. "If you must know, she gets les migraines and did not sleep last night." Elena flicked her hands at them. "*S'il vous plaîtes*, leave."

The officers exchanged glances, perhaps weighing the wisdom of challenging the older but formidable woman who stood before them.

In the end, they chose to retreat, unwilling to push the issue further. As they begrudgingly filed out of the room, I caught Elena's eye, silently conveying my gratitude for her quick thinking and unwavering loyalty.

As the search wound down and the officers began to reassemble in the foyer, the frustration on Detective Flanagan's face grew more apparent. Despite his best efforts, he had found absolutely nothing to support his suspicions, not one shred of evidence. It was a small victory, but one that I savored, even though I had no doubt Detective Flanagan would return soon, armed with a search warrant.

Once the detective and his team had departed, I turned

my attention to Keir and Costin, my gaze hardening as I studied their expressions.

"Now why don't you two tell me the real reason you're here? And please spare me the fairy tale about overhearing the commotion. One of you tipped off the police. I want to know why."

Costin met my accusation with an unwavering stare, his voice dripping with self-righteousness. "A gentleman has to fulfill his civic duty, Angelo. Surely you can understand that."

The urge to wrap my hands around the headmaster's throat was nearly overwhelming, but I kept my arms firmly at my sides, refusing to give him the satisfaction of seeing me lose control. "I didn't kill her," I said through grit teeth, my jaw muscles twitching from the effort of containing my anger. I could feel the heat of my fury rising within me, my heart pounding in my ribcage as I fought to maintain my composure. My eyes drew to slits as I wished for all the world I could shoot lasers into the headmaster's eye sockets, melting his head like steel.

A slow, calculating smile spread across Costin's face. "So you say, Angelo. But let's not forget, this is the fourth victim. Dracula will undoubtedly learn of these events at this point, and then it's only a matter of time before he descends upon New Orleans." His gaze swept over my home, taking in every detail. "Tell me, did the Nephilim really destroy your home and then repair it again? Remarkable."

I met his question with a humorless chuckle. "Why bother asking when you already know the answer, Costin?"

The headmaster's eyes glittered with malice. "Perhaps I

simply want to hear you admit it, Angelo. The power of the Nephilim is not to be taken lightly—here you stand, your home miraculously restored. One can only imagine the heady implications."

I stood my ground, refusing to be baited by his insinuations. "The only thing not to be taken lightly here is that you've chosen to involve yourself in matters that don't concern you, Costin. I suggest you tread very carefully, or you may find yourself in over your head."

Keir, who had remained silent thus far, stepped forward, his face a neutral mask. "We're not here to make threats, Angelo. But you must understand the gravity of the situation. If Dracula comes to New Orleans, the consequences could be dire, not just for you but for all of us."

I met Keir's gaze head-on. "Then perhaps it's time we stopped playing games and started working together to find a solution."

Costin glanced at his watch, then gave me a cool, calculating look. "I'm afraid I must take my leave, Angelo. Classes at Red Rose will be breaking for lunch soon, and there are matters there that demand my attention."

As he spoke, his dark eyes glittered with an unsettling intensity, and for a brief moment something flashed behind them—a warning, or perhaps a promise of things to come. A power unlike anything I had encountered since my turning in Italy flowed from him, causing me to instinctively take a step back. The air around us crackled, and I could feel the hairs on the back of my neck standing on end.

Costin Tarus was an ancient vampire, centuries older than myself, but I had never thought he was anything like

Vlad. Suddenly, however, I found myself wondering if he was as powerful as my maker.

I clenched my jaw, fighting the urge to demand answers from him. The mysterious power radiating from him only added to the growing list of inexplicable events that had transpired since Serenity's arrival. But as much as I wanted to unravel all his secrets, I knew that time was of the essence.

My heartrate spiked as I thought of Serenity, still vulnerable and weakened by the stone's power. The memory of her lifeless body in my arms was still painfully fresh, and the fear of losing her again gnawed at my insides like a ravenous beast.

"Listen, Costin," I hissed, my voice low and urgent. "I don't have time for games. Serenity is up there, and I need to make sure she's all right. If there's something you know, something that can help us, you need to tell me now."

He regarded me silently for a moment, his expression unreadable. His lips curved into a thin, enigmatic smile. "Indeed, Angelo. There are forces at work here that you cannot begin to comprehend. Forces that were already in motion long before you or I walked this earth." With those cryptic words, he started to head for the exit.

"I don't care about ancient forces or hidden agendas," I growled, taking a step toward Costin. "All I care about is protecting the people I love. Right now, that means protecting Serenity. So either help me or get out of my way."

Costin's lips twitched, a hint of amusement flickering in his eyes. "Very well, Angelo. Go to your Nephilim. But know that this is only the beginning. The path ahead is fraught with danger, and the choices you make will have far-reaching consequences." Then he bowed slightly. "Now, if you'll excuse me, I must return to the academy." He strode out the door, his heels loud in the foyer.

I shut the door after Costin left and turned to Keir. "All right. Why are you here? Do you have news on who has been murdering the girls?"

"No...but I do have news about Jacques' death." Keir's words hung in the air, a mixture of solemnity and smug self-satisfaction in his tone.

I exchanged a wary glance with Enzo; the ache of Jacques' death was still raw in our hearts.

"And?" I prompted testily.

"My sources tell me there's a new player in town," Keir continued, his eyes sparkling. "Someone who has a score to settle."

My muscles tensed as I fought to keep my frustration in check. I fixed Keir with a hard stare as I leaned forward, invading his personal space. "My patience is wearing thin, Keir," I growled, my lips curling back slightly and baring my fangs. "If you have information, just spit it out."

Keir leaned forward, his voice lowered conspiratorially. "I've discovered that you have a traitor among your people, Angelo. Someone within your own organization is responsible for Jacques' death."

My blood ran cold. A traitor in the Santi family? The thought was almost too much to bear. I looked at Enzo and saw my own shock and disbelief mirrored in his eyes.

"A traitor?" I echoed blankly.

"Yes. Someone close to you, someone you trust, has been working against you," Keir continued, his tone grave. "My sources suggest this person's ultimate goal is to take over the Santi family, and they are willing to do whatever it takes to achieve that end."

A sickening wave of anger and betrayal washed over me. The idea that one of my own would turn against me, against the family, was a blow that struck at the very heart of everything I held dear.

Enzo, ever pragmatic, jumped in. "Do you have any proof of this, Keir? And any idea who the traitor might be?"

Keir shook his head. "Not yet, but I'm working on it. I thought it was important to bring this to your attention as soon as possible, so you could take the necessary precautions."

My mind raced, trying to piece together the puzzle. Who among my trusted inner circle would be capable of such treachery? And how long had this betrayal been going on right under my nose?

I took a deep breath, trying to calm the rage boiling within me. "Are you going to tell me the name of this source?"

He chuckled. "No. But they're very reliable. The threat of torture and possible death tends to be effective."

He wasn't wrong. The dark Fae were notorious torturers. The threat of being subjected to their methods would send even the toughest vampire into hiding.

Serenity's sweet face swam in front of my eyes, and my gut tightened. "I have one more question, Keir. Does this involve—"

Keir cut me off. "Your Nephilim? Yes. I'd keep her close,

Angelo. My informant hinted that if the Nephilim was captured, it would be the end of your reign."

My heart clenched at the thought of Serenity being used as a pawn in this twisted game. I would do anything to keep her out of this and safe from those who sought to harm her.

"We'll need to investigate these allegations fully," I said, my jaw clenching so hard I could feel my teeth grinding together. I took a deep breath, trying to rein in the white-hot rage charging through my veins. "We can't let the traitor know we're onto them." The vein in my temple started throbbing from the barely contained fury that threatened to consume me.

Enzo nodded in agreement. "We'll have to be observant, watch for any whiff of disloyalty or suspicious behavior."

Uncovering the traitor could be difficult, and a sense of unease gripped me like a fist as one name kept coming to mind—Dimitri. The thought of confronting him, of accusing him of betrayal, filled me with a sense of dread. It would put me at odds with my sister again too. She would never forgive me. But if he was the one responsible for Jacques' death and represented a threat to Serenity, I knew I would have to face him, no matter the cost. I didn't shrink from my responsibilities. That's why I was head of this family.

I turned back to Keir, my voice low and dangerous. "If your information is true, Keir, and it leads us to the traitor, I'll be in your debt. But if this is just some attempt to sow discord within my family, you'll wish you'd never set foot in New Orleans."

Keir held up his hands in a gesture of appeal. "I assure

you, Angelo, my information is sound. I would have no reason to deceive you, not when the stakes are this high."

I escorted him to the front door and opened it. Then I gave him a long, measured look before finally nodding. "We'll see. Keep me informed of any new developments and watch your back. If the traitor thinks you're onto him, you could be next on their hit list."

With that, Keir quietly left. If his information was true, I would owe him.

I turned to Enzo, my eyes steely with resolve. "We'll start with Dimitri. I want eyes on him at all times, and I want to know every single move he makes."

Enzo's face darkened, a shadow of concern passing over his features. "Dimitri? You really think he's the traitor?"

I nodded grimly. "He's had a history of playing both sides. Remember when he was supposedly aligned with his father and Grayson Allen, who were planning to overthrow King Nico?"

"Yes...but didn't it turn out in the end that he had been feeding information to his brother Valentin and his mate, Rose, the whole time?"

"Exactly," I said, my jaw clenching. "And now I'm wondering if he's doing the same to us."

Enzo's gaze sharpened, his focus intensifying. "You think he might be working with our enemies while pretending to be on our side?"

"It's certainly a possibility we can't ignore," I muttered grimly. "If he's the traitor, we'll find out and deal with him accordingly."

Enzo met my gaze, his expression hardening to match

my own. "Don't worry, Angelo. I'll put our best men on it. We'll watch him like hawks for any suspicious moves and get to the bottom of this. One way or another, we'll find out the truth."

"Good. Be vigilant." I clasped Enzo's shoulder, my grip firm. Gianna might never forgive me for this, but if Dimitri was the traitor, it meant he didn't truly love my sister...and he'd pay with his life.

Chapter Thirty-Four

Serenity

I woke up with a start, my eyes struggling to see in the darkness that shrouded the room. The window curtains were drawn tightly, giving me no hint as to the time of day. My throat felt dry as sandpaper, each swallow a painful effort, and an overwhelming weariness had settled deep in my bones, as if the Aeternum Stone had drained every last ounce of energy from my cells.

Usually when I felt tired or depressed, I would call Joy. She had her own magical way of chasing away the grumpy clouds hanging over my head. But I couldn't do that now. My chest tightened as a tear slid down my cheek.

Sudden movement in the shadows caught my attention, and my heart leaped as a pair of glowing red eyes emerged from the darkness.

"Don't be afraid, Serenity. It's me." Angelo's soothing voice cut through the gloom as he sat down on the edge of my bed.

The familiar spicy scent of his cologne washed over me, and I let out a happy sigh of relief. "You're alive," I croaked, my voice barely above a whisper.

He chuckled, the soft sound warming my heart. "Of course I'm alive. Why would you think otherwise?"

I struggled to sit up, my muscles protesting with every movement. My inner thigh muscles were still achy from making love with Angelo. "I...I thought I might have been too late. That Dracula might have..." I trailed off, unable to give voice to the terrible fear that had haunted me.

Angelo's strong arms encircled me, pulling me close to his chest. "Too late? Not at all. You saved me, Serenity. You risked everything to restore the Aeternum Stone to protect me and my family. I will never forget that."

I leaned into him, delighting in his steady heartbeat. "So Dracula's not coming?"

He hesitated, as if he was holding something back.

I put my finger on his tightly closed lips. "No secrets, remember?" I peered at him. "Have you heard anything about Joy?"

He sighed heavily, a soft curse escaping his lips. "No. I am sorry. And I'm afraid I have other worrying news that you need to hear. Costin Tarus, the headmaster of Red Rose Academy, showed up with the police. He claims that Dracula is on his way to New Orleans. Apparently, he's furious about the murdered girls...and he believes I'm responsible."

I shifted in his arms, tilting my head to look up at him. "But you're not, right? You couldn't be..."

Angelo brushed his lips against my furrowed brow, his touch gentle and reassuring. "No, my little Nephilim. I didn't kill those girls. I may have done many terrible things in my past, but I would never murder innocent women, especially those close to me."

His words plucked at my overly taut heartstrings, making me feel like just another in a long line of lovers. "Close to you? Does that mean what I think it does?"

He hesitated for a moment, his eyes searching mine. "I won't lie to you, Serenity. I had relationships with two of the victims. But they were before I met you, and they both ended long ago."

A sudden pang of jealousy twisted in my gut, catching me off guard. I knew it was irrational to feel this way, given Angelo's long history and the countless years he had lived before meeting me. And yet the idea of him with other women, even in the distant past, made my heart ache.

"How...how long were you with them?" My voice was barely above a whisper.

Angelo pressed a tender kiss to the top of my head, a soft chuckle rumbling in his chest. "Now, is that a hint of jealousy I hear in your voice, sweet Nephilim?"

"No..." I lied, the scorching rush that engulfed my cheeks betraying my true feelings.

He smiled, his fingers tracing looping, soothing circles on my back. "One of the women worked for me, and the other was a favorite at Simon's club. But they were never anything more than brief dalliances, Serenity. They could never compare to you."

I wanted to ask him exactly what that meant but didn't want to press the issue. Instead, I just nodded, doing my best to push aside the irrational twinge of envy. "I understand. I'm sorry. I didn't mean to—"

"Shh," he interrupted, tipping my chin up to meet his gaze. "You have nothing to apologize for, Serenity. Your feelings are valid, and I want you to always be honest with me. Yes?"

"Yes." I leaned into his touch, drawing strength from his unwavering support. After a moment I asked, "So...have you found out who is responsible for killing these women?"

"Not yet. I have men working on finding the killer even as we speak." Angelo's voice was low and urgent as he gently turned me to face him. "Serenity, I need you to promise me something."

The gravity in his tone sent a chill down my spine, and I searched his face, trying to interpret the emotions flickering in his eyes. "Anything, Angelo. What is it? What's wrong?"

He took a deep breath, his gaze intense and unwavering. "I've received word that there may be a traitor among us, within our inner circle. You must be careful who you trust, Serenity. Stay close to Elena, Enzo, or Lorenzo, always. And whatever you do, do not share this with Gianna."

His words sent a jolt of fear through me. "Gianna? Why not? She's your sister, Angelo. Surely, we can trust her..."

Angelo's grip on my shoulders tightened, his dark eyes boring into mine with an urgency I had never seen before.

"Please, Serenity. Trust me on this. Promise me you'll do as I ask, without question."

The seriousness of his plea left no room for argument, and I found myself nodding in agreement. "I promise I'll be careful, Angelo. And I won't say a word to Gianna."

He pulled me close, his lips brushing against my forehead in a whispery, featherlight kiss. "Thank you, my sweet Nephilim," he whispered, his voice thick with emotion. "I know it's a hard thing to ask, but I need to know you're safe. I couldn't bear it if anything happened to you."

I melted into his embrace, my chest tightening at the thought of the dangers that lurked in the shadows and the possibility of losing him.

Angelo was quickly becoming everything to me, and if Dracula was indeed coming, I needed to be at full strength to protect him. Mom had always said that love conquered all. How that applied to someone like Freddie was beyond me, but a sudden desire to forge an unbreakable connection with Angelo consumed me. The last time we had made love, it had unleashed my power. Now that my power had been drained by the Aeternum Stone, I wondered if intimacy could restore what I had lost.

I pulled away from him, my hands trembling as I reached for the hem of my shirt. I hesitated, my fingers clutching the fabric as a sudden wave of uncertainty washed over me. Was I really ready for this again? After everything I'd been through, the thought of being so vulnerable, even with Angelo, sent a flicker of fear through my heart.

But as I met his gaze, I saw love and tenderness shining in his eyes, and I knew that I trusted him completely. He had always been my rock, my safe haven, and I wanted to feel that connection with him now more than ever.

With a deep breath, I steeled my resolve and slowly pulled off my shirt, jeans, bra, and finally my lacy underwear, baring myself to him in every sense of the word.

Angelo's eyes widened in surprise, and he instinctively leaned back a little. "Serenity, what are you doing?"

I straddled his lap, my bare skin pressing against the fabric of his clothing. The contact sent a shiver down my spine as I felt the heat of his body seeping into mine. "I want you, Angelo," I whispered, my voice trembling slightly. "I need to feel something other than pain and fear. I need to feel alive."

He swallowed, his body already responding to my touch even as concern etched his features. "But you've been through so much, and you're still recovering..."

I silenced him with a finger on his lips, my eyes locked on his. "I know," I said softly, my heart pounding in my chest. "I also know that I trust you with every fiber of my being. I want this, Angelo. I want you."

He nodded, his hands skimming along my sides with a reverent touch. "Are you completely sure, Serenity?"

I ground my hips against his in answer, eliciting a low groan from his throat. The friction sent sparks of pleasure careening through my body, igniting a fire in my core that threatened to consume me entirely. My inner thighs still ached with a delicious soreness that reminded me of the passion we had already shared, and I knew that I would gladly bear any discomfort to feel so close to him again.

Leaning forward, I pressed my forehead against his, our

breath mingling in the scant space between us. "I've never been more sure of anything in my life, Angelo," I whispered, my voice raw with emotion. "I need you, in every way possible. I need to feel your skin against mine, to be one with you, body and soul."

I punctuated my words with a roll of my hips, gasping as the movement sent another wave of pleasure crashing over me. My hands slid up his chest, feeling the hard planes of muscle beneath my fingertips, before tangling in his hair and tugging gently.

"Make love to me, Angelo," I breathed, my eyes locked on his, blazing with intense desire. "Please. Show me that I'm alive and remind me that I'm yours, now and forever."

His fingers found my breasts, his thumbs brushing over my hardened nipples and sending sparks of pleasure through my body. "You are. Just as I am yours, Nephilim, now and forever." His husky words caressed my skin, making me grow hotter and more anxious for his touch everywhere.

Chapter Thirty-Five

Serenity

The room was dimly lit, the silvery glow of the moon casting a gentle light across the planes of his face. The air felt charged, crackling with the intensity of our desire and the unspoken emotions that hung in the space between us.

With supernatural speed, Angelo deftly removed his shirt and pants, his eyes never leaving mine. My breath caught in my throat as I took in the magnificent sight of his sculpted body, and I struggled to find my voice. "Sit on the bed," I managed to say, my tone wavering slightly despite the newfound confidence I was trying to project.

As Angelo complied, sitting down on the edge of the bed, I felt a sudden rush of uncertainty. My hands trembled at my sides, and I could feel the heat of his gaze on my skin, both thrilling and unnerving. Was I really ready for this?

Could I truly let go of my fears and give myself to him completely?

I took a step forward, then hesitated, my courage faltering. Angelo must have sensed my inner turmoil, because he reached out and gently took my hand, his touch warm and reassuring.

"Serenity," he murmured, his voice soft and tender. "We don't have to do this if you're not ready. I would never pressure you."

His words, filled with understanding and love, steadied me. I took a deep breath, letting the air fill my lungs and calm my racing heart. I knew, in that moment, that I wanted this—wanted him—more than anything. My hesitation stemmed from fear, but my love for Angelo was stronger than any fear could ever be.

With a small, determined nod, I stepped closer to him, my fingers intertwining with his. "I want this, Angelo," I whispered, my voice growing stronger with each word. "I want you. I'm ready."

Another flicker of surprise crossed Angelo's features, but he complied without hesitation, settling on the edge of the mattress. I straddled his hips, the blanket twisting around our bodies as I pressed close to him. The heat of his hard cock against my inner thigh sent a shiver of desire down my spine.

"I want you, Serenity," he breathed, his voice thick with passion. "Every day and every night, for all eternity."

All eternity? Surely someday we would be parted, since he was immortal and I was mortal. But for now at least, he was mine.

His lips traced a searing path down my throat, his hands roaming slowly over my body, exploring every curve and plane in a way that made me tremble with need. I arched into his touch, my fingers splaying across his back, marveling at the muscles that rippled beneath his smooth skin.

My body knew exactly what it wanted this time. I impaled myself on his enormous cock, moving up and down, taking him deeper and deeper. His flesh rippled against mine, sparking something deep within me. Friction moved against friction, flesh slid against flesh, igniting a fiery storm of passion.

As our bodies moved together in a timeless dance of desire, I could feel the power within me surging to the surface, strengthened by the intensity of our connection. Each kiss, each caress, each whispered word of devotion fueled the flames of my nascent magic, until I felt as though I might burst with the sheer force of it.

Angelo sensed the change in me, his eyes darkening with a mixture of awe and lust. "That's it, my love," he encouraged, his hands guiding my hips in a slow, deliberate rhythm as he plunged upward into my core. "Embrace your power. Let it flow through you. Let me see all of you, Serenity, every beautiful, incredible, wonderful, part of you."

I threw my head back, a cry of ecstasy escaping my lips as waves of pleasure crashed over me, mingling with the intoxicating rush of my magic. He ran his fangs over my throat, scratching me. Chills shivered through me, and a hunger built inside me, desperate for something only he could provide.

I remembered what he said about how much pleasure I would experience if he bit me. I was ready.

I panted as I clutched at the back of his neck with my fingers. "Angelo, I want you to bite me."

He jerked his head up. "What?"

I dragged my fingers through his hair. "You heard me."

He hesitated, as if he wasn't sure what to do.

I kissed him, nipping at his lower lip. "Don't make me beg, Angelo."

He paused for only a breath before he smiled, revealing sharp fangs, and then bit down on my neck. As his fangs sank into my tender flesh, a sudden jolt of electricity shot through my body, setting every nerve ending ablaze. I gasped, my back arching involuntarily, and then the initial sting gave way to a flood of warm, tingling pleasure that emanated directly from the very point where his teeth pierced my skin.

With each pull of his mouth, I could feel my blood flowing into him, a sacred offering that bound us together in ways that transcended mere physical intimacy. It was as if he was not just drawing out my life force, but also replenishing the power that the Aeternum Stone had stolen from me.

As he drank more deeply, he rocked up into me harder and harder. A surging wave of desire built inside me, pulsing in time with the rhythm of his lips pulling on my throat. It was like a fire had been ignited in my veins, its flames licking at my insides with an intensity that bordered on the unbearable.

I writhed in Angelo's embrace, my fingers tangling in his

hair as I held him close, silently urging him to take me deeper, harder, to consume me entirely.

Through the haze of pleasure, I could sense my power rising up to meet his—our two spirits twined together in a dance as old as time itself. With each heartbeat, I felt my magic growing stronger, fed by the force of our connection and the potent sensation of my blood on his tongue.

The world around us fell away, narrowing to a point that was nothing but the exquisite pleasure of his mouth on my skin and the throbbing ache that threatened to consume me entirely. I was lost in the sensations, drowning in an ocean of ecstasy that seemed to stretch on forever.

Just when I thought I couldn't take any more, Angelo pulled back, his eyes blazing hungrily. As he licked the last crimson droplets of my blood from his lips, I saw my power reflected in his gaze, glowing brighter than ever before.

He grabbed my thighs and lifted me up, rolling us over on the bed.

I took control of our rhythm, guiding Angelo's hungry hands and mouth to every place my skin craved his touch. Each caress, each kiss, sent new sparks of electricity dancing across my nerve endings, igniting a fire in my veins that burned hotter with every passing second. I could feel the tension building within him as well, his muscles tightening beneath my fingers as he fought to maintain his self-control.

Suddenly, I felt an extreme power burst outward from my center, like a supernova explosion. A brilliant aura of shimmering energy enveloped us both, pulsing in time with our beating hearts. It was as if the very air around us was charged with the force of our connection, our love made manifest in a dazzling display of light and magic.

As the wave of ecstasy crashed over me and I reached the pinnacle of my pleasure, the aura around us exploded into a kaleidoscope of swirling colors, bathing the room in a mesmerizing glow. I could feel the power rushing through every cell of my being, electrifying and invigorating me like never before. I felt a second surge of energy explode outward, radiating into the very air around us. Books flew off shelves, their pages fluttering wildly as they swirled around the room in a chaotic dance. The doors to the balcony banged open and shut, their glass panes rattling in their frames as if they, too, were caught up in the throes of our passion.

The curtains billowed like sails, the fabric whipping and snapping in a sudden gust of wind that came from our joined bodies. Loose papers scattered across the floor, and the lamp on the bedside table flickered erratically.

Angelo's movements became more urgent, his breathing turning ragged as he chased his own release. I clung to him, my nails digging into his back as I urged him on with whispered words of encouragement. "Let go, Angelo," I breathed, my lips brushing against his ear. "I want to feel you come undone."

With a final, powerful thrust of his hips, Angelo cried out my name, his voice wild with ecstasy. I felt his flesh pulsing deep within me as he spilled his seed, his body shuddering against mine as he climaxed. The sensation pushed me over the edge once more, and I joined him in blissful oblivion, our bodies and souls joined in a moment of perfect unity.

As our twin waves of pleasure gradually subsided, Angelo collapsed onto me, his weight a comforting pressure that returned me to the present. We lay there, bodies tangled up in each other, our hearts pounding in sync as we melted into the afterglow of our lovemaking. The shimmering aura around us slowly faded, but the warmth of our connection remained, a glowing ember that would never be extinguished.

Through heavily lidded eyes, I watched tendrils of power weave themselves around Angelo's body, caressing his skin like ethereal fingers. I could feel my own energy intertwining with his, our essences blending and merging until it was impossible to tell where one left off and the other began.

As I lay there, I could feel my strength returning, my magic burning brighter and hotter until it was a raging inferno inside me. The Aeternum Stone's draining effects were being reversed, and the void the stone had left behind was filling up again thanks to the sheer force of our passion.

In that perfect, timeless moment, I understood the true depth of my connection with Angelo. My feelings were clear for this vampire Mafia king. In his dark world, he was my guiding light.

Cradling my face in his hands, Angelo gazed deep into my eyes, his expression filled with a tenderness that took my breath away. "Serenity," he whispered, his voice raw with emotion. "I...I love you. I don't know how it happened, or when, but somewhere along the way, you became everything to me. You're my light in the darkness, my reason for living. You're mine to protect, always."

Tears sprang to my eyes as the magnitude of his words sank in. For so long, I had been afraid to put a name to the feelings that had been growing inside me, but hearing Angelo say those three precious words out loud made everything crystal clear.

"I love you too, Angelo," I breathed, my voice trembling with the force of my emotions.

Angelo's eyes shone with unshed tears as he pulled me into a fierce embrace, his strong arms enveloping me in a warm cocoon of love and protection. "You are my everything, Serenity," he murmured into my hair. "I will spend every day for all eternity showing you just how much you mean to me. Together, we will weather any storm, conquer any obstacle. Our love is a force that nothing can destroy."

With a soft sigh of contentment, I tilted my face up to his, our lips meeting in a kiss that felt like a promise, a seal on the declaration we had just made. As the kiss deepened and our bodies began to undulate together once more, I lost myself in the exquisite perfection of this moment.

I had found my mate. My other half. Nothing would ever tear us apart. Come what may, our love would be the light that guided us home.

Chapter Thirty-Six

Serenity

I woke the next morning to find Angelo was gone. My thighs ached from the night of lovemaking. I sat up, the covers falling away from me, and looked for any sign of him again. Had he really meant what he said last night? Did he really love me?

"Angelo?" Silence answered me back and disappointment gripped me.

I flicked the covers off and climbed out of bed naked. He wasn't in the bathroom. I glanced at my reflection in the mirror. My hair was a tangled mess. I looked like I stuck my finger into a light socket.

I turned on the shower, hoping Angelo would return and join me, but after steam swirled around in the bathroom, that hope died.

I washed my hair and glided shower gel over my sensitive skin as I thought about our night of lovemaking and declarations of love. I didn't know if he meant it, but I meant every word. He was the love of my life. Someone I trusted and never wanted to be parted from.

The water pulsing over me turned cold, and I shut off the faucets. I towel dried my hair and my body. I put on lavender lotion then blow dried my hair. Within a few minutes, I looked normal, but I felt different. Not because my power had been restored, but I was in love. The feeling pushed over my doubts and any other negative ones.

I threw on a red sundress and headed downstairs. Angelo liked sundresses, and I wanted to please him. Maybe he had gone downstairs to eat breakfast and didn't want to disturb me while I was sleeping.

I followed the smells of frying bacon, my stomach grumbling and my mouth watering. Happy voices echoed through the dining room. I thought heard Gianna and Elena talking and was eager to join them. I was about to enter the dining room when Petar, one of Angelo's men, stood in front of me. He was Dimitri's father, but he didn't look anything like him. Dimitri had an undeniable presence to him that drew others in like a moth to flame, but his father had a slimy presence like an oily salesman that you just want to kick out the door.

The corners of his mouth curled up into a Cheshire Cat smile. "Serenity, I was just about to find you. Angelo sends word. He found Joy."

For a moment, the world seemed to stand still as his triumphant words hung in the air between us like a bugle call.

My heart leaped with a surge of relief and happiness so intense it nearly brought me to my knees. But before I could fully process the joyous news, he continued, his expression sobering.

"She's with her father and brother now, but she's hurt. Angelo says you can heal her."

The joy that had filled my chest suddenly twisted into a knot of worry and fear. Joy was hurt. The thought of her suffering, of the pain she must be enduring, sent a chill down my spine. I swallowed hard, fighting back the tears that threatened to spill down my cheeks.

"How badly is she hurt?" I asked, my voice trembling slightly. "What happened to her?"

He shook his head, his brow furrowing with concern. "I don't have all the details, but Angelo seemed to think it was serious. He said you were the only one who could help her."

A fierce determination rose within me, pushing aside the fear and worry. If Joy needed me, if I had the power to heal her, then nothing would stand in my way. I squared my shoulders, meeting his gaze with a resolute stare.

"Take me to her," I said, my voice steady and strong. "I'll do whatever it takes to make sure she's okay."

"Come, follow me." He clasped my arm a little too tight, but it just had to be the desperation to save Joy.

As we hurried through the halls, my heart raced with a potent mix of anxiety and determination. Hold on, Joy, I thought, sending a silent prayer out into the universe. I'm coming. You're going to be alright.

As the reality of the situation began to sink in, tears clouded my eyes. How badly was she injured? Joy was out there, hurt, waiting for me, and I knew that I would move mountains to get to her, to wrap her in my arms and never let go again.

As we set off, my steps quickening with every passing moment, I sent up a silent prayer of hope to the universe that I could heal her. She was my family, and I couldn't lose her. Not after Angelo had found her. Who had hurt her and why?

Doubt that I wouldn't be able to save her haunted me, but then I kept telling myself I healed Enzo, and he was a vampire, so I could heal her.

He guided me through the house, away from the delicious aroma of crackling bacon that wafted from the kitchen. I expected him to lead me to the front door or the courtyard that opened onto Bourbon Street, but instead, he veered down an unfamiliar hallway, his steps quick and purposeful.

As we navigated the twists and turns of the corridor, I couldn't shake the nagging feeling that something wasn't quite right. The air seemed to grow colder with each step, and the once comforting walls of the house suddenly felt oppressive, almost menacing.

I kept looking over my shoulder for Angelo or Enzo or Gianna, or even Elena, but there was no one behind us. Despite my uneasiness, I forced myself to keep going. Joy was in trouble. I'd walk through fire to save her.

Just as I opened my mouth to voice my concerns, Petar came to an abrupt halt before a nondescript door, half hidden in the shadows. With a furtive glance over his shoulder, he reached out and pressed his palm against a seemingly unremarkable panel on the wall.

To my surprise, the panel slid aside, revealing a sophisticated keypad. Petar's fingers flew over the numbers, inputting a complex code with practiced ease. A soft click echoed in the stillness, and the door swung open, revealing an alley.

We had come to the alley next to Crescent Manor where all the deliveries were made. There was a truck parked in the alleyway. I looked around for guards but there didn't seem to be any there. The morning sun hadn't reached the alley, and a dark shadow fell over us like a black mist.

"Petar, why are we here? Where're Joy and Angelo?" I whispered, my heart pounding in my chest as I strained to make out my surroundings in the feeble light. Angelo's words haunted me. He said only to trust him, Elena, Enzo, or Lorenzo. He hadn't mentioned oily Petar who suddenly reminded me of Freaky Freddie. I cursed my stupidity.

"Quickly, inside. Joy and Angelo are inside," Petar urged, his voice low and urgent as he clamped his hand down on my arm, ushering me up the ramp of the truck. "We mustn't be seen."

Angelo would not be hiding in the back of a delivery truck, especially if Joy was wounded.

I twisted my arm. "Let go of me." As he dragged me up the ramp, the sense of foreboding grew stronger, a cold dread seeping into my bones.

As I stepped over the threshold, I looked wildly around. "Where's Joy? Angelo, are you in here?"

A soft, menacing laugh sent a flicker of unease dancing up my spine. Something about this felt wrong, dangerous even. But before I could give voice to my doubts, Petar had closed the door behind us, plunging the truck's interior into near darkness.

And then, without warning, a door slammed shut and the truck started up. Petar released me abruptly and I stumbled. I could hear his dark laughter but couldn't see him. As my vision adjusted, I felt the blood drain from my face, my breath catching in my throat as I took in the scene before me.

For there, in the center of the truck, stood a figure cloaked in shadows, a figure whose very presence radiated malevolence and barely contained rage. And in that moment, I knew with chilling certainty that I had walked straight into a trap, led astray by my own eagerness to save Joy, and ignoring Angelo's dire warning.

Gianna wasn't the traitor. It was Petar, and he'd turned me over to the enemy.

"It's so nice to finally meet you, Nephilim," the dark figure said as he approached me, his voice dripping with a sickening mixture of anticipation and contempt. Yellow eyes, filled with a hatred that seemed to burn with the intensity of a thousand suns, glowed from beneath his hood. As I met his gaze, I saw my own death reflected in those merciless orbs, and a cold realization washed over me. I was about to become victim number five, joining the ranks of the murdered girls.

Instinctively, I stepped away, my back pressing against the cold metal wall of the rumbling truck. "Who are you?" I managed to ask, my voice sounding small and fragile in the face of such an overbearing menace.

"Someone who has wanted to meet you for a very long time," he replied, his words laced with a dark promise that filled me with an icy terror, freezing me to the core.

As he closed the distance between us, my heart hammered in my chest, a frantic beat that seemed to echo the relentless pounding of the tires against the road. "Why?" I whispered, my thoughts spinning in a dizzying whirlwind as I tried to make sense of this nightmare unfolding before me.

In a flash, he was beside me, his movements so swift and fluid that my eyes couldn't track them. His fist buried itself in my hair, twisting the strands painfully as he wrenched my head back, forcing me to meet his gaze.

"Because I want Angelo to feel the pain I endured," he snarled, his breath hot against my face. "I want him to know what it's like to lose a mate, to have his heart ripped from his chest and crushed before his very eyes. I want Angelo to suffer as I have suffered, to experience the agony of a love torn asunder."

Fear gripped me, its icy tendrils wrapping around my heart and squeezing with ruthless intensity. But even in the face of such terror, a desperate need to understand burned within me. Who was this creature, this being of shadow and rage, who sought to destroy Angelo through me? What vampire could possess such golden eyes, so different from the crimson hue I had come to associate with their kind?

Mustering every ounce of courage I possessed, I squared my shoulders, determined not to give him the satisfaction of seeing me beg for mercy. "Tell me who you are," I demanded this time. My voice was steady despite the tremors that wracked my body. "Are you a vampire?" The questions fell from my lips like a final prayer, the last words I might ever speak.

A cruel smile curved his lips, a flash of gleaming white in the darkness. "No, Nephilim," he chuckled, the sound devoid of any warmth or humanity. "I'm a wolf, and you, my dear, are my prisoner."

As the horror of his words sank in, a scream bubbled up in my throat, a primal, desperate cry that never made it past my lips. For in that moment, the world went black, and I knew no more.

* * *

Do you want to find out more about Serenity and Angelo? Here's a bonus scene for you!!!

There's more to this series! If you want to read more about the vampire mafia series, check these out!

The next book this exciting vampire mafia trilogy is Curse of Blood and Silence!

I'm the key to an ancient power. Now everyone wants to possess me.

If you want to find out more about Dimitri and Gianna, then you want to read their story in Kiss of Blood and Sin!

Mafia princess by force, rebel by choice.

<h1 style="text-align:center">Dear Reader</h1>

I am so glad that you took a new chance on my vampire mafia book! I really enjoyed writing this and love being a Vampire Vixen! I didn't know if I could write mafia romance until I joined this group. I hadn't even read a mafia romance. I dove into reading mafia romance and I was hooked.

My favorite tropes in these books are touch-her-and-die and morally grey heroes! I've always liked heroes that had a dark past but in the end do what's right like Damon Salvatore did in Vampire Diaries. He is the hero of morally grey heroes. Although he's done some really bad things, he's always makes the choice to make the sacrifice to save the ones he loves. Dean Winchester fits that bill too. They are probably my favorite heroes. What makes me laugh is that Captain America is my favorite hero in The Marvel Series. He's the complete opposite of Dean and Damon.

I have to admit its more fun to write about the morally grey hero like Angelo and Dimitri. As you discovered with this book and if you read Kiss of Blood and Sin, these heroes are not Captain America. They are true vampires, but they will do anything for the people they love, revenge, sacrifice, vulnerability. That's what makes them such heroes.

Neither Angelo nor Dimitri thought they would find love, but the Fates had ideas for both of them.

Chains of Blood and Darkness is part of a vampire mafia trilogy. I'm considering writing Enzo and Joy's story next. That will depend on you!

My editor fell in love with Enzo and thinks he deserves his own tale!

I hope you like these, because they are as easy as silk to write! Once again, thanks for taking a chance on me.

You can join my newsletter if you want to find out about new releases: https://authormguida.com/join-my-news letter/ You'll never miss another release and you'll find out how Angelo and Gianna became vampires! You'll get Throne of Blood and Night for free!

Have a wonderful day!

M Guida

Vampire Vixens

Do you want to become a vampire vixen? Are you lusting for more vampire mafia books? Check out the other books on the Vampire Vixens website!

Seven authors, seven cities, one vampire mafia world!

Each book starts in a familiar setting before venturing into new territory. Characters may cross over between books. We each rule a city - mine's New Orleans. You'll meet other city-ruling kings, some in couples, others in polyamorous groups.

Dive into these vampire romances that will keep you turning pages into the wee hours of night.

Become a Vampire Vixen:

Join the Newsletter

Join us on Facebook

About the Author

M Guida has always loved fantasy and romance, especially dragons. Growing up, she devoured fantasy books and all kinds of young adult books. And then she found romance and a whole new world opened up to her.

Now as an adult, she fell in love with academy romance and has blended all of her past loves into one compelling series. Dragons, vampires, elves, demons, and wolves all live in her world.

When she's not writing, she lives in the colorful Rocky Mountains with her fur baby, Raven, and enjoys taking her for walks.

Would you like to become a Legacy? Sign up for her mailing list and enter a world of the supernatural at her website authormguida.

You can also join her private Facebook page–M Guida's Legacy Academy. You'll become a Legacy and find out about your special power and maybe even find some romance!

Ebony's Legacy Year One

Ebony's Legacy Year Two

Ebony's Legacy Year Three

Ebony's Legacy Year Four

Collections:

Legacy Academy Collection One

Legacy Academy Collection Two

Academy for Reapers Collection

Wolf Princess Collection

Before Legacy Series:

Before Legacy: Armond

Before Legacy: Gunnar

Before Legacy: Valentin

The Defenders

Wolf Defender

Vella Story:

Bite Me: Vampire's Forbidden Romance

Kiss of Blood and Sin

www.ingramcontent.com/pod-product-compliance
Lightning Source LLC
Chambersburg PA
CBHW060901140726
47996CB00001B/62